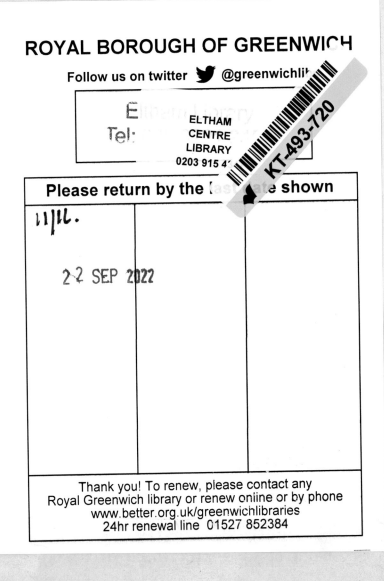

ROYAL BOROUGH OF GREENWICH

Follow us on twitter @greenwichli...

E
Tel:

ELTHAM
CENTRE
LIBRARY
0203 915 4...

KT-493-720

Please return by the last date shown

11|12.

2·2 SEP 2022

Thank you! To renew, please contact any
Royal Greenwich library or renew online or by phone
www.better.org.uk/greenwichlibraries
24hr renewal line 01527 852384

Praise for other books

Struck:

'The first young work to win the Romantic Novel of the Year Award' - Nick Clark, *The Independent*

'...the whole book is bursting with energy – it's fun and fresh and exuberant and, yes, romantic' - Alison Flood, *Guardian*

'...a provocative read which delivered on the romance' - Judges of Romantic Novel of the Year

'Attention grabbing and nail biting in the best kind of way' - *Everything Alyce* Blog

available in the series:

For Nigel Pearson,
the real missionary doctor who often
saves the day like Damien's parents

OXFORD
UNIVERSITY PRESS

Great Clarendon Street, Oxford OX2 6DP

Oxford University Press is a department of the University of Oxford.
It furthers the University's objective of excellence in research, scholarship,
and education by publishing worldwide. Oxford is a registered trade mark of
Oxford University Press in the UK and in certain other countries

Copyright © Joss Stirling 2016

The moral rights of the author have been asserted

Database right Oxford University Press (maker)

First published 2016

British Library Cataloguing in Publication Data

Data available

ISBN: 978-0-19-274598-9

1 3 5 7 9 10 8 6 4 2

Printed in Great Britain

Paper used in the production of this book is a natural,
recyclable product made from wood grown in sustainable forests.
The manufacturing process conforms to the environmental
regulations of the country of origin.

SHAKEN

Joss Stirling

OXFORD
UNIVERSITY PRESS

Prologue

Kennington, South London

A man was being held at knifepoint—that's what they'd been told to expect. Damien Castle crouched by the recycle bin at the side entrance to the newsagents. His friend and partner on this mission, Nathan Hunter, knelt beside him. The overripe smell of rubbish filled the air—and something worse that Damien preferred not to name. They exchanged a wry look.

'Didn't I say we get all the glamorous jobs?' murmured Damien.

Nathan narrowed his eyes and flicked a chip wrapper off the toe of his shoe.

'Any change?' Damien spoke softly into his tiny microphone taped just under his collar.

'Negative.' The police officer in charge of this operation described the situation in a crisp professional tone. Her team was spread out, occupying various vantage points along the cordoned-off street. A police marksman had taken position on a roof opposite but had no clear shot as the assailant had his arm around the chest of the elderly owner of Ali's Corner Shop. 'The suspect is standing behind the counter with a knife on Mr Shah—though locals all call him Mr Ali. Two other customers lying on the floor. There's a child strapped in a pushchair but it looks like he's beginning to make a fuss. That might spook our target. The doctor thinks our suspect's behaviour could rapidly deteriorate. I say it's a "go".'

Isaac's voice joined the conversation. 'I agree. Don't take unnecessary risks, Damien. Stick to the plan.'

With the go-ahead from their boss, Colonel Isaac Hampton, head of the Young Detective Agency, Damien double-checked his anti-stab vest under his jacket. He wasn't expecting to need it. The seventeen-year-old knife wielder was no hardened criminal but a disturbed teen who had neglected to take his anti-psychotic medicine. Kyle Channer had spiralled out of control and entered a dangerous paranoid phase, worse than anything his doctors had seen before. He had decided this afternoon that a gate to an alternate reality had opened up in Ali's shop and was about to let in an invasion of extraterrestrials.

'Ready to go face the alien-spotter, Nat?' asked Damien, touching his bead wristband for good luck.

'Yeah, before he harms anyone or gets taken out by that sniper.' Nathan completed his own checks.

'Let's hope they're right that he won't realize we're with the police and let us get close. Ready?'

His friend nodded and pulled up his hood over his dark hair. They were both dressed in scruffy black jeans and zip-up hoodies, bulky headphones hanging round their necks.

'Watch my six,' Damien murmured, switching on his music so it thumped from the headset.

'You know I have your back covered, but I can lead.' Nathan was definitely not pleased to be relegated to backup on this mission.

Damien grinned, enjoying the zing of adrenaline as they prepared to go in. 'Yeah, and Kate would so give me grief if you got a scratch on you. Stick to the plan.'

Bumping fists, they rose out from their cover and strolled towards the entrance, acting as if they were too intent on their argument to notice anything was wrong in the shop. To any onlooker they just looked like two ordinary teens, one blond, one dark, a little taller than average but otherwise just part of the street.

Damien burst through the door, which emitted a sharp electronic bleep, startling everyone inside. 'Get us a couple of Red Bull, will ya, Mr Ali.' He strode on down the aisle stepping over the prone customers, pretending his music was all he could hear. Nathan followed him, discreetly pushing the pushchair behind the protection of a shelf while all attention was on Damien.

'Stay back!' squawked Kyle, flicking the knife in Damien's direction. A strung-out looking boy with untidy brown hair, he had a wiry, desperate strength that didn't bode well for his frail hostage.

Damien slid off the headphones and held up his empty hands. 'OK, OK, mate. I'll stay here. But what's up?'

'They're coming. Can't you see them?' Kyle's bloodshot brown eyes darted to all corners of the store in frantic fear.

'No worries, they told me it was too cold for them here so they've gone back. Emergency over.'

'You know about them?' Kyle's face relaxed for a second from his terror. 'You understand?'

'Sure. I understand everything. Now, why don't you let Mr Ali go so he can get me those drinks and we can talk about the situation.'

Damien thought for a second his ploy had worked but Kyle suddenly stiffened, his brain having conjured up another phantom. 'No, you're one of them—you're all aliens!' He threw back his head and gave a grating laugh. 'Why didn't I see it? We've already been invaded. I'm the only one left. It's up to me to stop you.'

Uh-oh, not so good. The knife was far too close to the old man's neck. Mr Ali's eyes were glazed with a mixture of shock and pain. The toddler's wails had reached ear-splitting levels, shoes thumping on the footboard. Damien had to persuade Kyle to move the knife so that Nathan could sneak round the side and disarm him—all this before the boy lost it completely.

'I'm not one of them,' Damien said quickly. 'And I can prove it to you.'

This took Kyle by surprise. 'How?'

Damien pushed up his sleeve and rested his arm on the counter. Isaac was going to love this deviation from his orders. 'If you make a little cut with that knife, I'll bleed red. Everyone knows that aliens have blue or green blood.'

Kyle nodded, that somehow making perfect sense to him. On his right-hand side, Damien could sense Nathan's opposition to this risky variation on their plan. Damien gave a low hand signal to Nathan to get ready.

'OK, show me.' Kyle loosened his grip on Mr Ali and took a step towards Damien. The moment he did so, Nathan came in from the right and kicked the knife from Kyle's hand. It twirled in the air and fell with a clatter behind a display of drinks. Kyle screamed and jumped over the counter away from Nathan. He grabbed up a pair of scissors from beside the till and swiped at the boys. Damien swore under his breath, annoyed that he'd not spotted the alternative weapon. The two female customers on the floor had the sense to scuttle out of his path, one retreating behind the counter, the other to protect her kid in the buggy.

'Stay back!' Damien ordered the shop owner, who had risen to his feet. 'Now, calm down, Kyle. We're not here to hurt you.'

Kyle slashed with the scissors. 'Alien! You've got to die.'

'I'm not an alien. How can I be? I support Arsenal.'

Kyle shrieked with fury.

'OK, you're a Tottenham supporter.' Damien hoped his silly banter would get through but the boy was lost in his nightmare. The swipes were getting wilder. If he carried on this way, Kyle was going to end up with a bullet in the chest. 'Nat, get the others clear.'

Now the area behind the counter was freed up, Nathan ushered the shop owner, the women, and the toddler through to the safety of the stockroom.

'You can't go in there! That's the portal!' screamed Kyle. 'No, I won't allow you to destroy humanity.'

Trust them to get a mission with a guy who had watched too many sci-fi films.

'But Kyle,' Damien said calmly, hiding the fact his heart was racing, 'I'm here to help you. I won't let the bad guys take over. In fact, I'll let you into a little secret: I'm Tony Stark's younger brother.'

Turning from the stockroom, Kyle cut towards him, disbelief clear. 'Where's your Iron Man suit then?'

'At the cleaners getting oiled.' He had to get Kyle's mind off aliens. 'Hey, Kyle, do you like magic?'

The boy's eyes widened in confusion at this sharp left turn off the road of their conversation.

'I'll take that as a "yes". Wanna see a trick?' Damien ploughed on even though his audience seemed more likely to stick a pair of scissors in him than applaud. 'See this gold coin?' He picked up a large chocolate one wrapped in golden foil from the sweet display. It was nice and shiny, enough to catch anyone's eye. He passed his hand over it and made it disappear. 'See: it's gone. No, don't look back there—keep your eye on my hands.' He reversed the move producing it from behind his ear. 'And now it's back.'

A little bit of the tension went from Kyle's shoulders, the scissors dropped to waist height. 'Yeah, I like magic.'

Damien moved a little closer. 'Want to see how I did that? First, you pass the coin over to your palm.' While he was occupying Kyle's attention on the coin in his right hand, he reached out with his left and slipped the scissors out of the boy's grip, dropping them into his own pocket. He flicked his gaze to Nathan, giving him the sign to approach. 'Then you make it vanish.'

Kyle's mouth tipped up in a surprised smile. 'Where's it gone?'

'Hey, it's in your ear all this time.' Damien pretended to pull it from Kyle's left ear. 'Would you look at that. There: you have it.' He pressed the coin in the boy's empty hands.

As Nathan came up from behind and gripped Kyle firmly by the upper arms, the boy realized he was missing his weapon. 'No!' he yelped. The chocolate coin dropped to the ground as he struggled to free himself. 'Let go!'

'Target locked down,' Damien told the listeners.

Police officers rushed in from the street. Two took over from Nathan, securing Kyle's hands behind him in cuffs. A doctor followed, ready with a syringe to calm the patient.

Kyle was pressed to the ground. He drummed his feet very much like the toddler had been doing. 'No, no—I've got to stop the aliens!'

Damien knelt down beside him and slipped the chocolate coin in Kyle's pocket. 'They'll stop, mate, as soon as you're back on your pills. Take it easy.' Patting him on the back, Damien got up and brushed off his knees.

Chapter 1

West Village, New York

Another demand had arrived overnight. Feeling shaky with fear, Rose Knight picked it up off the mat. It had been pushed under the front door like its predecessors. They could have emailed it but they preferred the personal touch with its message of 'we know where you live'. She slid her finger under the flap of the cheap envelope and pulled out the single piece of folded paper. This time they'd printed off a photo of her father chained to a heating pipe by his ankle; he was holding a newspaper from the day before.

Take comfort from the proof of life, she told herself.

Don Knight appeared tired but otherwise unharmed. He needed better looking after though: his rusty brown hair was rumpled, shirt dirty, strain telling on his face. Were they letting him free to shower or even walk about? The message was like the others: a simple sum and a date by which she had to produce the cash. One million dollars by Friday. Our final demand. That gave her six days.

Dumping the letter in the box file on her desk, Rose strode to the window and pushed aside the white gauze curtain patterned with golden Egyptian sphinx. She leaned against the cool pane, trying to quieten the storm raging inside her head. She had little hope this really was the last they'd ask of her. She wasn't going to think about how she was going to achieve the impossible, she would just do it. That was how she had got through the other three demands, coming up with the cash in time and buying another lease of life for her father. A Knight could do anything if they put their mind to it, that was the family motto. She just had to live up to it.

A scatter of autumn leaves fell on the damp pavement like fragments of singed parchment. Another gust lifted them and made them dance along the gutter. Before the message arrived, she had been reading about Egypt under the Greeks and Romans. Was that what the streets had looked like when the great ancient library in Alexandria had been destroyed? Irreplaceable fragments of knowledge wheeling up into the air to fall into the mud? New York morphed briefly into Ptolemaic Egypt in her imagination, then back to New York as a fire truck screamed by. If only she could wrap her thoughts up in the settled story of the past, dwell on the wonders and hazards of history where she felt she fitted in, and not have to deal with the unstable, impossible present.

A familiar car drew up at the kerb outside her family's brownstone house on Bank Street. Her neighbours, Mr and Mrs Masters and their son, Joe, got out of the vehicle, followed by a fourth person, a boy of Joe's age, not someone she recognized. The twitch of the curtain must have caught their attention because Joe looked up at her window and waved, his smile as engaging as ever. Better to pretend all was normal. She leaned forward to acknowledge him then turned away, but not before she saw him say something to the blond friend at his side. What was Joe saying? *That's Rose, the weird girl next door, keep clear.* Maybe. Even nice guys like Joe didn't understand her eccentric ways and strange home life. How could they? It defied her understanding and she was supposed to have a genius IQ. A girl who liked nothing better than to study archaeology but instead had to spend all her time raising money to free her small-time crook of a father from

8

the big bad guys. She felt like screaming at the unfairness of it all.

No more delays. She had to get down to work. Her dad's life depended on her and all she could do was keep him on this cash life-support until she could think of a way of transplanting him from his situation. Sitting down in front of her computer, she felt a pang of envy for Joe with his regular family. When she was little, he had featured in many of her daydreams about her future, imagining them both partnered up, he the Indiana Jones to her Lara Croft, hacking through jungles and discovering golden caskets—her brilliance and his brawn solving the puzzles. He'd never known about her infant hero worship as she had played out the drama purely in her mind. Just as well no one suspected geeky Rose of ever looking at the opposite sex. She would curl up with embarrassment if they knew.

She entered her passwords in her encryption programme. Joe and his family had been neighbours ever since she could remember and they had gone to the same local schools until Joe opted to go to London to finish college. Of course, she had looked up the place: the YDA on the South Bank of the Thames. It had taken a while to break through the rings of security but finally she'd found out the truth about his course: he was studying at the Young Detective Agency, an establishment that trained those in British sixth form—Junior and Senior year of high school—to pursue careers in law enforcement or related studies at university. She hadn't been able to hack into the internal system though; someone with serious programming skills had to be running their firewall and she had never enjoyed the jousting with another programmer that such a hack would entail. Leave that to the boys and their digital toys.

Rose opened the web browser and put on her reading

glasses. Good for Joe: the YDA would suit his character as he had a track record of defending the vulnerable at school. Looking back with the benefit of hindsight, she realized he'd always been less of the roguish rule-breaking Indiana Jones of her imagination and more of a Captain America type; he'd make an excellent police officer. Unfortunately, his choice had meant he was the last person she could confide in as all the men in her family fell far on the wrong side of the law.

Rose was in the middle of liquidating the last assets in her family account to invest in some high yield but risky shares in Japan when the front door bell rang. She was tempted to ignore it but the person pressed the buzzer again in three short bursts, clearly not going to go away.

'Shoot,' Rose muttered under her breath as she switched to her screensaver of Tutankhamun. 'Coming!' Checking the spy hole in the door, she saw that Carol Masters, Joe's mother, was waiting on the step. Stifling a sigh, she took off the bolts and chains. 'Hello, Mrs Masters, how are you?'

'Hi, honey. I'm fine, thank you. And how are you?' Her neighbour was wearing a striking dress of bright orange trimmed with green, home sewn as usual. She looked like a glorious Halloween pumpkin decoration, a black afro halo around her jolly face.

Rose managed a smile but doubted it reached her eyes. 'I'm OK, thanks.'

'And your father? I've not seen him for a while.'

She shrugged. 'He's busy at work. You know what he's like.'

'He works too hard—you can tell him that from me. I don't like the way he leaves you for such long hours.'

'I will.' Rose fidgeted with the latch chain, desperate to get back to her task. 'Can I help you?'

Mrs Masters handed over a home-made card decorated with British and American flags. 'I just came by with an invitation for you and your family. We're holding a little neighbourhood party tomorrow for Joe's friend, Damien. They go to school together in London.'

'Oh . . . that's nice.'

'Six thirty. Drinks and a barbecue in the yard if it's warm enough. So if you and your family are free, we'd love to see you.'

If her family was free. Well, sorry, but her dad was chained to a wall and big brother Ryan was who knew where, hanging out with his dubious associates. Rose feared the next time she heard from him would be when the police rang to ask her to bail him out. None of this could be shared with Mrs Masters. Rose had worked hard to convince her kindly neighbour that all was sweetness and light next door.

'Oh, I think Ryan and Dad will be busy.' Rose tucked a strand of her hair behind an ear, catching it back with her blue-rimmed glasses.

'But you won't be, will you, honey?' Mrs Masters treated her to her glowing smile, showing from where her son got his killer grin, brown eyes glowing with genial warmth.

Rose prided herself on her stubbornness but Mrs Masters beat her hands down at persistence. 'I guess not.'

'So then, we'll see you tomorrow?'

'Yes, thank you.' Rose made to close the door but she couldn't shut it until Mrs Masters had left. She wouldn't stoop to being rude.

Mrs Masters paused on the step, gaze going to the empty hallway behind Rose. 'Are you sure you are all right, Rose, honey? Nothing you want to tell me?'

A lump formed in her throat. Mrs Masters had always been there for her, stepping in when a female touch was needed, taking over the role abandoned by Rose's mother, who'd left soon after she was born. Carol had baked her birthday

11

cakes and explained how to handle puberty when no one else stepped up to the plate. Rose felt awful lying.

'Everything's fine, Mrs Masters.'

The neighbour bit her lip but then nodded, electing not to push. 'If you say so, Rose. But we're just next door if you need us.'

'Yes, I know. Thank you.' Rose was finally able to close the door. She leaned back against it, listening to the muffled sounds of the street—Mrs Masters walking away, a passing car, a distant siren, a dog barking. She didn't have time to wilt if she was to make a million dollars by Friday.

Forcing herself to stand up straight, Rose went back to her computer.

After having taken a quick shower in the bathroom off the guest bedroom, Damien came down with a sneaky slide on the banister from the top floor of the narrow town house to the kitchen. His jet lag wasn't too bad. He was looking forward to a couple of weeks with Joe on this working holiday in New York, possibly with some time for rock climbing upstate if their official task was soon over. His eighteenth birthday fell towards the middle of his stay so he hoped to mark it with Joe on a mountain top somewhere. After the intense episode in London with the Scorpion gang, followed by the Kyle incident, he was more than ready for a few weeks in the slow lane.

'Thank you for collecting me from the airport, Mr Masters,' Damien said as he joined the family at the table for a late breakfast. 'You really didn't need to do that. I'd've been fine jumping in a taxi.'

Mr Masters looked at him over the top of the *New York Times*. 'We wouldn't let a guest find their own way. You're a stranger in our city and the cabbies at JFK are sharks.'

'Now, now, Pat, your brother-in-law's cousin drives a cab,'

said Mrs Masters ladling pancake batter into a heavy frying pan. A wonderful smell and sizzle filled the kitchen.

'You're not talking about Richie, are you? Then I rest my case,' said Mr Masters with a smile at his wife.

'Oh, you! He's not so bad.'

'Honey, he's not so good neither.'

Damien chuckled at this easy byplay and helped himself to some orange juice from the carton on the table. Joe had warned him that Mr and Mrs Masters would treat him like one of their children rather than a well-trained detective in his final year at college. It wasn't an age thing with them but the family culture. *Mom and Dad would be Mother and Father to the whole world if we let them*, Joe had said. Damien now understood what he meant.

Joe came in with the mail and put it between the salt and pepper shakers. 'Feeling OK, Damien? Not too tired?'

'I'm fine. What've you got planned for me?' Damien slid further along the bench in the breakfast nook to make room for his friend.

'Eat your breakfast first, sugar,' said Mrs Masters, placing a big stack of pancakes in front of him. 'Maple syrup or honey?'

'Syrup, thanks.' Damien got the message he was expected not to talk about business with Joe until after he had eaten. He drenched his pancakes in amber-coloured syrup and dug in. 'These are great, Mrs Masters.'

She placed two more plates in front of her menfolk then joined them at the table. 'Joe, would you do something for me, hon?'

'Of course, Mom.' Joe sliced banana in little pale discs over his breakfast.

'I'm worried about Rose. Will you go visit her later—get her out of that house? I swear she's not ventured out at a weekend for months. She goes to school and comes home—that's all.' Mrs

Masters spooned yoghurt and blueberries over her pancakes, making a neat mound. 'And I've not seen her father for ages. She says he's working but I know her too well to fall for that.'

'Oh, come on: how do you know for sure she's lying, Mom?' asked Joe. 'Maybe he really is just busy?'

'Uh-huh, no way. She should never play poker, she has this tell—she tucks her hair behind her ear when she's nervous—she's done it since she was little. Believe me, that poor girl is a bundle of nerves at the moment. I wouldn't be surprised if Don's had to hide from his creditors—she acts as if she expects the debt collectors each time I call round. Ask her to go out with you and Damien—see if you can find out what's going on, will you, Joe?'

Damien didn't like the sound of his visit being hijacked by babysitting a neurotic housebound neighbour but kept that thought to himself. He had promised his friends back home to be on his best behaviour for Joe's sake.

'Sure, I'll see what I can do,' said Joe at once.

'Perfect.' Mrs Masters patted his hand.

'Someone should teach Don a lesson for neglecting that girl,' grumbled Mr Masters, folding up the newspaper so he could do justice to his pancakes. As a retired school principal, he appeared frustrated he couldn't be the one to set the punishments any more. 'And Rose's older brother's no better. Only time I expect to see him is when I watch *New York's Most Wanted*.'

Now that was more promising. 'You live next door to crooks?' asked Damien, thinking it would be entertaining to spy on them for a few weeks to get an insight as to how crime worked American-style.

Mrs Masters pursed her lips. 'We don't like to speak of it—for the sake of that poor girl.'

'Yes, they're crooked.' Mr Masters was clearly less inhibited about the matter than his wife. 'Neither Don nor Ryan choose the straight and narrow way if there's a winding devious route on offer. Both are charming, can talk themselves in and out of trouble most days, but I'm sorry to say they're rotten.'

'No one is beyond salvation, Pat,' said Mrs Masters reprovingly, nodding to the little white statue of the Virgin Mary that presided over her kitchen from the ledge above the sink.

Mr Masters shook his head. 'Carol, why do you have to be so generous to everyone? You should save your efforts for Rose. She's the only one who deserves it.'

Mrs Masters waved off her husband's cynicism. 'Which takes me back to my request. You'll call by, will you, Joe?'

Joe swallowed his mouthful, used to spectating while his parents had one of their usual discussions. 'I said I would, Mom. I've always looked out for Rose—you know that.'

'Thank you.' Pleased to have arranged the world to her liking that morning, Mrs Masters settled down to eat. 'It's so lovely to have a British guest. What do your parents do, Damien, dear?'

'They're not crooks, if that's what you're asking,' Damien replied with a smile at Mr Masters.

'Oh, you!' Mrs Masters chuckled. 'I never suggested such a thing.'

'They're doctors. They work with a medical charity in northern Uganda.'

'Oh, how wonderful! What lovely people they must be.' She balanced her chin on the back of her folded hands, elbows propped on the table, contemplating such cheering self-sacrifice.

Lovely for all their patients, not so great for their son. Damien had been told numerous times that the emergency just rushed into hospital was so much more important than his needs. It was OK to hear that once or twice maybe, but in their line of work it became an everyday brush-off. Tough for a five-year-old to understand when left to celebrate his birthday alone with just a babysitter. He didn't think he'd ever really had their attention when he was little. Nothing wrong with what they did, but they shouldn't have thrown a child into the mix. 'Yeah, they're saints, that's for sure.' He could not entirely hide his note of scorn.

'And how long have they been serving abroad?'

'Ever since I remember. I grew up in East Africa with them until I came back for high school in the UK. I see my parents maybe once a year. I live with my Uncle Julian in the holidays. He's got a flat in London—Greenwich. You know: where the international time zones are measured from?'

'I'm glad there's someone at home for you.'

'Yeah, he's a cool guy.'

Every plate at the table was polished clean. Joe got up to clear and Damien joined him, ignoring Mrs Masters' protests that he was a guest.

Once out of earshot of his parents, Joe flicked the tea towel at the back of Damien's legs. 'You're looking a bit out of condition. Wanna go for a run?'

Knowing he was at peak fitness and Joe was just yanking his chain, Damien flicked Joe back, getting one in on his ribs. 'Yeah, if you think you can keep up.'

Now in running gear, Damien followed Joe to the boardwalk that curved along the edge of the Hudson River. It felt good to be out in the air even if it was tainted with car fumes. At least the open water blew some of that away. The river was a blue-grey, strikingly wild in the middle of a city, the huge weight of water seeming to tug at the shore, giving the sense that nothing was fixed. A fringe of parkland trees along the boardwalk

16

made the surface slippery underfoot as the leaves had started to drop. The two friends ran at a brisk pace, settling in time with each other, their feet pounding on the pavement, kicking up twigs and crunching on sycamore seeds. Tiny spits of rain blew in from the sea, the sky unable to decide if it would bring sunshine or showers. Sleek yachts and humbler fishing boats bobbed restlessly in the local marina, ropes ringing on masts that swayed like metronomes counting out the city's upbeat time signature. The weather reminded Damien of London. As they headed south, Damien caught glimpses between buildings of the iconic skyline of Manhattan—the Empire State and the financial district. This was a city after his own heart: slick, wise-cracking, and shiny. From here the gathering of skyscrapers looked like a Cadillac engine stripped down for some sky mechanic to tinker with the sparkplugs.

Damien drew level with his friend. 'So, Joe, how are you really?' Joe had taken a few months off after a bruising mission undercover in an English boarding school. He'd been drugged and brainwashed before he was able to get out. Damien had been out of his mind with worry for his friend but he didn't normally do touchy-feely stuff like talking about emotions.

Joe gave him a firm look, no shadows in the expression of his brown eyes, his skin in good condition with a healthy dark glow. 'I'm fine now, thanks for asking.'

Enough said. Damien couldn't afford people to suspect he had a softer side, not if he was going to be any good at his job. The boys ran on in silence, leaving unspoken how disturbed Joe had been that he had almost let down his friend and colleague, Kieran Storm, under the intense pressure exerted by his captors.

Damien gratefully changed the subject. 'So what's the deal over here? Isaac said he'd had you working on something for him?'

'Yeah, that's right. Isaac's been talking to someone in the

FBI who's interested in setting up a branch of the YDA over here, a sister organization to the one he established in London. He wants you to meet her so she can ask you about your training.'

'So you've met her already? What's she like?'

Joe thought for a moment. 'Impressive.'

'In what way? Is she an Owl, Cobra, Cat, or Wolf?' The students at YDA had renamed the four streams of detective training after the characters of these animals and used them as a shorthand to assess people. Damien's own stream—the Cobras—considered themselves the sharpest operators, able to make the tough calls and balance risk. Joe's Cats were better at blending and getting close to the mission target. Isaac said the YDA had no elite stream; difference was welcome as members of each group balanced the other when paired on a mission.

Joe wiped his wrist over his brow. 'I'd say she's more Cobra than anything else.'

'Then I'm looking forward to meeting her already.'

'Thought you would like that. I've set it up for Monday when she does a career talk at my old school. That way you get the weekend to settle in and you can hear the standard pitch made to high school kids considering a career in law enforcement.'

They turned for home. As they crossed between parked cars, Damien recalled Mrs Masters' request. 'So, Joe, what do you think is going on next door?'

'Dad's right: the Knights are trouble. The son, Ryan, has always been bad news. Anyone with a grain of sense round here knew to steer clear of him.' They headed away from the river, pausing on the pavement to let a police car go past. 'The mom lit out soon after Rose was born to return to her career as a dancer in Vegas.'

Damien choked on that image. 'You lived next door to a showgirl?'

'Briefly. Shame I was too young for her to make an impression.' Joe gave him a mischievous grin. 'Mom says Belle Knight looked as sweet as candy but inside was as tough as nails. In that house, Rose is the exception—like she's been put in the wrong family entirely—a flamingo in a pack of jackals.'

Damien wiped a wrist over his brow, enjoying the glow brought by exercise. 'How's she different?'

'You'll recognize the father and brother: standard crooks—too bright to be happy in a regular job but not bright enough to make something of themselves, always after the shortcut to a fortune. But Rose, well, she's amazing—unique. It's her ability that keeps a roof over their head.'

'I guess the rents round here are pretty high?'

'Astronomical. Rose handles the family share portfolio and pays the bills with the dividends. You can bet her family have also tried to exploit her talent but she's just not interested and doesn't want to get dragged over to the shady side of the street.'

'She could make a mint.'

'Yeah, and she'd give Kieran a run for his money on computers if she could be bothered, but she prefers history—ancient history.'

Damien laughed.

'Last time I asked her what she wanted to do on graduation, she told me she'd just turned down a place for Computer Science at MIT—talent scouts had offered her a full scholarship and were going to advance her a year. They want more bright girls to take up computing.'

'Serious stuff. Is she insane?'

'No, she said she wanted to study Archaeology and Anthropology. She'll probably find some way of qualifying for a scholarship for that too. She'd prefer to dig around in the dirt finding bits of broken pottery than sit at a keyboard manipulating code.'

Neither option appealed to Damien. 'Weird.'

Joe shrugged. 'Just Rose. She's not your usual kind of girl, Damien, so try to be nice to her when you meet her.'

Damien felt a tinge of hurt that his friend doubted him. 'What do you mean? I can be nice.'

Joe slowed down outside his house to stretch. 'She needs handling with care.'

Damien didn't have time for whingeing females. 'Joe, girls get treated as equals round me. If they have a problem with that, then tough.'

'Then keep your distance as a favour to me. You two would be oil and water.'

'OK, fine. I'll be a model of diplomacy. Keep at arm's length.' Damien didn't think that was too big an ask. A geeky girl who liked old pottery was hardly a huge temptation. They'd have nothing in common.

'I'll ring on her doorbell to see if we can get her to come out with us later. And you, just look friendly or something.'

Fixing on what he hoped was an amicable smile, Damien trailed Joe up the steps to the neighbour's brownstone, curious now to see the fragile flower his friend was making such a fuss about. Did Joe fancy her? His remarks hadn't suggested that but he obviously had a major blind spot where the manipulating damsel-in-distress was concerned. Joe might even need protecting from her if she was going to abuse his concern.

Joe cast him a warning look over his shoulder. 'Be nice.' He pressed the buzzer.

No answer.

He pressed it again.

Nothing.

Knocking sharply, Joe called out. 'Hey, Rose, are you all right in there?' He pressed his ear to the door. He must've heard something this time because he stood up. 'She's coming.'

The door opened, chain still on. A pair of deep chocolate brown eyes peered through the gap, framed by a creamy complexioned face dotted with a scatter of pale golden freckles. Damien had to admit she was surprisingly gorgeous. 'Hey, Joe.' She took off the chain and opened the door.

First positive impression flew out the window. She was very pretty but, frankly, even that could not distract from the fact that she was extremely oddly dressed. Her long red hair was bundled up in—was that a sock she'd tied round it? She was wearing a ratty old man's cardigan over a T-shirt that had a maths equation across the front—obviously a message to those who could decipher the signs. Damien had thrown a party when he had given up maths after GCSEs.

Joe stepped closer to give her a hug. She pulled away quickly. Amused by this eccentric neighbour, Damien had to shift to one side of Joe to keep his view of her.

'You OK, Rose?' asked Joe. 'I was worried there for a moment when you didn't answer.'

Her gaze lifted over Joe's shoulder to met Damien's eyes. Her expression shuttered from pleased to neutral. 'I'm fine, Joe. Why wouldn't I be?'

'Cool. My friend and I were wondering,' Joe said, gesturing to Damien who was standing at his back, 'if you'd like to come out with us later to catch a movie or something?'

'No, thank you.' Her voice was a softened version of the distinctive New York accent Damien could hear everywhere.

'It doesn't have to be a movie. You can say what you'd prefer to do—Damien won't mind.'

'Sorry—I really can't.' She folded her arms revealing a bangle of paperclips around her wrist.

21

'Mom says you've not taken a break for weeks,' pressed Joe. 'I'm sure you're ahead of your schoolwork; you can take a night off.'

'I can't. I've got an assignment to finish.' A lock of glossy red hair got loose from the sock and fell over her cheek. It was an amazing colour, like the shine on a chestnut fresh from the husk. She tucked it back.

'Aw, come on, Rosie, come keep two guys company for just a few hours. Damien's never been to New York before. He'd like to be shown around by a local.' Joe rested a hand on the door frame, leaning in.

'I'm sure you'll do just fine on your own, Joe, showing your friend the sights. You've only been away a year so you won't have forgotten. Oh, there's the phone. I really have to go.' She shut the door in their faces. Joe had to move his fingers quickly so as not to get them pinched.

Back on the pavement, Joe paused, scanning the blank house front for clues. 'There was no phone call. She's in trouble.'

Damien grinned. 'You didn't tell me she was . . .' He sought for a kind word to describe the weird mixture of good looks and downright eccentricity and couldn't find one. 'Like that.'

Joe rubbed the back of his neck with both hands, elbows out. 'Yeah, well, I did mention the showgirl mother. Great genes.'

'But what's with the sock?'

'She just doesn't notice that stuff.' Joe dropped his arms. 'Why do you think I had to spend most of my Junior High years defending her?' He gave Damien a meaningful look. 'I worry I'm not around any more. She's definitely got more unique while I've been away.'

'Unique? Is that would you call howlingly eccentric? At least she's very easy on the eye—if you can get past the charity shop clothes, that is.'

22

Joe shook his head. 'You really do plumb the shallows, don't you, Damien?'

'I never understood the attraction of the deep.'

Joe got out his front door key. 'I'd've thought now you've seen Kieran with Raven—and Nathan with Kate—that would've taught you something about girls—about not judging books by covers.'

'Yeah, that I'm not going to get caught like them. Those two are no fun any more—they're so happy and devoted. We're way too young to be tied down. Me, I intend to be free to sample widely.'

Joe was no poster boy for going steady either. 'Fine, but no sampling next door, OK?'

Damien almost choked on his laughter. 'No chance of that. She's nice looking but I'm not really into making a move on someone with her kind of accessories. Did you notice the paperclips?'

Joe tried not to smile. 'Don't mock her. She's a friend.'

'Your instructions are noted, Commander.' Damien tapped his forehead in an ironic salute. 'I'll treat your neighbour with absolute respect.'

Joe gave him a dubious look. 'OK, we'll see how that goes.'

Chapter 2

Sunday evening arrived too quickly. Rose pushed away the keyboard. As much as she would like to ditch the party next door to get on with her task, Rose knew that Mrs Masters wouldn't let her get away with it. Looking on the bright side, if she went to the party and stayed up then she'd be awake for the opening of the Asian markets and then the London stock exchange. She'd made half the amount needed but still had to decide her strategy to double it in short order. She could then bring her gains over to Wall Street and still make it in time for registration. It was essential her school didn't get wind of the fact she had effectively been abandoned at home. Official interest in her predicament would sign her father's death warrant, his captors had been very clear about that.

Stretching cramped muscles, she turned her thoughts to what she might wear for the party. Her stomach rumbled, reminding her she hadn't eaten since a hasty breakfast of a stale bagel after a few hours' sleep last night. A shower was a must. Voices in the backyard next door told her she was already running late; the party was starting without her.

In the bathroom, she caught sight of herself in the mirror. Oh heck, she'd opened the door with her ponytail tied up by a white sock! She only vaguely remembered grabbing the first thing to hand when her hair had got into her eyes. And her dad's cardigan—she'd been wearing it so she was surrounded by his comforting smell but even she could see it was dowdy in the extreme. No wonder that boy had been smirking.

Diving under the cold shower—something was wrong with the boiler but she didn't have time to fix it—she briskly soaped herself and washed her hair. She then towelled herself dry, bundled her hair in a terrycloth turban and yanked open the doors to her wardrobe. The meagre selection reminded her that she hadn't bought anything for herself for a very long time. Mrs Masters liked girls to dress up for her parties so it would have to be a dress or a skirt. She had a green one that used to reach her knees. It now hit her mid-thigh, shorter than she liked, but really there was no other choice. She was nervous about her legs—they were too long. Normally she'd hide them under calf-length skirts and jeans. Was the dress too short? She thought she remembered seeing other girls wearing skirts like that so it might not matter. Oh why, oh why, didn't she understand these things? What was in and what was out made absolutely no sense to her and she was endlessly making mistakes. If she'd performed as badly in her chemistry practical exam, she would have blown herself up. That was her dress sense: a combination of unstable elements.

Rummaging in the back of a drawer, she found some nylons without holes—a minor miracle in itself—and then finished the outfit with a three-quarter-sleeved white and purple polka dot cardigan and black pumps. Black went with everything, didn't it? Blasting her hair upside down with the hairdryer, she then pulled a quick brush through it. Her hair was the only reliable thing about her appearance: she could mistreat it but it always seemed to fall OK in the end. Her hairdresser said she had compliant hair—Rose regarded it as the only part of her life under control. She made a quick pass with some basic make-up in the mirror. Last touches were her hieroglyph gold earrings and matching necklace—the eye of Horus—that Ryan had given her last birthday in a rare fit of brotherly inspiration. She hoped he hadn't stolen them. She took a final look in the mirror. She looked awful. Was it the cardigan or the dress—or both?

The buzzer rang. As expected Mrs Masters had sent someone to extract her out of the house. Going to the door, she saw that the messenger this time was Mr Masters.

'Good evening, Rose. My, don't you look charming. I see my visit was unnecessary but Carol thought you might have forgotten.'

'Hello, Mr Masters. Sorry, I was just running late.' Did she really look nice or was he just being polite?

He held out his arm with old-fashioned gallantry. 'Then may I escort you to the ball, my lady.'

'Oh, thank you.'

Pausing only to grab her keys, she set the alarm before shutting the door and then accepted his arm. He patted the back of her hand, a silent offer of comfort, a promise that everything would be all right. Though he didn't cross-examine her like his wife, his kind of persuasion to trust was even more dangerous. She had to lighten the mood before she confessed how scared she was—how she feared she wouldn't be able to come through this time with the ransom.

'Is Joe's friend enjoying his visit?' she asked. *The smirking Brit*, she added silently. She had already decided she didn't like him. He'd seen her at her very worst and even she had enough vanity to be embarrassed about that.

'Damien? I think he's having a fine time. The boys are talking about going rock climbing upstate next week. But why don't you ask him yourself?' Mr Masters conducted her into the small backyard and pushed her gently towards Joe and his friend. 'I've duties at the barbecue. You have fun now, sweetheart.'

Rose hesitated on the wooden decking of the terrace. This was just the kind of event she hated. People expected her to make small talk, whatever that was. Joe had spotted her and smiled but his friend still had his back to her. A flicker of self-directed anger flared. The two were the kind of boys her high school friends swooned over: one tall and dark, the other tall and fair, standing so confidently like two gods visiting from the underworld, Ra and Amun, both kings of kings in god terms. Those girls would mob them at the least encouragement to make their offerings but Rose just felt inadequate, a lesser handmaiden not allowed to approach the shrine. She looked for another person to talk to but the other people at the party were either older or far younger, a point made forcefully by a neighbourhood toddler colliding with her legs and making her stagger forward.

'Jimmy!' called his mother from the other end of the terrace.

Joe reached her in an instant and swooped down to catch up the little boy. 'Careful, Tiger: you mustn't manhandle the ladies. It's not cool.'

Jimmy chuckled and patted Joe's cheeks with flat and possibly sticky hands.

Rose squinted down at her legs. Two chocolate coloured handprints now decorated her calves.

'At least he missed your dress,' said Joe's friend with a swift smile. His ice-blue eyes twinkled with amusement as he swept her green and purple-white combination and lingered a little on the handprints.

'Maybe he's just pointing out that nylons are one of life's more idiotic creations.' Rose bent down to try and repair the damage. She wanted to extract herself quickly from the conversation but Joe had moved off to return the toddler to his parents, leaving her stranded. She sought something relevant and interesting to say to fill the pause. 'I blame Wallace Carothers.'

The British boy's smile froze, body tensing, eyes scanning the company. 'Who? I don't think I've met him yet.'

'Inventor of nylon through condensation polymerisation.'

His alert stance relaxing, the Brit looked a little bemused as people often did when she dropped interesting facts into conversation. Did people not do that normally? 'Yeah, he sounds a real villain. So, er, Rose, we didn't get introduced yesterday, did we? I'm Damien—a friend of Joe's from London.'

'Nice to meet you.' Chin down, Rose was conscious that she was staring at the toecaps of his shoes. They looked very smart—probably some designer brand she would know if she paid attention to that kind of thing.

'Joe says you like ancient history?'

Was that small talk? She could see Joe standing close by chatting to the toddler's mother while the woman cleaned the boy's hands. He was angled to keep an eye on his friend and her at the same time. 'Yes, I do.' Rose could tell her tone was overly defensive for an innocuous comment.

'Any particular period?' Damien gestured that they should take a seat on the garden bench.

'You really want to know?' She shivered in her thin dress.

'Are you cold? Let me get you a warm drink.' Proving the tradition of the English gentleman was not dead, he snagged some hot apple juice from the bar by the barbecue, returning swiftly to her seat. 'Here. Mr Masters said he thought it was too cold to eat out but Joe's mum was not to be stopped.'

Rose cradled the glass sitting in a pretty silver holder, allowing the warmth to seep into her palms. Her embarrassment over the Carothers mistake faded. 'I'm not surprised. I can't believe it's almost Halloween.' That sounded like small talk, didn't it?

'So what's your favourite era?'

'I don't have one.' Rose sipped. The juice was still too hot to drink and she regretted it the moment she put the cup to her lips. 'I like it all.'

'But you must have a favourite aspect. Ancient pottery maybe?' He really was working really hard to make conversation with her, Rose realized. Was she being chatted up or subtly mocked?

'Pottery? Not so much, though it's vital for dating sites.' A mischievous impulse awoke inside her. She couldn't resist the temptation of seeing how long it would be before smug Damien's eyes glazed over. 'But if I have to pick a favourite I think I like forensic examination of burials the most.'

He stretched an arm along the back of the seat. 'Awesome.'

'We can do so much now with technology, seeing inside the outer wrappings of mummies without even having to unwind them, analysing teeth and bones to find out what the ancient people ate and what they died of.'

Rose was surprised to find that his eyes didn't glaze over; they actually latched on to her face with more acuity. 'That sounds really cool—like police work. They can do virtual autopsies these days with some of the best equipment.'

'But these are very, very cold cases I'm afraid.'

He laughed, a wonderful rich sound quite at odds with his disturbing self-possession. 'Yes, I guess they would be. Tell me more about them.'

Was he laughing with or at her? 'Well, they've done scans of Tutankhamen recently—you know, the boy pharaoh?—and discovered he probably had a genetic illness.'

He rubbed a fleck of dirt off the knee of his jeans. 'All that intermarrying—couldn't have been good for the pharaohs.'

'That's right.' She gave him credit for making the link so rapidly. 'They had thought until then that he'd died in a chariot accident.'

'That sounds far more interesting.'

'And a definite chance for foul play, but maybe after all he died in his bed.'

'A case for CSI Luxor.'

Whatever the British visitor's motives, she was beginning to feel at ease with him. 'Wouldn't that be a great programme? Something I might actually watch, unlike most of the programmes on TV where people eat beetles and such.' She had never understood the attraction of witnessing people suffer like some Grand Guignol drama, which seemed to sum up half the reality TV programmes she had caught her dad and Ryan watching.

'No, I don't see you as someone who's keen on TV.'

'How right you are. I like dancing programmes though—watching someone learn a new skill. Oh, I think Joe wants you.' Joe was standing by the barbecue gesturing at his friend with a rather scary looking fork. Rose was rather disappointed because she had never managed so long an exchange with anyone before. She was even revising her 'smug' verdict, dialling down to 'smooth'.

'And here I was thinking I was a guest,' Damien said wryly. 'Looks as if they want me to work. Well, it's been nice talking to you. See you later.' Damien got up to join his friend. Rose watched in amusement as Joe loaded him down with a tray and gave him some terse orders. She wasn't an idiot. She could guess that Joe was worried that his friend would find out what an odd creature lived next door. Too late, Joe, they'd already discussed ancient autopsies.

For the next ten minutes, Rose hung around at the edge of other girls' conversations, filling up on the snacks and trying to look as if she fitted in. The yard was getting busy and it was hard to see who else was there. Most of the people her age gathered around Joe and Damien, the loudest and most lively spot in the whole party. Rose moved a little closer. Some clown—oh, big surprise: Marco Andreotti, a boy from her year at school—had a bag of chillies that a cousin had bought in Mexico and was challenging others to try them. Rose had forgotten that Joe played baseball with Marco and so naturally would invite him. Marco was a good-looking guy despite his slightly wonky nose. He'd been hit by a ball in the face in fourth grade. Unfortunately her brother Ryan had been the one pitching and she'd been paying for it ever since.

'Come on, guys, are you all wimping out on me?' crowed Marco as Akim, another baseball player, gagged on the first bite and backed off.

Akim pushed away the fatal red pepper Marco was thrusting under his nose. 'That's really lethal. Can't do it, Marco. No one can eat a whole one of those.'

Marco smiled, making sure his little group of girlfriends could see him. 'I could.'

'Go on, Marco. Prove it,' said Akim.

'Only if someone else takes up my challenge, or what does that prove?'

That you're monumentally stupid, thought Rose. The chilli was stacked full of capsaicinoids designed to deter mammals from eating it—why pit yourself against a natural force?

'I don't think you've eaten one,' grumbled Akim. 'It's impossible. You are so full of it, Marco.'

'If no one takes up my challenge, then you'll never know, will you?' Marco put an arm around his date, Lindy Baker, one of the most popular girls in their class. She was sleek and pretty, with a great river of plaited black hair extensions. Rose thought Lindy could do much better than Marco but unaccountably Lindy seemed to like him. At some point, Rose decided, she really must investigate the elements that went into human attraction; whatever they were, they certainly weren't logical.

'I'll do it.' Sir Smoothness of London Town had stepped forward.

Joe tried to hold him back. 'Damien, these aren't your normal kind of chillies.'

'Yeah, I got that, Joe. Let's see if your friend here will go through with it.'

Marco pulled a mocking sad face. 'Look, you're from England, right, Damien? I doubt you know much about hot chillies.'

'And you've clearly never been to Bradford and had a curry.' Damien's remark went over everyone's head, apart from Rose who knew, thanks to her photographic memory for facts and figures, that the city had a reputation for the spicy cuisine of its large Asian minority.

'Aw, man, this is a nuclear weapon of a pepper.' Marco didn't seem so confident now someone had taken up his challenge.

'Bring it on.' Damien held out a hand.

Marco measured out two of equal length from his grocery bag. Rose wondered if Joe was going to intervene but saw that he was leaning against the porch fence with a resigned expression on his face.

'So it's bite for bite?' asked Damien.

Marco swallowed. 'Yes. And the first one to chicken out loses.'

'Fair enough. Joe, give us a count down.'

The little crowd went quiet as Joe counted down from three. On one, Damien took a bite of his pepper, eyes fixed on Marco who was taking longer about his mouthful as if uncertain which end to start. Rose expected Damien at least to howl and complain but he kept chewing, the only sign of suffering the slightly reddened colour of his face and teary look to his eyes. Marco took a bite and chewed quickly.

'Oh man, oh man,' Marco hissed.

'That was fun. Again.' Damien's tone was relentless.

Joe counted down and the boys bit down. Marco immediately spat out his and dived for his soda. 'I can't. You win. Whoa-whoa-whoa, that h . . . hurts!'

Coolly, Damien swallowed. 'A little hot, I grant you. Nothing a real man can't handle.'

Joe punched him on the shoulder. 'Yeah and you just have to prove you're the man each and every time don't you, you moron.'

The crowd applauded and whistled his achievement. *And what had he achieved?* thought Rose. *Proof that he was as idiotic as Marco.*

'What do I win?' Damien asked.

Marco was still gasping so his reply was to thrust the remaining chillies at Damien who laughed. 'Great. I get the nuclear weapon vegetable. I'll put these inside.' He walked off.

I bet he's going inside to weep, thought Rose with some satisfaction. Damien might act cool but even he couldn't defeat chemistry.

Mrs Masters bustled into the middle of the group, a plate of sliced carrots and an avocado dip in hand. 'Are you all having a lovely time?' she asked, quite oblivious to the scene that had just played out.

'Yes, thank you,' replied Lindy, grabbing a handful of carrots and shoving them at Marco. 'Here: these will help.'

'Good, good.' Mrs Masters beamed at the young people around her. 'Joe, give me a hand with the burgers, please, so your father can take a break.'

Amused by Marco's undoing, Rose found a wooden toadstool seat on the edge of the flower border, allowing herself a little breather. She had made an effort, talked to one person, and soon it would be OK to leave without offending her neighbours. She was entering the home straight in her social marathon. So, occupied with thoughts of freedom, she failed to anticipate that her presence had not gone unnoticed, and it was too late to take evasive action.

'Hey, Ginger, how're you doing?' asked Marco, his voice a little hoarse, eyes bloodshot. Lindy was by his side, patting his arm consolingly.

'Don't call me that.' Rose stood up.

Lindy's eyes swept her outfit and came to rest on the handprints on her legs. She didn't need to say anything. Lindy wasn't bitchy or anything, she just didn't understand Rose and struggled to find things to talk about. 'Nice weekend, Rose?' she asked finally.

'Just great, thanks. When I'm not being used as a climbing frame by the under-fives.' Neither Lindy or Marco laughed, taking it as a serious statement. They weren't used to her making jokes. Why, oh why, didn't they teach you social banter at school? She'd have more real use for that class than many of the others.

'Have you done your assignment from calculus?' asked Marco.

'Not yet.' Schoolwork was the last thing on her mind.

'Aw, Ginger, I was counting on you. I'm stuck at number four.'

'I said don't call me that. And I haven't done it yet.' She wished she was a pharaoh who could click her fingers and have Marco sent off to build pyramids. The little drama played out in her mind, ending with Marco heaving granite blocks up impossible slopes.

He gave her one of his insincere smiles. 'I can't believe that. You've never failed to turn in a homework since first grade. You gotta help me.'

'Sorry, can't. You'll just have to use your own brain this

time, not zombie feed off mine—that's if the chilli eating hasn't burned out the remaining cells.'

Lindy giggled. She had no idea about the strength of the animosity between Marco and Rose. 'Aw, poor Marco. I think he's sorry he ever offered that challenge, don't you, Rose?'

Marco dropped his arm from Lindy's shoulder and gave his girlfriend a stiff little smile. 'Sorry, Linds, gotta talk to Ginger alone a sec.'

'OK, Marco.' Lindy turned away to speak to her friends. 'Be nice now. Don't bug her.'

'I'm just asking for a few pointers—nothing major.' Waiting till Lindy was out of earshot, Marco crowded Rose towards the flowering border. 'About that homework. You don't get it, Ginge: you've got to help me or I might just let the school know that you're home alone.'

'I'm not,' she said quickly. One step back and she'd crush Mrs Masters' dahlias.

'Really? That's not what Ryan told me.' Rose felt a swoop of despair. Ryan hung out with Marco's older brothers and it would be like him to blurt out something that got back to her classmate.

Go on the attack, she told herself, *don't let him bully you*. 'Ryan hasn't a clue what goes on at home—he's never there. Anyway I'm sixteen—it shouldn't matter to anyone.' She tugged the hem of her dress down, annoyed to find it riding up.

Marco shrugged. 'Fine. Then you won't mind the school counsellor checking on you?'

Desperation swirled inside her. 'You really are the lowest form of life aren't you, Marco? Just a cell division away from the primordial soup. I really haven't done the homework yet.'

'Then you'd better come to school early so we can compare notes tomorrow morning.'

She wanted to tell him where to stick his notes but dramatic free-spirited Lara-Croft-Rose, the Rose that walked rope bridges and snatched precious artefacts from the bad guys, was talked down by wary sleuth Nancy-Drew-Rose all too aware of the reality of her situation. 'Look, all right. OK. I'll help you tomorrow.'

He patted her cheek in a patronizing manner. 'Thanks, Ginger.'

Rose finally broke away at the expense of some pansies, retreating behind a spiky mahonia bush with its topknot of yellow flowers. She was furious with herself for allowing Marco to get to her. When her dad was back home, she'd think of a way of getting even. He'd certainly never get one more equation's worth of help from her once Don Knight was safe.

Her phone beeped. Checking the display, her heart sank. An earthquake in Kyoto—the Nikkei would be in free fall. Her investments. She had to go.

Without saying goodbye to her hosts, she hurried back to her computer to see if she could salvage anything from the disaster.

Damien was struggling to keep smiling but his throat felt like he'd drunk acid. Why did he always put himself through things like that? He had been so annoyed at the cocky attitude of that Marco guy that he'd given in to the impulse to take him down a peg or two. Training had helped hide the fact that he was hurting—he'd known he wouldn't have to eat the whole damn pepper before his opponent bottled out—but it was still a stupid thing to do. Though also very satisfying to emerge the clear winner.

'You are a complete headcase, you know?' said Joe, restocking his tray with meat from the barbecue.

Damien sipped the milk he had sneaked from the kitchen,

watching the guests from the party mingle. Marco had cornered Rose. She was hugging that awful purple spotted cardigan to her waist. How did she choose her clothes? With her eyes shut? He hadn't missed the world-class legs though, even while he was making completely respectful small talk about her odd affection for ancient stuff. She had been far more interesting than he expected, especially when her eyes lit up as she described the hunt for forensic clues. He had promised Joe not to bother Rose again even though their conversation had been totally innocent and actually not that boring. It seemed Joe didn't trust him to resist mocking his eccentric neighbour. 'Yeah, but you love me anyway.'

'I figured that the deed is its own punishment both now and tomorrow.'

'Don't remind me.'

'And you shut Marco up for once. That guy's more annoying than I remember.'

'You asked him to the party.'

'Habit—one I should break. He's now going to be pissed off and take it out on some poor sucker.'

Damien hadn't taken his eyes off the couple by the flower border. Rose was being told something she really didn't like by Marco.

'You mean like Rose?' he asked.

Joe craned his neck and swore. 'Damn. He's always hounding her to do his work for him. I told him to cut it out last year. I'd better go help.' He passed his tray of burgers into the hands of a startled guest. 'Congratulations, Lee: you've just been hired,' he told the boy, patting him on the back.

Pushing through the crowd, Joe made his way over to Marco. Intrigued to see how his friend dealt with the 'protect the neighbour' agenda, Damien tagged along. Could Rose not just stuff a sock in the guy's mouth; she seemed to have one on

hand at most times. Damien grinned at the thought but he'd
lost sight of Rose in the crush and was disappointed to find she
had gone by the time they arrived. Still, Joe looked as if he was
still on mission to put Marco right about a few things.

'Hey, Marco, can I have a word?' called Joe.

'Sure, Joe. Let's get another drink. Still feeling the after-
effects.' Marco rubbed his throat.

'Yeah, me too,' admitted Damien.

Marco gave him a sneer of a smile. 'Good—or I was going
to ask if you weren't an android the way you swallowed that
without a whimper.'

'I don't whimper.'

Marco's smile dimmed. 'Yeah, you're the man. I get it.'

Joe took him over to a table of drinks and selected another
Coke. Damien stepped in behind Marco, smoothly cutting
him off from his friends. Joe levered off the lid. 'It's about
Rose.'

Marco gave him a bemused look, too stupid to worry. 'You
mean Ginger?'

'Her name's Rose.'

'She's been Ginger to me since grade school.'

From the tense muscles of his back, Joe appeared close to
rearranging the smirking features in front of him. 'And even
then she asked you again and again not to call her that.'

'But I guess that nickname must be tempting for someone
with no originality,' said Damien with fake understanding. It
took Marco a second to realize he was being insulted.

'Hey, it's sweet. She likes it!'

Was this guy really as obnoxious as he sounded? 'She didn't
look too thrilled talking to you a moment ago.'

Marco shrugged. 'What's your angle, guys?' He swigged his
drink nervously.

Joe took a step closer. 'Marco, this is getting old. I've

warned you before. You need to back off Rose, OK? Do your own work.'

Marco put down his drink. 'You seriously still going on about that? Look, the girl's got more brains than the rest of us put together: it's her civic duty to share.'

The joke fell flat. Joe just looked at him. Beneath Mr Nice Guy Joe, Damien was pleased to see something a hell of a lot tougher lurked.

Marco gulped. 'Did she ask you to do this?'

'No.' Joe rubbed his chin. 'But it's interesting that you think she did.'

From the ticking muscle in his jaw, Damien could tell that Marco was annoyed but didn't dare escalate the encounter. He tried to shrug it off. 'Her family owes me.' He pointed to his broken nose. 'What's it to you if she helps me?'

'If it were just help, then I'd be cool with it, but we both know you're using her. And Rose is in no way to blame for what Ryan did to you—something that was just a sporting injury in the first place. If you mess with her again, I'll know— even in the UK.'

Damien could see the idiot was thinking 'out of sight, out of mind'. 'Funny thing about living in England is that it's just like here. Internet—airports. And I guess Joe also has holidays where he has nothing better to do than check up on folks back home. Isn't that right, Joe?'

'Now you come to mention it, Damien, I do. Christmas vacation isn't that far away now. I'll only be gone a few weeks.'

'So if some moron was upsetting a girl he thinks of like a sister, he wouldn't be too pleased.'

'Got it in one.'

'Do you think Marco's got the message?'

'Hard to tell. How about we drop in on my old high school tomorrow to see how Rose is doing?'

39

'Sounds a plan.' Clinking their bottles together, they walked off, leaving Marco alone with some decisions to make.

Rose was weeping. She'd started when she saw the news reports and then found she couldn't stop. She felt a complete cow that she wasn't crying primarily for the victims of the earthquake; she feared that her tears were mainly for the huge losses she had incurred. There was fading hope now of reclaiming the capital she needed to invest in time to multiply it for Friday's deadline. The news kept scrolling pictures of victims, dusty and shocked as they staggered around the ruins of their home. She was a horrid person not to care more for them.

By the time the sun came up, she had managed to recoup a hundred thousand. In order to live with herself, she sent a thousand to the disaster fund then shovelled the rest into energy shares in London, knowing it would be relatively safe there while she figured out what to do.

Up in her bedroom her alarm clock went off by the bed she hadn't slept in. A shower would have to suffice to keep her awake. After a quick cold soaking, she pulled on her usual school clothes of jersey and jeans. Looking in the mirror, she saw that she had huge dark shadows under her eyes; it would be an appropriate Halloween look on Friday but not so good for a Monday at school in front of astute teachers. She didn't have the make-up know-how to disguise it so she didn't even try. Grabbing a piece of toast and slathering it in peanut butter, she was out of the house before she even remembered her homework. Marco was going to kill her. If she hurried to school, maybe she'd have time to do it in the library before registration? Bypassing her usual coffee stop, she got on the subway and travelled the two stops to her school. Avoiding everyone's eyes, she fast-walked through the gates, crossed the yard to the library and sought out her usual study carrel in the history section. Her calculus was where she had stowed it in her bag on Friday, textbook unopened, list of questions stretching the length of the worksheet. Her brain felt like mush. Usually she would zip through problems like this like an aerial dancer roping down from the ceiling at the Cirque du Soleil; today she sat like a chump in the clown-car, wheels blown off. Resting her head on her crossed forearms, she took a couple of breaths in the quiet dark of the little cocoon she had made. Before she knew it, she was asleep.

Her doze was shattered by the bell for registration. She jerked upright. Oh Lord. All that she had managed to do was leave dribble marks on her empty sheet of paper. Stuffing her things back in her bag, she stumbled to her classroom. From the odd looks she attracted, she guessed she must be a wreck. She collapsed into a chair at the back and pulled out a folding brush with a mirror in the handle from her bag. Her nose had picked up a black tip from the pen she had slept on. Taking a tissue she tried to scrub it away but she feared she still had a grey mark.

Marco came in with his usual swagger. Rose hunched in her chair but his eyes skated over her and he sat on the other side of the room. Had he forgotten?

Lindy leant over from the next desk, holding out a wet wipe. 'Hey, Rose, you look like you need this.'

'Thanks, Lindy.' She took the offering and rubbed her nose.

'What did you do? Have a fight with a mascara wand?'

'Um, no.' Her reflection now looked almost normal. 'Had one with my pen.'

Lindy smiled. 'That figures. Did you enjoy Joe's party?'

'Oh, yes, I guess.'

'Marco so regrets bringing those chillies. You didn't stay

long?' Lindy got out her compact and checked her faultless make-up as if Rose's messiness might be catching.

'No, I had things to do.'

'Isn't Joe's friend gorgeous? He must be made of steel to eat that pepper. I'd really go for all that golden hair and skin and accent if I weren't already with Marco.'

'I guess he is . . . um . . . hot.' Rose knew she was terrible at this kind of conversation. She was surprised Lindy still kept on trying with her. She really was too nice for Marco. 'Didn't you think he was a bit smug though?'

'Oh, I don't know. I thought he smiled like he had a delicious secret. And that accent!'

Maybe when he looked at Lindy he appeared mysterious but not when he was smirking at Rose's appearance.

Mrs Fallon entered. 'Good morning, students.' She called up the register on the laptop and ran through their names, entering any absences on the database. 'Before you head off to class, there's just one announcement. Don't forget the career talk after school. We've a speaker from the Federal Bureau of Investigation—a real privilege for the school—so I expect to see all of you there.'

Rose would normally have been interested but she couldn't spare the time today. She kept her head down.

'It's our class's turn to provide student hosts so, Rose and Lindy, would you please be in the entrance hall to meet our guest at three. The principal wants you to show her around our science block.'

This couldn't be happening.

'Yes, Mrs Fallon.' Lindy preened, liking that she had been picked out. She was the best in the school at biology.

'Rose?'

'Yes, Mrs Fallon.' Rose felt the opportunities to recoup her losses rapidly disappearing.

The teacher gave her a second silent look before dismissing the class. As Rose passed her desk, Mrs Fallon put out a hand to stop her.

'Is something the matter, Rose?'

'Just didn't sleep very well last night.' Like not at all.

'I see. Something worrying you?'

'I'm fine.'

'Well, if you need to talk to someone, you know where to find me.'

Rose could not complain about the number of people offering to help her. If only it was a kind of problem that could be solved by confiding in a friend or teacher. 'Yes, I know. Thanks, Mrs Fallon.'

Seeing that her first class was calculus, Rose gave serious thought to cutting it but then decided it would raise more questions that the simple failure to do her homework. Other students forgot all the time. It shouldn't be a big deal. She slid into the last remaining seat at the front and prepared to duck attention.

Mr McGinty strode into the room and dropped his files on the teacher's desk with a thump. A heavyset man with a high complexion, he always looked as though he was in a bad mood even if he was feeling quite chipper; from the vibes rippling from him today, he definitely was not in his happy place. Rose got out her books and quickly scanned the problems wondering if she could scribble down a few answers to make her omission less of a sin. She read the first one and jotted down the workings.

'I won't say good morning,' he began. 'Because that would be a misnomer.' He swung round and slapped a book on Marco's desk. 'What does "misnomer" mean, Mr Andreotti?'

'Huh?' Marco gaped.

'Mr Graham?'

The next victim flushed. 'I thought this was calculus, not literature, sir.'

'Ignoramus. Miss Knight, can you explain?'

Normally she didn't mind Mr McGinty's intellectual bullying but just now she really didn't feel like playing his game. 'It means a name wrongly attributed to something.'

'Exactly. Thank goodness we have one student with a brain in the class. I've just endured the excuses of my sophomores lining up outside my form room to explain why they failed to complete their assignments over the weekend so I can tell you now no excuse will be allowed for my seniors.'

Not even working to save your father's life? thought Rose grimly, quickly scratching out the answer to number two.

'Who has the answer to number one?'

Rose joined the others in putting up her hand but he picked on another girl. She didn't listen to the answer as she was too busy trying to keep ahead of the pace of work like a railway worker desperately trying to lay the track in front of a train steaming down the line.

'I'm afraid that's wrong. Can you see where you went awry?' Mr McGinty had written the working down on the white board. 'No? Anyone? Miss Knight, can you help us out?'

Startled, Rose looked up at the board to see where they had reached. Number four. She hadn't got there yet. She ran her gaze over the workings and made a guess.

'Is there an error in the second line?'

Surprised, Mr McGinty checked his handwriting, so used to Rose being right. 'No, not there. What did you have for this one, Miss Knight?'

Rose glanced down at her half filled page, equations scrawled rather than neatly ruled as she would normally do. 'I . . . er . . . must've left that one out.'

A seasoned teacher, Mr McGinty scented student evasion.

'Show me.' He held out his hand for her pad. Swallowing, she passed it up to him. He scanned the page, eyebrows winging up. 'Stay behind after class, Miss Knight.'

Her fellow students were stunned. Rose had never got into trouble in any lesson before in her entire school career. Her embarrassment hit the red zone on her inner dial. Mr McGinty dropped the pad on her desk with a sniff of disdain. 'Anyone else?'

Marco reluctantly put up his hand. 'I think the value should be zero point five, not zero, zero point five.'

'Correct. Well done, Mr Andreotti. It seems none of us are quite ourselves today.' Mr McGinty ushered the lesson back on track.

Rose stared at her pad, deeply humiliated. Even Marco had done the work, which was bizarre considering how he had threatened her the day before. When the bell for the lesson rang, the class got up and hurried out, leaving her alone.

Mr McGinty returned to her desk. 'This isn't like you, Rose.' His finger rested on the scrappy work she had managed.

'I'm sorry, sir. I'll do it tonight.' She had to get home before the stock exchange closed.

'You'll do it in detention. No exceptions even for you.'

'I have to be student host to a visitor at three, sir.'

'Then come by after the career talk. I'll still be here as I've a parent–teacher consultation. You can explain then why my best student is acting like her GPA no longer matters to her. I'll expect you to have done the assignment by then too.'

'Yes, sir.' She got to her feet. Risking a quick glance at him, she saw his mouth was open to ask more. He was probably about to ask if everything was all right at home. 'I'll not let you down again, I promise.' She escaped before Mr McGinty could show he had a softer pastoral side under his bluster.

Chapter 3

Joe and Damien strolled through the school gates, Joe exchanging greetings with the older students hanging out in the concrete yard.

'No playing fields?' asked Damien, studying the late nineteenth century brick building with modern additions. It wouldn't be out of place in the East End of London, he decided, little flourishes gesturing to late Victorian whimsy in the arched windows and steeply pitched roof.

'No room here—real estate is too expensive in West Village. They bus the students out for field and track sports. Hey, Mr McGinty, how are you?' Joe stopped to shake hands with a red-faced man crossing the yard, whose furious expression only relaxed on recognizing his former student.

'Mr Masters—Joe—how are the British treating you?'

'Great, thanks. I've got one of them with me. Damien, meet Mr McGinty, my math teacher from way back.'

Damien held out his palm. 'Pleased to meet you, sir.'

Mr McGinty shook hands. 'Nice to meet you too. I'm glad I ran into you, Joe. I was wanting a word with you about Rose.'

Not another one. That girl had more people fretting over her than the most pampered pop princess.

'What's up?' asked Joe, brow wrinkled.

'You're neighbours, correct?'

'That's right.'

'Well, I'm worried about her. She's not herself. In class

today, she admitted that she neglected to do her homework.'
He announced it like it was a big deal. Damien couldn't count
the number of times he had come up with inventive excuses
for not having produced the goods. If it were a first offence, he
wondered why the teacher didn't cut her some slack.

Joe, however, looked shocked. 'Oh, yeah, I see.'

'I don't want to put her on report but I've given her
detention . . .'

'Do you want me to have a word with her?'

'Would you? That girl is so bright, she fairly dazzles us all.
I'd hate to see her throw it all away in the last few months of
high school.'

'I will. Thanks for letting me know.'

Mr McGinty gave a humph, relieved to have spoken his
piece. 'You're a good boy, Joe. We all miss you here.' He strode
off, returning to his usual spirits by barking at some loitering
students.

'Why has everyone got themselves in a twist about
her?' Damien asked. 'She's not the first person to dodge
homework.'

Joe headed for reception to sign in. 'You don't get it. She
would never leave schoolwork undone—not unless it was a
life or death situation. It's like Stephen Hawking flunking a
freshers' physics test.'

'Don't you think you're all making too much of it? Maybe
she just had an off couple of days. Maybe she just wants to
stop being so damned perfect and rebel against the Goody-
Two-Shoes image. Sounds like she needs it.'

'I've always thought that her rebellion was not to be such
a waste of space as the rest of her family. I'm going to get to
the bottom of this. Let's find her.' Joe stopped at the reception
desk. 'Hello, Mrs Trent.'

'Joe! Lovely to see you.' The grandmotherly receptionist

passed him a pen to fill in the visitors' log. 'Not coming back to us, are you?'

'Not this time. My friend and I have come for the career talk. We're guests of the speaker.'

'Then sign yourself in, dear. I'll get you some passes.'

'Would you know where Rose Knight is this lesson?' Joe scrawled Damien's name beneath his.

The receptionist checked her computer. 'She should be in Chemistry Lab Two.'

'Thanks, Mrs T.'

Amused, Damien followed his friend along a corridor lined with lockers. 'You know, I never get this kind of reception when I go back to my old school. The teachers usually heave a sigh of relief that they don't have to teach me any more.'

'What can I say? I'm just a nice guy.' Joe's eyes sparkled.

'Keep telling yourself that, mate, but I know you better. I've seen you in action.' Damien waited while Joe looked through the little window in the door into the lab. 'She there?'

'Yeah.'

'How long until the end of the lesson?'

A bell shattered the relative quiet of the corridor. 'No time at all.'

Doors flew open the length of the hall and students poured out of the classrooms. The noise was deafening. Damien stood back against the wall, watching as Joe went through another of his meet-and-greet sessions. Geez, all this adulation couldn't be good for the guy. If Joe wasn't careful, he'd miss Rose leaving her lesson. Just as anticipated, Joe was busy exchanging complicated handshakes with old friends as his neighbour slid out of her class, head down, course set in the opposite direction. Damien wove through the crowd and caught up.

'Hi, Rose. Good to see you again.'

'Oh. Hello, Damien.' She fiddled with the strap of her bag,

her slight frame weighed down by more than the load of her books. 'What are you doing here?'

'Just visiting. Let me take that.' He snagged it from her and slung it on his shoulder before she could refuse.

'I'm perfectly able to carry my own bag.'

'Humour me. I like to pretend I'm a nice guy sometimes.' And he didn't want her running off. 'Where are you going?'

'To the library. I've a free but I've got to catch up with some work.'

'Great. I'd love to see your library.'

'I don't have time to give you a tour.'

'Not asking for one.'

She massaged her forehead. 'Sorry—I didn't mean it to sound like that.'

'Bad day?'

'I've had better.' She checked her watch and doubled her pace.

Joe caught up with them. 'All OK, Rose?'

'Everything's fine and dandy.' She sounded irritated now. 'Your friend wants to see the library. Can't see why. It's just like your average school library—you know: books and computers. No surprises there.' She walked like a proud prisoner ascending the gallows, back ramrod straight.

'Did Marco leave you alone about the math homework?'

Her step faltered. 'Was that you?'

'I just told him to stop bugging you.'

'Thank you.' She rubbed her eyes wearily. 'I guess that will work for a while.'

'I told him that it was the end—no more stealing of your work. You tell me if he crosses the line again, Rose.'

'It's OK, Joe. When I've time, I'll deal with him. He's just a parasite.'

They'd reached the library but Joe held her back. 'Look, I

know you're busy but it's obvious to everyone that something's wrong. Can't you tell me?'

'Everyone?' She looked longingly at what she saw as the sanctuary of the library. 'Just money troubles—nothing important,' she admitted at last. Remembering Mrs Masters' observation, Damien waited for the tell of Rose tucking her hair behind her ear but it didn't come. Maybe they'd got the truth this time. 'Some investments have turned bad. I'll handle it.'

Joe frowned but had to accept her explanation. 'OK. Well, you know where to find us if you need help.'

'Yes.' She reached out to take her bag from Damien. 'Q and A finished?'

Reluctantly, Damien handed it over. Standing so close, he'd felt the tug of the light perfume she wore. He finally placed it: roses. Of course. Perfect for her. Funny, when she got so much else wrong about her appearance.

'Can we walk back with you after school?' asked Joe.

Rose blushed a furious shade of red. 'I've got a detention with Mr McGinty.'

'I know. We'll wait.'

'Fine. I can't seem to shake you off, can I?' She disappeared through the library doors.

'Why do I get the impression she only agreed to cut short an argument?' Joe and Damien followed her inside. 'So, Damien, this is the library.' He swept his hand to the high-roofed room.

'Yep. Books—tick—computers—tick.'

While Joe chatted to the librarian on duty in complete disregard of the notices demanding silence, Damien watched Rose set up her books in a study cubicle, slid on her reading glasses, and feverishly set to work. She had her phone on her lap and, in between writing down answers, she'd quickly look at her screen so that the librarian didn't see—and that was despite the poster in each section forbidding the use of mobiles in the strongest terms. He grinned. The little rebel. When she spotted him looking at her, she gave him a scowl which he returned with a smile. He was not the kind of guy to shop someone for chatting on Facebook illegally.

A bell rang in the hall accompanied by the thunder of students on the move again. Joe hooked Damien's arm, dragging his attention away from Rose. 'We've got to meet Agent Hammond. I'd said we'd see her in reception at two thirty.'

Reminded he was here on YDA business too, Damien joined Joe in battling against the tide of students outside the quiet haven of the library. Agent Hammond was already waiting for them in reception, a colleague standing behind her. Both were dressed in the FBI unofficial uniform of dark suits and white shirts. Damien received his first surprise when he noted that Hammond was in a wheelchair.

'Injured five years back protecting a senator,' Joe explained quickly.

Damien did not make the mistake of underestimating the agent because of that. He'd met enough army veterans in his training to know better. In his experience, the bigger the obstacle someone had to overcome, the more formidable the character. A dark-haired woman with almond shaped eyes, Hammond had an unlined face, making it very hard to guess her age. Her brown eyes held years of knowledge so Damien decided she might be late forties.

'Agent Hammond, this is my friend Damien Castle. I believe Isaac's told you about him?' Joe shook her hand.

'Hey, Joe, good to see you. And Damien.' She offered him a palm to shake. Damien noted the callouses which showed that she hadn't given up practising firearms. 'I've heard about you. Isaac describes you as quite the tough customer.'

Damien appreciated the character reference from his boss. 'We can't all be Good Cop like Joe.'

She smiled. 'And this is Jack Stevens, my driver for the day and a colleague with four years' experience. He's here to meet the kids at the career talk but also to help in my assessment of you two.'

Stevens removed his shades to greet them, before disappearing back behind them like Cyclops from the X-Men. Damien momentarily wondered if he should invest in a pair—it was a cool look.

'We've half an hour before the fun and games begin. The principal has arranged for coffee to be brought to a meeting room over there so let's get down to business.' Leading the way, Hammond propelled her chair into a brightly lit conference area decorated with trophies and photos of the school's teams. She gestured to them to take a seat at the long table as she moved a chair to make a space for herself. 'So, Damien, tell me why I should establish a branch of the YDA over here.'

Over the next thirty minutes, Damien enjoyed her expert grilling. She was particularly interested in the division into four types, testing his views as to whether that was really necessary or too restrictive. He assured her that the system was flexible to allow for movements between the different streams but that it did help distinguish different strengths and stopped students underestimating people who were not like them.

'To be honest, ma'am, I think a few years ago I would've totally not understood my friend Kieran without the system. I'd've dismissed him as a geek and not seen what he could add to a team. I would have been really wrong to do so and many missions would've suffered as a result, not to mention I'd've missed out on knowing a really great guy.'

'Ah, yes, Kieran Storm, Isaac mentioned him.' She checked her notes.

Joe smiled at Damien. 'We think he's Isaac's secret favourite—he's incredible.'

'But as you say, not an obvious candidate for training. An owl. In many places he would have been ushered off into an academic life and law enforcement would've lost a great asset. Hmm, yes, I see what you mean, Damien. The YDA system makes Isaac and his team look for diversity rather than a one-size-fits-all student. I think we weaken ourselves by narrowing our pool of talent.'

There came a knock at the door. Stevens went to answer. 'Come on in, Principal Chandler. Thanks for the loan of the room.'

'I guess we'll have to continue this later.' Hammond reversed away from the table as the headmistress entered. 'Ah, Mrs Chandler, I see you've brought us our student hosts. Hello, girls. I was told you were going to show us around the science facilities?'

The head teacher quickly introduced the girls before leaving to check on the arrangements for the talk. Damien wasn't that surprised to see Rose had been picked for the task of guide. A school would want to show off their brightest star. Pairing her with Lindy was a good move as the tall girl had the social ease the smaller redhead lacked.

'I'm so pleased to meet you, Mrs Hammond,' said Lindy.

'Agent Hammond, please. I'm on the job,' corrected the visitor.

'Oh sure. Sorry.'

'Don't apologize. You weren't to know the protocol.' Hammond made the introductions to the rest of the people in the room. When she reached Joe, he stopped her.

'It's fine, ma'am: we already know each other. Hi, Lindy, Rose: we've come for the talk too.'

'Good. Let's get going then.' Hammond fell in beside Lindy, Joe alongside Stevens, leaving Damien to walk with Rose.

'Get your work done?' Damien asked Rose as she hugged her bag to her chest. He made to take it again just to annoy her but she clearly wasn't going to surrender it this time.

'Yes, thanks.'

'And caught up with Facebook?'

'I wasn't . . .' She stopped. 'Yes.' She tucked a strand of hair behind an ear.

'So you weren't checking your messages. What were you doing?'

She glanced sideways at him.

'You can tell me the truth. I'm not the school internet police.'

'I was trying to salvage some investments.' She plucked at the frayed end of one of her bag's straps. 'It's not illegal.'

'But that must be hard with all the schoolwork you have to do. You do this kind of thing all the time?'

'No, I've just had a run of bad luck. Not that it's any of your business.'

He was just going to ask why she needed the money so urgently, but they'd arrived at the labs. As they gathered by the workbenches, Lindy directed the guests' attention to Rose.

'Agent Hammond, Rose Knight here is our top science student. She's top in everything. She can tell you about the facilities far better than me as she has had a say in the selection of the new equipment.'

'Oh?' Hammond spun her chair to look at Rose. 'That's unusual. Why was that?'

'Oh, I . . . um . . .' Rose laced her hands together, posture broadcasting her discomfort at being in the spotlight.

'She won a big science competition last year with her project on applying forensic techniques to archaeology,' said Lindy proudly. Damien found himself warming to Lindy. She

54

genuinely seemed to be fond of Rose and treated the gawky classmate like a little sister.

'It was nothing,' Rose demurred.

'In that case,' teased Lindy, 'it was ten thousand dollars of nothing.'

'Congratulations. So, Rose, tell me about this project of yours.' Hammond took Rose to one side and began to question her. Removed from a larger audience, Damien could see that Rose regained her confidence and had begun to talk animatedly, using her hands to gesture, a little like at the party when she had talked to him about CSI Luxor. He couldn't stop watching—which was ridiculous when he had a real FBI agent with him to talk to about his work. Damien gave himself a mental kick up the backside.

'So Agent Stevens, can you tell me anything about the kind of work you've been doing?'

The cyclops stare turned to him. 'I could but then . . .'

'You'd have to kill me?'

Stevens smiled, making his granite face much more approachable. 'No, I was going to say "disappoint you" as I've done public relations for the last few months since a case I worked on went pear-shaped.' Checking that Lindy and Joe were occupied listening in on Rose and Hammond, Stevens lowered his voice. 'Tell me, did I catch that girl's name right? Rose Knight?'

'Yeah, she's Joe's neighbour.'

'Is her dad Don Knight, do you know?'

Damien wondered where this was going but the truth wouldn't be hard to find out. 'I've only been here a day or two but I think so.'

'I knew one of his kids was in the school but I wouldn't have picked her out of a line-up for that dubious honour. I certainly wouldn't have pegged her as the top science student.'

'So I hear. Seems she's the law-abiding exception. Any reason why you wanted to know?'

Stevens gave a sour smile. 'I'll just say Don Knight is the reason I'm working public relations.'

Catching the resentment, Damien felt he had to put in a word for Rose. 'But the daughter's nothing like the father, Joe told me.'

'Don't worry, I had worked that out for myself. We aren't completely clueless in the Bureau.'

'Can you tell me what he did to you?'

Stevens flicked through a chemistry textbook stacked on a side bench. 'Why do you want to know?'

'Rose is having a rough time at the moment and Joe's worrying about her. I was wondering if it was relevant.'

Stevens rubbed his jaw. 'She is? I wonder . . . Maybe I should look into it.'

Damien hadn't meant to land Rose in trouble—and certainly not with the FBI. A quick bit of redirection was needed. 'Why not get Joe to do that? He knows her well.'

'Good idea. Ask him, would you?' Stevens handed over his business card. 'And if you hear anything else, let me know, OK?'

Damien slipped the card in his pocket. 'Sure. But I'm just a visitor.'

'You underestimate yourself. You are a product of YDA training, for the moment living next-door to the Knights. You could be very useful if you keep your eyes and ears open. If you come through with the goods on this one, my boss won't need much more persuasion that the YDA should go ahead over here.'

'Thanks.' Damien felt a sudden surge of excitement. He hadn't meant to volunteer but the FBI had just given him a mission which, if he did well, would really please Isaac and the team back in London. Rose was up to something, his instincts told him that much. If he explained it was for her benefit, Joe would understand.

Rose had found the career talk fascinating despite her expectation that the time would have better been spent sorting out her investment tangle. Agent Hammond had made much of the opportunities for science students to apply their knowledge in the support roles to field agents. Rose had never really given much thought to the many branches of forensic science, having convinced herself that she would prefer to study the past, but the idea of seeking justice for victims in the present did appeal to her desire to do something worthwhile with her life. Not everyone had to go into the grisly world of the morgue; technicians could also work on evidence gathering on crime scenes, in the lab analysing samples, and hunting down the digital trail left by many criminals.

With a sigh, she made a mental note to check her father wasn't leaving traces of his activities that would later catch up with him.

Her father.

The thought was like a punch in the gut. She had to get back to raising his ransom. She slipped out of the auditorium as the principal gave a vote of thanks to the visitors. She had hoped that no one noticed but she caught the cool blue gaze of Joe's British friend watching her.

She couldn't worry about that. One problem at a time. Knocking on Mr McGinty's door Rose waited for him to say she could enter. She found him in the middle of grading papers, cold cup of coffee on his desk.

'I really apologize for earlier, sir,' Rose said as she handed over her now completed assignment.

He ran his pen down the list of neatly written answers.

'That's more like it. But let's not go here again, Rose. Even a fraction of a reduction in your results could jeopardize your chances of a scholarship.'

Rose dismissed the thought that she would just make the money herself. Her pride wanted her to win the funding for which she knew she was amply qualified. 'I know, sir.'

'OK then, I won't keep you any longer. Off you go.'

With relief that she could finally get back to what she needed to do, Rose wondered if she could escape school without her escort of Joe and Damien but found they were waiting for her at the gates.

'You really needn't have stayed back for me.' As much as she loved Joe, she really couldn't handle his attention right now. And his friend was simply too much in her face every time they met.

'No problem.' Joe put an arm round her shoulder while his friend stole her bag off her again.

She made a vain attempt to snatch it back. 'You guys are impossible.'

'Glad you realize that,' said Damien, pulling the strap across his chest, 'beats wasting time on pointless arguments.'

'What did you think of the talk?' asked Joe as they headed down the steps into the subway.

Rose gave in for the moment, too tired to wrestle Damien for her bag. 'She's a good speaker.'

'I thought the part about the FBI labs might interest you.'
'It did.'

'They've got the best equipment in the world.' They passed single file through the gates to the platform.

'So she said. I'd like to get my hands on it.'

Damien bobbed up at her side now he guessed she wasn't going to lunge for the bag. 'Joe and I are going to see some of it later this week.'

Against her intention to keep conversation to a minimum, Rose began to imagine what it must be like to be able to trace a criminal from the merest scrap of DNA. 'Lucky you. I'd read that they are able to solve old crimes with less and less physical evidence. It makes you wonder if detectives are going to be needed in the future. Maybe everything will get solved on a microscope slide.'

'But you'll still need the muscle to bring the criminals to book, even if the brains like you nail the ba—' Damien caught himself and changed word choice, 'guilty parties.'

Joe chuckled.

Rose frowned at her neighbour. 'What's so funny?'

'Damien trying to be polite.'

The train rattled into the station and they took positions near the doors of their crowded car.

'He finds it funny because I'm on my best behaviour.' Damien gave her a charming lopsided smile. 'I promised Raven faithfully that I wouldn't let England down and lapse into my usual crude language.'

Rose found herself wondering who this Raven was, who had an influence over Damien. 'That's an unusual name.' *Don't fish for answers*, Rose berated herself. *It's none of your business*.

'Yeah. She goes to school with us,' said Joe. 'She keeps us all in line.'

'Especially Kieran.' Damien smirked.

'Kieran?' asked Rose.

'Her boyfriend,' said Joe.

Rose tried not to analyse why she was pleased by that answer.

'And our resident genius,' finished Damien. 'You'd have a lot in common with him. If you like, I could ask him to help you with those bad investments of yours.' He nudged her with his shoulder. 'He's brilliant at that kind of thing.'

'Oh, it's nothing. Just a little hiccup on the stock exchange,' said Rose quickly, wishing this journey home on the subway would end. 'Nothing I can't handle.'

'Damien's right—Kieran could help.' Joe glanced at his watch. 'He might still be up in the UK.'

Enough with the offers of help. 'Look, just leave me to sort out my own muddle, OK?'

The boys exchanged a look and Damien got out his phone. They weren't showing any signs of backing off. Why did no one listen to her wishes? Was she such a nothing of a person that everyone felt they could disregard her views? She wished she could have the kick-ass attitude of her inner Lara Croft, even the girl detective Nancy Drew—another favourite role model from childhood—would do at a pinch, but instead they continued to escort her, prisoner-under-guard style, all the way to her front door, Rose quietly seething.

'I've just texted Kieran. He'll be on Skype in fifteen minutes to help,' said Damien, tucking his phone away.

'That's great. I thought he'd be with Raven,' said Joe.

'No, she's out on a . . . er . . . school field trip with Kate and Nathan. He's lonely so welcomed the call. If you let us in, Rose, I'll just sign into my account on your computer and you can take it from there.'

Rose curled her hands into fists, channelling Lara. 'No.'

'Come on, Rose: be reasonable,' said Joe, using the coaxing tone she'd heard him use on tired toddlers and stubborn old people over the years.

She whirled round, using the extra height of the steps to get herself on eye-level with her two would-be Good Samaritans. 'Joseph Masters, listen to me! I said no. I don't need you to help me with this. I need to be left alone.' She poked her forefinger in his chest. 'Understood?'

'Rosie . . .' Joe shook his head in bemusement.

'Don't you "Rosie" me—it won't work. Just . . . just . . . go away.' She almost swore but shied at the final fence.

Joe started to laugh. 'Rose Isabelle Knight, did you *almost* say a bad word?'

His friend was grinning too. Neither of them got that her dad's life depended on her, that she had so much pressure on her, the almost use of a vulgarity was the least of her worries right now. She opened the door, meaning to slam it before she started to scream in frustration or, worse, weep.

Joe put his foot in the door. It got squashed by the force of her shove. 'Ouch.'

Damien leaned against the door to free his friend's foot. 'Sorry if Joe's being a persistent pillock—that's usually my role. But can't you give our friend Kieran a chance to help?'

As much as she'd love to share her burdens, she couldn't take a complete stranger into her confidence. He'd surely ask her why she needed so much money by Friday and what could she say to that?

'Remove your foot, Joe, or I'll take my Pyramid of Giza paperweight and drop it on your toes.'

'Not the Pyramid of Giza!' said Joe in mock terror, still not getting how serious she was with her threat.

'I think she means it,' said Damien, sounding as if he found her fury entertaining, which of course whipped up a further storm of feelings inside her. 'If she thinks she can manage, then we'd better leave her.' He gave a shrug as if to say they'd tried and the rest was on her.

Joe removed his foot and Rose pushed the door closed.

Chapter 4

Undeterred by having the door slammed in their faces, Damien put in the call to Kieran anyway, but on Joe's computer. As he logged in, Joe raided the kitchen and brought up a tray of snacks. He pulled over a second chair so they could share the screen.

'Hey, Kieran, how's life?' Joe asked as the video camera kicked in.

'Hello.' Kieran was in his room at the YDA, clearly deep in some project or other as his place was a mess. His girlfriend had obviously been away for a few days as she wouldn't put up with the amount of lab equipment snaking over desk, bed, and shelves. 'OK, I suppose.'

Joe smiled at his friend's depressed tone. 'Missing Raven?'

'Yeah.' Kieran rubbed his jaw.

'What's with the pirate look?' asked Damien, noting the rumpled dark hair, stubble, and shadows under his friend's pale green eyes.

'I've got an experiment running.'

'So?'

'My sink is currently in use.'

'For what?'

'I'm testing how long it takes printed matter to decompose if submerged in water at the temperature of eight degrees Celsius.'

'Almost instantly, I'd've guessed. I once put a girl's phone number through the wash by mistake and that was the end of a potentially beautiful friendship.'

Joe frowned. He knew Kieran even better than Damien, having shared rooms with him in the past. 'Printed *matter*, Key?'

Kieran's gaze scooted away from the screen. 'Yeah, well, there's this old case involving a sailor who had a tattoo.'

'Don't tell me you've samples of human skin in your sink!' Damien gave a horrified laugh.

'Of course not.' Kieran looked disgruntled by the suggestion. 'That's far too hard to source. No, I'm using the skin from a joint bought from a reputable butcher who sources his meat fresh from the abattoir.'

Damien shoved aside the picture of his friend tattooing the Sunday roast. 'How long has Raven been away?'

'Too long,' muttered Joe.

Kieran nodded glumly but Damien guessed his reasons weren't the same as his friends' for regretting his girlfriend's absence.

'Go shave in my room, you dumb clot,' said Damien. 'You could sleep there until you've removed your latest health hazard.'

'I didn't think of it. Yeah, I'll do that.' Kieran's eyes brightened. 'So where's this neighbour of yours that needs my help, Joe?'

'She wasn't receptive to the idea of bringing you in to sort out her financial problems,' said Joe wryly.

'But she's in some serious trouble.' Damien decided it was time to mention the suspicion that had grown since he spoke with Agent Stevens. 'Joe, do you think it's possible she didn't want help because what's she's doing is illegal?'

'What? Rose? No way!' Joe's face didn't agree with his denial. He was wondering for the first time whether Rose might not be as untouched by her family's criminal activities as he supposed.

Damien was more pessimistic about human nature. He didn't believe in purity; even if she looked like the nasty side of life had missed her in her geeky ivory tower, Rose was bound to have her dark side. Everyone had one, even his saintly parents. 'It's worth thinking about.'

Kieran had started typing furiously. 'No need to speculate. I can find out for you. What's her name and address? Do you know her IP number?'

Joe grabbed a handful of cashews. 'I've got an old email from her. Give me a moment and I'll forward it to you.'

'No need, I've already hacked your email account. You really need to use a less obvious password, my friend. There she is.' Kieran had that glint in his eyes which meant he was on the hunt. 'Ah, lovely little firewall here, much better than your normal. Joe, I'm pleased to report your neighbour is much more sensible about security than you. Oh you devious little programmer—thought I wouldn't see that trap, did you? Whoa, nice encryption!'

Damien helped himself to the bowl of M&Ms while Kieran muttered away to himself. Rose appeared to be giving the YDA's secret weapon a run for his money.

'Impressive,' Kieran stated at last.

'Has she beaten you?' asked Damien.

Kieran cocked an eyebrow in a 'ya think?' gesture. 'No, of course not. She has a high level of ability but I'd say she isn't really interested in the game—or perhaps she's distracted. Looks to me she's been too busy with her investments for the last two months to give much thought to updating her firewalls.'

'Two months?'

Kieran gave a low whistle. 'Clever girl: she's made three

million dollars in the last six weeks. I'm genuinely impressed—
I'd be pushed to do the same.'

'So she doesn't exactly have money trouble after all,' said
Joe thoughtfully.

'Maybe she does. She's made the money and taken it out—
in three one-million-dollar instalments. She's in the middle of
doing the same this week. Must be eating away at her capital.
Nasty hit on the Japanese stock exchange, should've tracked
the geological early warning system, but . . . yeah, she's back
on target now. She's just moved a large proportion of her
stake into an energy company that's about to announce a
new investment in shale gas. That should send the shares up
tomorrow.'

'And she knows this how?' asked Damien suspiciously.

Kieran shrugged. 'I guess she has a programme reading the
same scientific chatter as I do. I think I'll follow her lead. The
YDA could do with some money for a roof garden.'

'Paid for by controversial carbon-producing investments?'
asked Joe.

Kieran grimaced. 'Oh yeah. Maybe not then. I'll put the
shares in biogas instead.'

'And when did Isaac put you in charge of the YDA
investments, remind me?' asked Damien.

'Two years ago.'

'So you've enough experience to tell if she's doing anything
illegal?'

'Yeah.' Kieran studied her figures more closely, scrolling
back through the investment history. 'Nope. All looks fine
to me—apart from the fact that she's pretending to be her
father.'

'Is that a crime?' asked Joe.

'Technically perhaps, but there are plenty of parents who
tell their kids their PIN number. This is just a very impressive

example of that: she's making him money rather than spending it.'

Damien leaned back in his chair, folding his arms across his chest. 'But the big question is what does she need the money for? It could be going into her father's criminal activities.'

'Give me a moment.' Kieran tapped away, humming under his breath. 'Do you want the bad news or the bad news?'

'Bum choice,' said Joe.

'The first bad news is she is sending the money to an offshore account that looks very shady to me—Janus Enterprises. I'll need a lot more time to run that one back to source. The second piece of bad news is that Don Knight's credit cards show no activity for the last two months apart from standing orders. No coffee stops, no groceries, no petrol purchases, nothing.'

'He's gone underground?'

'Or he is underground—as in six feet under,' offered Damien.

'Then why is she still working so hard to raise all this money?' asked Kieran. 'My guess is that she is paying—or thinks she's paying—for his continued existence.'

'So who's holding him?'

'If I get behind Janus Enterprises I should be able to tell you the answer to that too. Leave it with me.' Kieran ended the call, not bothering to say goodbye. Not having Raven around had sent Kieran's social skills back a step or two but the boys didn't mind. Kieran was a genius and if he promised them an answer, he'd get it for them.

Joe put his head in hands and swore. 'No wonder she's been looking so strung out.'

Damien walked to the window to gaze down on the dark patch of garden at the back of the neighbour's house. 'But she doesn't want our help, Joe. She made that plain.'

'But what happens when she can no longer keep up this act of spinning straw into gold? She must realize these demands will never end.'

'I guess she can't see a way out of the trap.' Damien felt a twist of pity for the social misfit of a girl caught between a rock and a hard place. He couldn't afford to go soft over her; Joe was already too lenient so Damien's own brand of toughness was needed as a counterweight. That was why Isaac often paired them together.

'We've got to do something.' Joe picked up his set of juggling balls from the bowl on his desk and began to toss them, a habit to help him think. 'But with her dad's life on the line, we've got to be very careful what that "something" is.'

Excited by the prospect of investigating a complex and serious crime, Damien had to remind himself these people were special to Joe. 'Exactly. And also, since you mentioned it, I'm wondering how clean the money is that Rose is using to invest. If it's her dad's then . . .'

'She might be laundering his dirty funds to pay the demand?' Joe's face registered his dismay. 'She just might. She loves that deadbeat.'

'What about telling Agent Stevens?' He'd already filled Joe in about the FBI man's interest in Rose and her father.

'I suppose we could involve him,' said Joe dubiously. 'But he's no friend of the family.'

'I guess not.'

'So let's take a day or two to think it through. According to Kieran, Rose has this week's ransom in hand so we've got time—and we can wait to find out who is behind Janus.'

'OK. I'm cool with that. I didn't get the impression Stevens was expecting instant reports.'

'And I'd like to be sure we aren't going to do anything to get Rose arrested before we speak to him.'

Damien wanted to agree but he had to hang tough. 'We might have no choice, Joe.'

'I can't send Rose to prison for the sin of loyalty to her father.'

'But money laundering is not a victimless crime—it's what fuels people trafficking, drugs, corruption.'

'Yeah I know, but you've met her: she'd never survive a sentence. No one would understand her inside.'

'Surely it would be in a juvenile detention centre if it came to that? And besides, it wouldn't be our fault.' He refused to dwell on the mental picture of Rose in an orange jumpsuit thrown in with the toughest girls in New York. They'd shred her the moment she accessorised it with a polka dot sweater.

Joe raised anguished eyes to him. 'Wouldn't it?'

On Thursday night, Rose celebrated making her million with a jig along to 'Happy' in the kitchen. She'd pressed the send button and the money was now in the offshore account. Her dad was saved and maybe his captors were serious—maybe this was the last demand. She had included a message that she had no more capital reserves to raid so they had to know they had milked this particular cow dry. Banging a frozen meal into the microwave, she bobbed round the work surface, using a wooden spoon for a microphone, singing through her upbeat tracks while it cooked. With her earbuds in, she didn't hear the front door or notice the arrival of someone else in the kitchen until she was grabbed from behind. The wires were pulled from her ears as he lifted her from her feet. She shrieked in terror—then recognized the aftershave.

'Ryan!'

'Mop!' Her brother swung her round and sat her on the surface, grinning right in her face, his brown eyes a mirror of her own. His auburn hair was slicked back and his breath was slightly tinged with alcohol. In his snazzy silver-grey suit and thin tie, he looked a little like a barracuda, his features sharpened by his hairstyle.

She glared at him. 'Don't call me "Mop", you dimwit.' It was a pet name from when she was not much more than a little girl with an unruly head of copper ringlets. Ryan had teased her by holding her upside down and pretending to clean the floor with her. Thankfully, her hair had calmed down in colour and curliness as she grew up. 'I haven't seen you for weeks. I really need to talk to you.'

The microwave pinged. Their eyes met and they both lunged. Ryan got there first and snagged the meal out. 'Kind of you to cook for me.' He stole her fork and dug in. 'Ah, ow, hot!'

Scowling, Rose got out another meal from the freezer. 'You're supposed to wait. The microwaves carry on vibrating the water particles—basic physics, Ryan.'

He stirred the ratatouille, releasing the steam. 'Duly noted, Kid Genius.'

'Why are you here?' Wondering how to broach the subject of their father's kidnap, Rose got out some juice and poured two glasses. Ryan gratefully gulped his down to cool his burned tongue.

'Can't I call on my little sister just because I feel like it?'

'Of course. Yeah, I really believe that every time you say it—and my middle name is still Gullible.'

Ryan looked around the kitchen. 'Dad still away?'

Rose hesitated. Should she confide in him? Could she risk it?

He didn't wait for an answer. 'When you see him, tell him I need to talk to him.' Ryan perched on a bar stool to eat at the counter.

'I'm not expecting him back for a while. You see—'

'Then I'd best talk to you. You've got to take extra care for the next few weeks.' He refilled his glass, avoiding her eye.

This wasn't good. Thoughts of confiding in him died. 'Why do I have to do that, Ryan?'

'I've had a run of bad luck. Might've promised some people things I couldn't in the end deliver. They're angry with me and it's not impossible they'll try to get to me through . . .' he waved a vague hand at the room.

'Through us?' supplied Rose. She wanted to beat him over the head with her spoon. That's all she needed: not only her dad's trouble but Ryan's as well. 'Sometimes I just want to emigrate.'

His face lit up. 'You know, that might not be such a bad idea—go away for a few weeks, at least until this all passes.'

Was he for real? 'Ryan, I'm at school. I've got to graduate.'

He shrugged that off. 'You don't need to go to school. Everyone knows you're amazing.'

A bitter nub of resentment formed in her chest. 'I still have to finish. I seem to remember you didn't graduate, Ryan. How did that work out for you?'

His face hardened. 'I'm doing OK.'

'So why do you sneak back in here to warn me that I might be victim of some vendetta you've sparked off?' Oh, this was useless. One thing she knew about the infuriating men in her life is that they never saw things as their fault. They were unlucky; the other guy was to blame; it would've worked out if only . . .

The microwave pinged. No longer feeling hungry, Rose took out the second meal and upended it on a plate.

'You don't understand how hard it is for me,' grumbled Ryan. 'You—you've got all those brains. You'll be OK. I never had any luck at school. All the teachers hated me.'

He'd also never worked and frequently cut class. He'd

enjoyed his reputation for being a glamorous rebel but as the years passed that veneer was wearing thin. What seemed cool at eighteen was cold comfort at twenty-three. Rose couldn't see any route for him that didn't lead to jail—and that broke her heart. Taking the bar stool next to him, she squeezed his arm—it was either that or box his ears. He and Dad were all she had. 'I know, Rye. I don't mean to nag.'

He glanced sideways at her. 'So you'll take care?'

'I'm always careful.'

'You'll ring me if trouble comes calling? Don't let anyone in unless Dad's home, no matter the excuse.'

'I don't invite people home—you know that.'

'Not even a maintenance guy.'

'Yes, I get that. Oh, that reminds me, could you look at the water heater?' Ryan was actually very skilled at mechanical things but thought such work beneath him.

'Sure. How long's it been out?'

Rose nibbled at a piece of carrot. 'About a week.'

Ryan groaned. 'You and Dad are hopeless.' He shoved his empty plate aside. 'I'll get the tools.'

Even though he was trouble, Rose enjoyed having Ryan about the house. He stripped off his suit jacket and rolled up his sleeves, looking much more like the big brother she remembered from years back before things went wrong. He'd run that side of the house while she managed the bills and groceries. Dad had done the yard and decorating. They'd been a team—for a brief time. Loneliness swept her. Ryan would breeze out in a few minutes, leaving her to cope. He hadn't even asked her more questions about their father. Likely he realized there were problems but didn't want to know. Maybe he couldn't imagine how bad it had become? He'd help if he knew, wouldn't he?

Wouldn't he?

Not wanting her last family illusion stripped from her, she held her tongue.

Half an hour later, Ryan came back into the kitchen. She'd had time to bake some cookies as a 'thank you'.

'All done. It was just a fuse and luckily I'd stocked up on spares last winter.'

She gave him a hug, clinging on far too long for a simple fix.

He patted her back but didn't ask. Instead he changed the subject. 'You made those for me?'

'Uh-huh.' She forced herself to step back.

'So what's the news round here?'

'Oh, not much.' She searched for a neutral topic. 'Joe's got a friend to stay. From the UK. Mrs Masters had one of her yard parties.'

Ryan grimaced. He had never got on with Mr and Mrs Masters. They asked too much of him, things like living up to his responsibilities, going straight, being a decent upstanding member of the community. 'Poor you.'

'I heard a good career talk from the FBI at school.'

He gave a mocking laugh. 'Don't you dare, Rose.'

'Dare what?'

'Work for that pack of wolves.' He selected the largest cookie. 'They're why Dad and I have such a hard time.'

'How do you mean?'

'They consider us people of interest in their investigations into Roman Melescanu, but we've only ever been on the very edge of anything that crazy guy does. They've poisoned the well for us. Everyone knows the Feds have eyes on the Knights and now they all think twice about working with us.' His expression turned inward. 'Maybe that's the real reason I've not had a good break for months now.'

She didn't want him to spiral back into his self-pity. 'Who's Roman Melescanu?'

'Not someone you'd want to know. He controls things round here—him and his gladiators—that's what he calls his thugs, the pretentious jerk. He runs a business down on the waterfront offering construction services for big international projects but that's a cover for other stuff, people trafficking mainly, drugs too, from Mexico. He has half the police department in his pocket.' Ryan gave a 'what can you do?' shrug. 'Forget I mentioned him.'

Was he the man who had kidnapped their father? When all this started, Rose had tried to find out who was behind Janus Enterprises but their security had been too tight and she hadn't been able to get behind it.

'Is he . . . is he someone you can cut a deal with?'

Ryan gave a dark laugh. 'Like you can cut a deal with a rabid bear. He's a little loco. The rumour is that he was in prison back in Romania in the eighties. He emerged in the nineties to set up his little organization untroubled by such things as conscience.'

'So why do you and Dad even get involved with him in a distant way? Sounds like he should be avoided like the plague.'

Ryan gave her one of his patronizing half smiles. 'It's complex out there. You don't know how lucky you are that Dad and I have sheltered you, but you can't avoid guys like him if you want to do anything in this part of New York.'

She wanted to shake him, tell him that if he'd gone to technical college and taken a useful qualification he would own his own business by now and have no need to walk on the wild side. In rich areas like this, a local handyman was like gold dust. He'd be beating off clients with a stick. He would have plenty of legitimate work and be employing others to get their hands dirty. But that argument had been lost years ago. 'If you say so.'

Ryan put his suit jacket back on. 'So take care, OK?' He tapped her nose.

'I will.'

'I'll come by again soon.'

'OK.' She hugged herself, rubbing her palms up and down on her upper arms.

'Come here.' Ryan tugged her to his chest. 'Just keep your head down, Rosie. It'll all work out.'

The philosophy of the Knight men. 'Sure it will.'

'Love you.'

'Love you too.'

With that, he was gone, back to his life dodging the guys he owed money to, the police sniffing around his deals, the girlfriends who had once given him a place to stay before he two-timed them.

Rose sighed and began to clean up the kitchen.

Chapter 5

Arriving on time for school, Rose unpacked her books at her desk, checking she was prepared for the morning's lessons. Finally, a day when she felt on top of things after a hellish week.

'Are you coming to my Halloween party? You haven't replied to the text,' asked Lindy, settling into the chair next to her in a cloud of sweet-scented perfume.

'It's Halloween?' So caught up in her own troubles, Rose hadn't even noticed the date, but, of course, it was Friday already.

Lindy laughed. 'Earth to Rose, yes, it's Halloween. Didn't you notice the earrings?' She tapped her skull danglers. 'So, the party?'

'Um . . .'

'We're going to do one of my dad's cryptic treasure hunts, remember, and oh my gosh, you can join in now!' Lindy jingled her bangles, a little peel of fairy bells. 'I've just worked it out: your two-year-ban has expired. And Joe's coming—with his friend.'

'Oh.'

'I think his friend likes you.' Lindy grinned at her.

'He does? How do you know that?'

'He watches you. Didn't you notice? All the time we were with that FBI lady, he was manoeuvring to be next to you. So you'll come?'

'I'm not sure.' Rose didn't think Damien liked her; she felt he watched her like a TV show that he found mildly amusing.

'I should warn you.' Lindy dug in her bag, took out a red tube, and passed lip gloss over her perfect lips.

Not another warning. 'Of what?'

'I've decided to make you my latest project. Joe mentioned he thought you looked lonely.'

Joe again.

'You don't realize how many of us would be happy to be friends with you, do you? You need to mingle more, Rose. We want to get to know you, get you to loosen up—and if you're going to go to college next year you'll need to make friends— might as well get into the swing now.'

Rose couldn't fault Lindy's reasoning. She wanted to be more like Lindy at school but somehow her awkwardness won out every time. She always ended up putting people off by acting strange or saying something odd. So often she felt like a foreigner taught the wrong words for things everyone else understood. 'I guess.'

'Great, so Joe'll bring you. I've already asked him.'

Put like that, how could she say no without sounding churlish? 'Thanks.'

'And don't forget you'll need a costume.' Lindy flicked her hair over her shoulder as she got up to go to class.

'A costume? Oh yes.' Could she back out now?

'I'm expecting something clever from you. Don't let me down.'

Rose did not have much experience of 'clever' fancy dress but, on the other hand, it felt good to spend the next few hours agonizing over something as simple as a costume choice rather than keeping her father alive. Consulting the oracle of Google produced nothing helpful but, by the end of the day,

Rose thought she'd come up with an idea that would impress Lindy and her friends, though a niggling doubt inside suggested that maybe it was a little too obscure. She shrugged it off. The benefit of the brainwave was that she had all she needed at home to make the outfit.

Opening her front door, her spirits sank. No Dad. She hadn't spelt it out to herself but she'd been able to enjoy the day because she'd hoped against hope that the money had been enough and he'd be there, wanting to catch up on the last two months, promising never to get himself in such a fix again. That was too much to expect. On the bright side, there was no further demand on the doormat either. All she could do was wait. They still might let him go.

'Costume,' she muttered. If she had to wait, then she wouldn't do it sitting in an empty house. Taking the pruning shears, she went out into the yard and began to attack one of the neglected bushes.

Damien looked out of Joe's window. 'Hey, Joe, do you know why Rose would be hacking at the garden at this time of the evening?'

Joe joined him. He was half way through applying his Dr Death make-up, face well on the way to becoming a skeleton. 'Nope.'

'Looks therapeutic.' Damien chuckled as he saw Rose yank a great long tendril of ivy off the wall, almost toppling over as it gave way. Dusting off her hands, she did a little victory jig before disappearing back into the house, which he thought extremely sweet. He enjoyed watching her: she was always showing new sides to her personality, things that you rarely glimpsed when she thought anyone was there to see her. He kept forgetting she was a target. He had to remember his mission now was to get her to confide what was going on in the Knight household so the FBI could get their man. 'Does she like dancing?'

'Never seen her dance in front of other people—she's more a stay-in-a-corner-and-solve-the-mystery-of-the-universe kind of girl. So, Damien, do I need any more white?' Joe angled his chin so his friend could examine his make-up, raided from his mother's Sunday school face-painting supplies.

'You need a bit more on the left side.'

Having surrendered the mirror over the bathroom sink to Joe, Damien checked his vampire outfit in the wall-length mirror on the landing. 'Are you sure this isn't too clichéd?'

'I thought you Brits invented the gentleman vampire?' called Joe from the bathroom.

'Did we? OK then, but . . . I dunno.' Damien passed his fingers over his slicked-back blond hair.

'And Lindy did put in a special request.'

'I draw the line at wearing plastic teeth all evening.'

'Relax: I've got you some very upmarket stick-on fangs. Can't have you ruining the effect.' Joe chucked him a little plastic box.

With a grunt of agreement, Damien read the instructions then fitted the teeth over his canines. Face paled with white powder, a strategic drip of red paint, and now white fangs, he had to allow he looked the part. Nudging Joe aside, he bared his teeth at the mirror.

'Go on, say it,' teased Joe.

'Absolutely not.'

'You have to. *I vant to suck your blood.*'

'No thanks. I only suck blood from pretty vampire brides, not six-foot skeletons. Grant me some taste.'

'Speaking of pretty vampire brides, we'd better get going. I told Rose I'd pick her up at seven. No biting.'

She would probably stake him if he dared try, but he

couldn't resist teasing Joe. 'Are you suggesting I don't put her on my menu?'

Joe tapped his top hat in place. 'Absolutely off the menu. As far as she is concerned, you are a vegetarian vampire like the *Twilight* ones.'

'Yeah, and look how that turned out,' murmured Damien, following his friend down the stairs.

'We're to get her to spill the beans, not break her heart.'

But sometimes, thought Damien, the only way to get a target's trust was to get them to let down their barriers. Falling a little in love made anyone less guarded. It would be for Rose's own good in the end. Maybe he could charm the Geek Princess?

Mrs Masters gave a gratifying shriek as Joe swooped on her in the kitchen.

'We're just off out, Mom.' Joe kissed her cheek.

'Keep your phone switched on!' Catching sight of Damien, she patted her chest. 'My, don't you look to-die-for gorgeous, young man.'

Damien grinned, revealing his teeth. 'That's good because I'm already dead.'

Mrs Masters gave another shriek, this time of delighted laughter. 'Oh, what it would be to be your age again!'

Mr Masters entered the kitchen and put his arms around his wife. 'But I like you just the way you are—the right vintage for me.'

Looking pleased, Mrs Masters pretended to bat him away. 'Oh, you!'

Joe and Damien went out into the cold crisp air. Most of the privately owned houses were decorated with pumpkin lights artfully sculpted into grinning faces. Mrs Masters had made a large one with a little squash in its mouth—a cannibal pumpkin—which Damien thought very cool. Rose's house was the only one without any decorations.

Joe rang the bell. 'Remember: be nice to her and you've no dining rights.'

When Rose opened the door, Damien was stumped. He was all ready to compliment her on her Halloween costume no matter what she had chosen, but she was dressed in a white toga wrapped around with ivy. An evergreen crown sat on her head. She looked more like a Christmas angel than anything, apart from the disconcerting animal skull suspended around her neck.

'Oh, you guys look great!' Rose reached behind the door to take her coat off the hook.

Having known her all her life, Joe was able to be blunter than Damien. 'Rose, what the heck are you wearing?'

'Half the back yard.' She gave him a worried smile. 'Don't you get it?'

'You've come as what? Some kind of wood sprite?'

'No, that's not very Halloween, is it?' She set the alarm then locked the door behind her. 'Damien, you get it, don't you, being from the UK?'

'I do?' Damien spotted her disappointment so quickly changed his tone. 'I mean, I do.'

'Oh yeah? So what is she?' asked Joe, eyebrow arched. A light rain began to fall, misting Rose's crown with amber droplets in the orange glare of the street lighting. Joe put up a big black umbrella to cover her.

'She's clearly come as . . . as something very suited to Halloween that's so obvious we'll kick ourselves when she tells us.' Damien squeezed under the shelter, welcoming the excuse to huddle close.

Rose brushed the rain off the end of her nose, her expression telling them that her initial confidence was withering. 'I'm Samhain,' she said awkwardly.

'Sam who?' asked Joe.

At least Damien had heard of this. 'It's the Celtic name for the pagan festival before the Church invented Halloween. So you're a Celtic priestess, right?'

'Yes.'

'The skull?' He put an arm round her, pretending he just wanted to straighten the strap from which it hung.

'It should be a horse skull but we only had this deer one from my granddad's hunting days and I thought it would do. The horse skull was part of the ritual procession. Have I gone a little too obscure?' she appealed to Joe. 'Lindy told me to be clever.'

'No, no,' lied Joe. 'I'm sure other people will be quicker off the mark than us. Won't they, Damien?'

'Oh yeah,' Damien said with certainty, because he and Joe were going to go around the party dropping a few hints so others would know and the Geek Princess wouldn't be embarrassed.

It was only a short walk to Lindy's house. The party was already in full swing when they got there, kids from school spilling out onto the covered entry steps and silhouetted in the ground floor windows.

'You're here! Great!' exclaimed Lindy, pouncing on the three of them as they entered. She was dressed as a witch's cat in a black leotard and leggings, with ears and a very tempting tail. She went up on tiptoes to kiss Joe, who whispered something in her ear as Damien helped Rose with her coat. 'Oh Rose: you don't disappoint, do you? Celtic priestess, isn't it?'

'For Samhain, yes,' agreed Rose, a suspicious look in her eyes as she glanced at Joe.

'So clever!' Lindy gave Damien a welcoming hug, then linked her arm through his. 'Come on: now you're here we can start the treasure hunt.'

'Treasure hunt?' asked Damien.

Lindy squeezed her hands together in excitement, looking much younger and more adorable than usual. 'You'll love it. It's a family tradition. When we were little, Dad didn't like us to go Trick or Treating without a challenge. We had to go round the local area on a path he had worked out for us in a series of clues. Now we're older we've dumped the Trick or Treating and just do the treasure hunt. He always stumps up for an amazing prize.'

'A bag of sweets?' Damien gave a sardonic smile.

Lindy laughed. 'Listen to you! *A bag of sweets.*' She did a poor imitation of his accent. 'No candy this year but tickets to the next Giants home game at the MetLife Stadium.'

Now she was talking! 'That's American football, right? Sounds awesome.'

'Of course, it's football.' Lindy patted his arm. 'Where've you been for the last few centuries? Oh yeah, in your coffin.' She leaned closer. 'Go on, say it: *I vant . . .*'

She was pretty enough for a vampire bride but somehow she wasn't the special he wanted on his menu. 'I'm saving it for my chosen victim. I'm strictly a one–meal-a-night guy.'

Lindy gave a little shiver and grinned at Rose. 'Ooo, lucky girl.'

They had arrived in the large open plan living room kitchen full of Halloween characters. Lindy clapped her hands and, when that didn't work, put her fingers in her mouth and produced an impressive whistle.

'Hey guys: I'm about to start the treasure hunt. For those of you who haven't been to one of my parties before, I separate you into couples. The clues will take you to local landmarks. You text my dad the answer you find there and he'll send you the next clue. The first pair to solve them all wins the treasure.' She waved two tickets in her hand. 'Sorry, Jets fans but these are for the Giants.'

'Shame!' jeered a boy in the back row before being bundled upon by his Giants supporting mates.

'Now, I promise you, I don't know any of the clues—Dad's been working on this all week locked up in his study—so let me introduce you to the mastermind behind this game.' Her father, who was standing by the kitchen counter serving a fruit punch, waved a hand. He was a strange contrast to his glamorous daughter: small and earnest with white-speckled black hair. 'Among other things, Dad teaches cryptography at NYU—just saying.'

The crowd groaned.

'Right: here are the pairs, chosen totally at random.' Lindy winked as she picked up a witch's hat stuffed full of paper slips and started pulling out names. There was more laughter and a few jokes as couples were put together. Joe was paired early on with a girl with an impressively bountiful figure, dressed as a ghost in a capacious white sheet. He tried to look pleased but Damien could see from the strain around Joe's mouth that the two had a history. Damien wondered how much the girl had bribed Lindy as he could see their hostess had a special pocket inside the hat for certain names. He knew what to look for as he'd learnt the same trick himself from a conjuror who had come to the YDA one summer to teach them circus skills. It was a beginner's trick for sleight of hand but it got results.

Lindy paired herself with Marco. Her boyfriend, dressed as Frankenstein's monster, gave her a squeeze around the waist, happy with the result. Looking around the room, Damien could see that very few people were left. Rose was trying to blend with the wallpaper—a feat helped by the fact that it was a patterned William Morris design of birds on a trellis. Her ivy fitted right in. He sidled over to her.

'Like being chosen last at PE, isn't it?'

She turned her big chocolate-drop eyes to him, expression wary. 'I'm always picked last for teams.'

'No good at sport?' Somehow he wasn't surprised.

She scowled. 'I'll have you know I'm not a complete failure.'

He couldn't resist baiting her. 'But the data suggests otherwise, or why are you picked last?'

'It's more that I lose my temper.'

Now he could imagine that—there was fire under the intellectual surface. 'You do?'

'I'm very competitive. I get annoyed that I've no hand-eye coordination and then I get mad. They tend to keep me on the bench.'

Damien swallowed a laugh. 'I see.'

'I bet you always get chosen first,' she said, a wistful note in her voice.

'Not quite first but yeah, I usually don't have to wait till last. Not this time though—I'll be a massive handicap to my partner, whoever they are.'

'Oh, I think I can guess.' She watched Lindy with an ironic gleam in her eyes.

'So you've seen that our hostess doesn't deal from the top of the pack?'

'Yes.'

'And the last couple,' declared Lindy with a sly smile in their direction, 'is Rose Knight and Damien Castle!'

There was another groan. Damien couldn't tell if it was for him or Rose. No matter: he was just pleased with the outcome. It gave him a chance to see how far he could charm his way into her trust.

Thank you, Lindy. Damien gave Rose a sheepish grin. 'Sorry. Please don't lose your temper with me.'

She smiled back, a slightly mysterious expression that he couldn't quite read. 'Don't worry about that.'

'Have you played this treasure hunt game before?'

'Not for two years. I was banned.'

'Did you have some kind of temper tantrum?'

'Not for a tantrum. I just wasn't very popular because of the way I played.'

'Uh-oh, you play dirty, do you?'

'No!' She sounded quite offended by the suggestion. He'd meant it as a compliment.

'So why don't we just go for a nice stroll together and not worry too much about the clues?' He imagined snuggling up to her in a warm cafe somewhere and listening to her tell him all the weird stuff she knew about ancient Celtic culture—oddly appealing. Oh yeah, and he could also gain her confidence. *You're on a mission*, he reminded himself.

Lindy's dad stepped into the centre of the room. 'The first clue is on these sheets of paper. On the back is my mobile number. Text me when you solve it and I'll send you the next one.'

He handed out the slips of paper. While others had already started on the clue, people seemed to be blocking Rose and Damien from getting theirs. Damien finally had to snatch their copy from Marco. He stared down at it: the clue was on squared maths paper but all that was inked on it right in the middle was a tiny square. Some clue.

'OK, on my mark: go!' Lindy's dad blew a whistle and the party spilt out into the night. The room was emptying rapidly, some of the pairs casting Rose dark looks and muttering about getting a head start. Joe gave Damien a half-pleading look as he was dragged off by his partner. Rose took her time getting back into her coat.

'So, shall we go for coffee and just pretend we tried?' asked Damien, following her out.

'We could—or we could win those tickets.' She watched

the street carefully then, keeping to the shadows, headed off in the opposite direction to most of the participants. Some of them did indeed seem to be watching for them but she doubled back, eluding them like a professional. 'Come on, keep up.'

Damien was amused to find himself in the unaccustomed role of trailing behind a girl who was supposed to be the amateur in this kind of evasion technique. 'Where are we going?'

'Back route. Don't want anyone following us.'

Her competitive streak was showing. 'You know what the answer is?'

Rose stopped behind a parked truck. 'Of course. It's obvious.'

'It is?' Damien moved closer so the folds of his cloak flirted with the skirt of her costume.

She wrinkled her brow. 'Oh, I suppose you don't get it because you're not local.'

'That's a generous interpretation. So enlighten me.' He held back on his urge to trace the line of her cheek and throat. Had to be his costume getting to him.

'The square—it's drawn one by one. That's the name of a singles bar a few blocks away.'

Damien suddenly saw the evening wasn't going to go the way he had expected at all. Lindy had paired him with a genius for whom such puzzles were laughably easy. He took her hand. 'You were banned for being too good, weren't you?'

Her lips curved. 'Might've been.'

'I always wanted to go to an American football game.'

'Come on then: let's go get those tickets before they exclude me for another two years.' She began to run.

Rose was having a ball: the competition was child's play. Even

86

the third clue that required a basic understanding of code breaking over two layers of encrypted information didn't hold her up once they called up a copy of the King James' Bible on Damien's phone. After that it was a simple letter substitution. Damien was flatteringly in awe of her talents and kept looking at her in a funny way—part admiration and part something else. She wasn't sure what the something else was but it was making her spine tingle. They had occasionally bumped into others roaming the streets, usually way back solving earlier clues. Damien had been outrageous, pretending to Joe that they were getting nowhere, just wandering in circles.

'You've got to save me from her. She just won't listen to me,' he had moaned to Joe and his partner. 'Here I am—dead for centuries—and she ignores my advice. Insists she knows best.'

'But as a Celtic priestess, I'm two thousand years old, so I trump a few vampire centuries any day,' she had reasoned.

Laughing, Damien had dragged her off out of sight before Joe twigged that they were nearly at the end of the hunt. It was easy to get lost in the crowds as the roads were very busy with younger trick-or-treaters out in packs, extorting candy from neighbours. Parent escorts carried festive lanterns and the chatter was at full volume—the West Village at its best.

The seventh and last clue was outside a fast food restaurant that sold 'giant' burgers.

'That's it: the last number is fifteen—the order number for the super-sized meal,' said Rose tapping at the glass window containing the menu.

Damien sent the text and received back a *congratulations— wow that was fast* message. The next text was a general one to all those on the hunt announcing that the clues had been solved in record time. The phone then pinged with various incredulous messages, even suggestions of cheating, until Lindy announced that Rose had been on the winning team. The complainers subsided with a 'no fair' last protest. Lindy sent out a call back, promising more games and food back at hers.

Damien held up the messages so Rose could read the screen. 'Why no fair? We didn't cheat.'

Rose shrugged. 'My classmates all think I'm infallible—like the pope taking a quiz on Catholic doctrine.'

Damien smiled. 'If you've got it, flaunt it.' He took her hand and brushed his thumb over her knuckles. 'Out of interest, what's your IQ?'

She shrugged. 'It's a flawed test—doesn't tell you much.'

'So I'm guessing your result is probably off the charts?'

'Intelligence isn't everything.' Some days she'd prefer not to be so book clever and understand more about how to mend boilers—or fix her family.

'But it goes a long way.'

'As far as a Giants game at least.'

'Exactly.' He leaned over and gave her a quick kiss. 'Well done, partner.'

Unnerved, she touched her mouth, still feeling the shimmering sensation of the brief contact. Few people ever touched her. 'Thank you.'

'I'm happy to be Watson to your Sherlock any day.'

'I'm no Sherlock Holmes!' she protested.

'Good—because I'd feel conflicted about wanting to kiss him.'

She lifted her gaze to meet his intense blue eyes. 'And you don't feel conflicted about me?'

'Oh, I'm conflicted all right, just not about the kissing part.' He leaned down and kissed her again, this time letting his fangs sink a little into her lip. 'Sweet,' he whispered. 'So sweet.' He stayed there, his arms around her, his mouth close to hers but not touching. 'What am I going to do with you?' He sounded a little exasperated at himself.

She didn't hear his answer to his own question as Lindy and Marco caught up with them.

'Hey, you two: well done!' called Lindy. 'Exactly the result I expected.'

Rose wasn't sure if she meant the competition or the kiss—or both.

Damien stood up and turned so his hand now rested on her hip. 'Thanks, but it was all Rose.'

Still reeling from the kiss, Rose leaned against her partner. Wondering how much Lindy and Marco had seen, she looked up and saw that Marco was giving Damien a strange look—and not a friendly one.

'Oh, we know it was her brains but you kept her company. Let's get back so you can claim your prize.' Lindy linked arms with Rose, hurrying her away from the boys. 'You wicked girl: kissing on the streets on Halloween! What has come over you, you devil?'

Rose was sure her cheeks must be scarlet. 'He kissed me,' she said defensively.

'I saw. I'm so proud of you!' Lindy gave a snort of laughter. 'You can thank me later for putting you together and keeping Joe out of your hair.'

Things fell into place. Lindy might not have the numerical skill of her father but she had inherited the strategizing instinct. 'You did that on purpose—put Joe with Miley.'

Lindy giggled. 'I know. Poor Joe. But at least Miley is ecstatic.'

'You're the wicked one, Lindy Baker.'

'Aw, hon, I've only just started.' She threw a significant look back at Damien.

'Don't feel you've got to interfere with my life.' It came out more as a plea than a refusal.

'Too late. I've just arranged a date for two at the Giants game, haven't I?'

Chapter 6

When they first got back to Lindy's, Damien was amazed to find that quite a few of the partygoers still wanted to dispute what he knew to be a clear win. He soon realized he had landed in the middle of a long-running dispute about what to do with the sparkling genius in their midst. Rose coped with it by retreating into aloof silence. Damien decided to go around cooling resentment by accentuating his hobbling role on Rose's natural brilliance.

'Man, it's amazing we came anywhere, what with me insisting on going the wrong way half the time,' he assured a couple of Giants fans, playing up the clueless stranger act. Despite this being far out of his real character, they swallowed it whole. He gave himself a pat on the back when he managed to charm the most outspoken complainers with the suggestion that, rather than banning Rose the following year, they should ask her to team up with Lindy's dad to set the clues.

It also helped that Rose was clearly terrible at all the other games, coming nowhere near winning a prize. For apple bobbing, she half-drowned without getting a bite, muttering darkly about the forces in water being too complicated to be scientifically predictable. In Twenty Questions she picked such an obscure character that no one guessed her choice and she was bemused when they still didn't know who Ada Lovelace was (daughter of Byron and an early pioneer of the maths that led to computer programming—Damien had to google it). She didn't know any of the pop culture characters the others chose, completely ignorant of anything to do with SpongeBob. Damien tried explaining to her who the cartoon character was but dissolved into laughter when he saw her incredulous expression.

'People actually watch that?' she asked.

He nodded and wiped his eyes. 'Yep.'

'That's so weird.'

'It's life, Rose, but not as you know it.'

The *Star Trek* reference seemed to pass her by too. 'I guess it is,' she said with a serious frown creating two creases between her eyebrows. 'But not one that gives us any evolutionary advantage. Maybe it'll be bred out of us in a few generations.' He wasn't entirely sure she was joking.

Fortunately for Damien's ribs, already aching from laughing so much, Lindy decided they had had enough games and should turn up the music. Leaving Rose, at her insistence, in a corner to watch, Damien dived in among the other dancers. He loved dancing. There was something about losing himself in the music that released a whole new side to his character. Joe joined him, the two of them falling into one of their jokey routines worked out at YDA parties where they danced in synch. Their performance attracted shouts and whistles from the onlookers, and that just spurred them on to be more and more outrageous. Then some joker dressed as a mummy put on 'Walk Like an Egyptian' and lumbered onto the floor, bandages trailing.

'Rose has got to dance to this one,' Damien shouted at Joe.

Joe began to protest but Damien had already plunged back into the crowd to find her. She was still in her corner, watching the dancing with what he decided to interpret as a yearning expression. It could have been scorn but he wasn't going there.

'They're playing your song.' He held out a hand. 'Come on, dance with me.'

She shook her head. 'No, I'll look stupid.'

'That's the point of this song: everyone looks stupid.' He pulled her up to her feet. He could feel from the tension in her arm that her body was fighting an intriguing battle with itself, only part reluctant.

'Egyptians didn't walk like that.'

He tugged her away from the chair. 'Only you would base your case against dancing to a party song on a failure of historical accuracy.'

She took a worried look around her. 'But people will see!'

'No one is looking at you—except me.' He grinned. He almost had her. 'And I know you like to dance: I saw you in the garden earlier when you were attacking that bush.'

'That was private—you shouldn't have been watching!'

With a sudden tug on her wrists, he got her in his arms. 'Then please do spend the rest of the night telling me off. I like it when you lecture me.'

She went quiet. He pretended not to notice her reaction to his closeness: that would be the quickest way to spook her. 'Now, you put your hand up sideways like that . . .'

She gave him one of her adorable frowns. 'What are you doing?'

'Baby, you may be the archaeological expert but I'm way ahead of you in this field.'

'What field?'

'Walking like an Egyptian.' He pushed her back a little. 'Now just do what I do.' She watched him with a puzzled expression, like a zoologist observing the antics of some new species of ape. He began laughing. 'C'mon—it's not hard.'

'But they're only painted sideways because they didn't know how to create perspective . . . oh!'

The last yelp was because he'd seized her hands and started moving her like a marionette. 'That's it—you're walking like a completely erroneous idea of an Egyptian!'

She laughed and that made her loosen up. 'Damien, this is ridiculous! I'm ridiculous!'

'Exactly! Priestess, you spend far too much time being the ultra-brain, time to remember you've a body too!' He dropped his grip on her arms and circled her, bending his knees in the silliest of silly walks. He was pleased to see she hadn't stopped dancing, though her moves were elegant compared to his. She had a nice fluid action that signalled there was much more dance inside her just waiting to get out. She spun with him, adding the head jerk so they both looked like pecking roosters. No one was watching—well, if they were, he wasn't going to let on. He suspected that quite a few of her friends were observing them out of the corner of their eye and approving of his attempts to get her to lighten up a little.

The song finished and she surprised him by not taking his head off for getting her out of her corner. 'Thanks: that was fun.'

The next song came on, an upbeat track whose driving pulse seemed to beg in Damien's mind for some kind of mock-tango moves. 'Do you only dance to historically related songs?' he coaxed.

She shook her head. 'I don't dance to any.'

'You just have so that's a theory you've got to revise. *Quod erat demonstrandum.*' He could thank Kieran for the little Latin he knew—thus it is demonstrated. 'Come, my little vampire bride.' He took her hands and guided her dramatically through the crowd, steering her through the melodramatic moves of his approximation of the tango, his vampire cloak swirling to create space around them. His prowling Dracula routine caused yet more laughter from the others. Rose let him bend and turn her like she was indeed in his thrall but all the time

93

her eyes glittered with excitement. She was laughing, looking astonishingly beautiful, and he loved that he had provoked that reaction. Knowing it would provoke more hilarity he flashed his fangs, pretending on a lunge to nip her neck. She surprised him by returning his teasing with a brush of her fingers down his arm, the move hidden by the folds of his cloak.

She's mine. The unexpected thought was a dangerous one to have in the middle of a dance floor with scores of people watching. Smiling wickedly, he ended the duet with a wild spin before making a flourishing bow to the applauding crowd. The playlist clicked to another Halloween classic, so he made way for the influx of zombies doing the living dead routine to 'Thriller'. He tucked Rose under his arm and steered her away from the dancers.

'Come with me?' he asked in a low voice.

Rose nodded and let him lead her out onto the back porch.

As much as she didn't want to admit it aloud, Rose was having the best time. Secretly inside, she was still crowing for the victory in the treasure hunt, pleasure made all the more acute because it had taken place in front of such an admiring audience. Damien had watched her unravel the clues with a wondering smile, cheering on her more inspired leaps of logic and obscure connections. And now the smooth Brit, the last person she would have thought would coax a wallflower off her wall, had helped her fulfil one of her all time dreams: dancing right in the centre of a room at a party, past caring who saw. Before today she might have occasionally risked a little jig and sway on the margins, but he had marched her right into the middle and then proceeded to do an amazing *Dancing with the Stars* type routine. He had created a space where she could momentarily be like other girls and it had felt wonderful.

But now he wanted to talk.

That never sounded good, did it? Confidence ebbing, she readied herself to go on attack first. Was he going to tell her she was embarrassing him, that she should stop clinging to his arm? But if that was the case, he was far more to blame. He'd started it. Or—even worse—had he found out something about her predicament?

Once outside on the back porch, Damien took off his cloak and folded it around her. The red silk lining took a moment to warm up as it settled against the bare skin of her arms but then it felt wonderful, smelling of dressing-up boxes, talcum powder, and a little hint of Damien's aftershave.

OK, Rose, tackle him head on, advised her inner kick-ass Lara. 'Is something the matter, Damien?'

He leaned next to her on the porch rail. Now he had her here he seemed less certain what he wanted to say. 'What gave you that idea?'

'Well, you did the cutting the target from the herd thing— for lions that signals you're going in for the kill.'

He laughed. 'You think I'm a lion?'

Oh yes—it was all that golden hair and skin suggesting it to her imagination. 'It's just a metaphor.'

He edged closer so his upper arm pressed against hers. 'I just wanted to tell you . . . I've had the best night with you.'

'Oh. Thanks.' She turned a little towards him and smiled up into his eyes, no longer cold blue but mysterious in the darkness, like the sparkle of a distant galaxy. 'Did you know that when you look at Andromeda, you're really looking at four hundred billion stars, can you imagine that?'

He smiled and tucked a lock of her hair behind her ear. 'I can't but if there is anyone on earth who can, it would be you. Rose, are you . . . er . . . seeing anyone?'

She wasn't sure if he meant that the way people did when talking to normal girls so decided to take it literally. 'Well, I'm seeing you right now.' She waved her hand in front of her eyes. 'I might not be able to make out a single star in Andromeda but I can spot what's right in front of me.'

He caught her hand and kissed the fingertips, warming each with his breath. 'Would you consider seeing a little more of me while I'm here?'

He was asking her out? No, surely not. People didn't ask her out, they asked her *for* things—help with homework, the rent, money miracles. 'What kind of seeing are you talking about, Damien?'

He pressed her fingers lightly against his cheek. 'The usual kind of seeing—dating.'

She checked all her collected data for a comparison to this situation and came up blank. 'But why do you want to do that with me?'

He looked briefly over her head, swallowing a smile. His gaze doubled in intensity when he turned back. 'Because there's something about you that speaks to something in me. I want to spend a little more time listening.'

That sounded cryptic—and not a puzzle she was sure she could solve with her usual logic. One thing was plain though: this was a time-limited deal. 'How long are you here for?'

'A fortnight.'

'That's two weeks in American, right?'

'Yeah.'

Two weeks. They were likely to be filled with yet more Dad-inspired misery. The idea of a boy taking her out and making her feel good about herself sounded very attractive. And the fact that it was going to end was also a bonus as he wouldn't have time to get too interested in her home life or pry into the absence of her parent. Dating happened outside the home, didn't it? At cinemas and parties. At least that's what her observation of other girls suggested.

And, she realized, she wanted an excuse to say 'yes'. 'OK.'

'Only OK?'

She could feel her cheeks flushing. 'Yes, that would be nice.'

'Only nice? I'd better get to work on that, bump it up another level.'

Surprising her, he closed the distance and threaded his hand through the hair at the back of her neck, cradling her head in his warm palm. The other hand rose to her waist and tugged her nearer so she was leaning against him. He then bent down and kissed her with gentle persuasion, mouth cruising along hers, the vampire fangs tugging a little at her lower lip. He paused and smiled.

'Shall I take those things off?'

Rose was lost for a moment then realized he meant the fake teeth. 'No, I . . . I quite like them,' she admitted.

'Then, for one night only you get your vampire fantasy.' He resumed the kiss.

Rose could have sunk through the floor right there. He guessed she had a vampire fantasy? But then embarrassment was the last thing on her mind as she let the kiss sweep her away. It felt so wonderful to be close to someone, to be held with care as if she was worth something. The wonderful moment was brought to a sudden end by a series of loud pops and the descent of multi-coloured streamers. Joe and Lindy had appeared in the doorway, Joe holding several empty party poppers in a clenched fist.

'Good—that finally got your attention,' said Joe.

Rose felt Damien stiffen and stand her up until her legs could do the job of holding her steady, but he still kept a protective arm around her. 'What do you want, Joe?' he asked.

'Just saying the party's ending. Time to get Cinderella home.' Joe was clearly annoyed but Rose wasn't sure why. She was hardly the first girl to kiss one of his friends in a corner of a party.

Lindy was watching the exchange with amusement. 'You're a braver person than me, Joe, disturbing Dracula at his supper.'

That seemed to make Joe's mood even darker. 'And when was it, Dracula, that you were going to remember you're vegetarian?'

Rose looked confusedly between the two friends. There seemed to be volumes spoken in the gaze passing between Joe and Damien.

'Joe, it's not what you think—' began Damien.

'No, it is exactly what I think. Time to go, Rose.' Joe removed the cloak with a quick flick of the clasp and chucked it at Damien. 'You had a coat, right? In the house?'

Rose nodded dumbly, wondering what the right thing was to say in the event of being caught mid-clinch. Joe was acting as if she had been insulted whereas in fact she had just lived through the finest few minutes of her entire life.

Joe took her arm in a firm grip. 'Let's go then. Epic party, Lindy, as ever.'

Lindy kissed Joe's cheek as he bent down to say goodbye. 'Thanks for bringing the entertainment. Bye, Rose, bye, Damien.'

Joe efficiently located her coat and bundled her into it like she was a four-year-old being dressed at kindergarten. In a stony silence, the three emerged onto the street. Parents were queuing up outside in their cars to collect their offspring. Rose briefly looked for her dad then remembered. Her spirits dipped.

'If he upset you, you can tell me,' Joe said fiercely, glowering over his shoulder at Damien who was wisely keeping a couple of steps back from his friend's bad mood.

'Who? Damien? No, no, it wasn't like that.' Rose wondered

how to rescue the feel-good factor from the party. 'I wanted to kiss him, Joe.'

If anything, Joe got even angrier at that admission. 'I know—that's what he's good at. I'm sorry: I told him to keep away from you even before I knew he had you in his sights. He normally keeps his word.'

Rose began to get annoyed now. What right did Joe have to police her love life? How was she ever going to have an ordinary girl's experiences if he planted great big 'No trespassing' signs around her? It wasn't as if he even wanted her for himself. 'What if I didn't want you to warn him off, Joe?'

He shook his head. 'Rose, you don't know what you're saying.'

'Don't you patronize me, Joseph Masters. Why can't I m . . . make out with someone at a party if I want?'

She was pleased to see that he at least looked a little embarrassed by this mortifying conversation. So he should for spoiling her fun. He acted as if she were still a little girl in pigtails.

'You can, just not with him.'

'Why not him?' She risked giving Damien a quick smile which he returned with a rueful look. 'He's your friend. Doesn't that mean he's a good guy?'

'I'm not so sure about that. He's not for you.'

'You don't get to make that call, Joe.' They had arrived at her doorstep, the dark windows not the least bit welcoming. Rose sighed, giving up on the argument as the weight of the burdens she was carrying thumped back down on her. It hardly seemed relevant. 'Thank you for walking me home. Goodnight, Joe.'

He glanced up at the frontage, dismal next to the blaze of lights that was his home. 'Want me to check the house for you?'

'No, no need.' A cheeky impulse made her turn to his friend. 'Damien, would you do a quick walk-through for me?'

Damien elbowed Joe out the way. 'My pleasure.'

'I'll be waiting right here,' said Joe menacingly.

Smiling at the blank door, Rose fitted the key into the lock and opened up. Tapping in the security code on the illuminated control board, she then switched on all the lights. She was no fan of spending nights alone in her big house but had found keeping the lights on helped. Damien pushed the door shut behind her.

'Do you want to stay in the hall while I check?' he asked.

She watched in surprise as he started a methodical survey of the ground floor. 'I just said that to get back at Joe. I'm fine—really. Nothing's tripped the alarm.'

'There are ways of bypassing that kind of alarm.' Damien's matter-of-fact tone wasn't reassuring.

'Oh.' She hurried to catch up with him, not liking this new piece of information at all. 'Then I'll come with you.'

He took her hand without needing her to ask. 'This floor is clear. Basement next.'

The laundry room, store cupboard, and den were all declared free of intruders in rapid succession.

'Sorry, there's a lot of house to check,' admitted Rose.

Damien relaxed his intent look for a second as he smiled at her. 'That's fine. I get to spend more time with you and Joe gets time to cool off.'

'Or work himself up even more.'

'That's a distinct possibility.' Damien seemed to be enjoying the thought.

The living room, bathrooms, and bedrooms on the next floor were also given the all clear. Damien didn't mention the cold, uninhabited feel to all but her bedroom and ensuite. To save money, she'd switched off the radiators in all the other rooms—something she regretted now.

'Nice curtains,' he remarked instead, peering down at the street from her window.

'Thanks.' She leaned with her back to the computer, hoping he hadn't noticed the open box file on the desk with the picture of her dad on the last demand. Surreptitiously she flicked it closed behind her back.

'Now we know we're alone, I get to say goodnight.' Damien moved in and gently caressed her cheek.

'Back to your coffin?' Her voice sounded surprisingly husky.

'That's right.' His gaze was transfixed by the pulse beating double time in her neck, his finger resting lightly on it. He probably knew, as she did, that this was one of the classic signs of attraction as well as fear. She wondered if he realized which feeling was uppermost. She knew it wasn't fear.

'Thanks, for everything, Damien.'

'Thank *you*. So our deal stands despite Joe?' He brushed a thumb over her lips as if mesmerized by the texture.

'Which deal?'

'The dating one.'

'But Joe—'

'But Joe nothing. I'll put him right about this.'

Feeling a little wild, a little reckless, her face broke into a grin. 'Tell him from me to butt out.'

'Absolutely will do. So, goodnight.' He leant down and kissed her, lingering over her mouth as if he couldn't quite get enough of her. 'Be good.'

'I could say the same to you but I fear it would be wasted.'

'You know me so well already.' With a last brush of his fingers on her neck, he headed back downstairs. 'Make sure you double lock the door behind me. Your security's not bad, by the way. No need to worry about anyone breaking in but remember to set the alarm before you go to bed. Joe and I will hear if it gets tripped and we'll be with you before you know it.'

Hugging herself, Rose found those words very reassuring. 'I will. I'm careful about that kind of thing.'

Darting over for a final quick kiss, he opened the front door and gave Joe a shove in the back, catching his friend unawares as he texted on the step.

'Night, beautiful.' Damien grinned, a last flash of fangs.

'Goodnight, Damien. See you, Joe.' Rose closed the door, locking it as promised. She waited, hearing the sound of a grumbling argument kicking off outside. Shaking her head, she floated on her delicious memories up to her bedroom, going to bed with something other than grim thoughts for the first time in a very long while.

Chapter 7

Damien knew Joe was spoiling for a fight so wasn't surprised when his friend followed him into the bathroom between their bedrooms. Reminding himself to keep his temper and let Joe say his piece, Damien started to ease off the fangs as if he didn't have an irate guy at his shoulder.

'What the hell do you think you're doing, Damien?' Joe grabbed a flannel and began scrubbing off his make-up, passing through an ashen phase to return to his usual dark complexion. 'I gave you one rule—no messing with Rose—and you break it on the first opportunity.'

'I'm not messing with her.' Damien placed the first of the teeth back in its box, running his tongue over his now normal canine.

'So making out in a dark corner with her at the party is not messing with her? Somehow your definition and mine have gotten way out of agreement.'

Damien shrugged. Joe could make of it what he wanted. He'd not committed a crime.

Joe balled up the flannel, squeezing dirty water down the sink. 'Can't you think straight for one second? She's not the kind of girl you do that stuff with. I told you—and you promised.' Damien put the second fang away then reached for his toothbrush. Joe slapped his hand down. 'No, you're going to answer me—not pretend nothing's happening.'

'I'm not pretending.'

'Like hell you're not!' Exasperated, Joe found release in throwing the flannel, hitting him square on the chest.

Damien was getting pissed off now—he was giving Joe a pass as his concerned friend, but there were limits. 'Watch it!'

Undaunted, Joe got right up in his grill. 'Part of me really wants to beat the crap out of you right now.'

Temper flared. 'Then by all means, let's take this outside.'

Joe growled at the baiting tone but ignored Damien's ironic sweep of the arm to the door. 'I'll say it for the last time: Rose is special—she won't cope well with your love-'em-and-leave-'em style.'

Overreacting or what? 'Joe, you're making far too much of this. All I asked was to date her—for two weeks—and she said she was OK with that. In fact, she went so far to tell me to tell you to butt out. She's a lot stronger than you make out. We need to find out what's going on and her taking me into her confidence is much more likely if we date.' Maybe from Joe's perspective it would seem as if he had broken his word. He had to explain he wasn't being heartless. 'I like her a lot, Joe—that haughty genius thing she does really works for me. I like that she gives as good as she gets. And I really think this is the best way of protecting her long term interests. I don't want to leave her to the FBI to investigate.'

Joe curled his hands into fists, leaning on one against the wall, probably to stop himself throttling his friend. He shoved the other into his pocket. 'We've been here before. Isaac's had to tell you not to use what people feel for you to do the job.'

Damien rubbed a flannel over his face, trying not to think about the suspension from missions he'd earned in London eighteen months ago for cosying up to a diplomat's daughter. This wasn't the same, was it?

'How do you think she'll feel when she finds out the guy she's been kissing has been telling tales to the Bureau?'

'It's not telling tales—it's investigating. It's our job.'

Joe didn't look the least sympathetic. 'Damien, I'm one of your best friends, right?'

'Yeah, right,' he said sardonically. This conversation was exactly the kind he hated and Joe wasn't that much of a fan either of all this examine-your-motives stuff. He had to be in serious trouble for Joe to do this.

'You might think you are doing the best you can for Rose but you've never had the experience of betrayal or rejection, have you?'

From his parents all the time, but Damien kept quiet and confined his answer to a shrug.

'How's she going to feel when she discovers she was just a mission to you?'

'That's not what it's like.'

'Isn't it?' Joe turned and walked out. 'You can use the shower first. I'm going to check our messages.'

Needing space from Joe right now, Damien stripped off his vampire gear and stood under the shower, letting the hot water pummel him. His anger faded and turned to a much cooler assessment of Joe's concerns. As much as he hated to admit it, Joe had a point. The YDA had rules about no relationships while on a mission. Could he dial back on the dating and still carry out his promise to Stevens that he would investigate her? He wanted to impress the Americans. Yet he'd seen both Nathan and Kieran bend the exact same rule and he had been less than generous in his reaction when they introduced the conflict of interests into an already complex situation. Strange how different it felt to be on the other side of the argument. He really should've cut the guys more slack. He rubbed shampoo into his hair punishingly, removing the last of the vampire gel. As for himself though, he didn't deserve slack. He was supposed to be the tough one, the cobra. He needed to

105

stop mooning about because a clever, pretty girl had dug her way past his defences.

And yet . . .

He swore and slapped the tiled wall, welcoming the sting on his palm. He'd not done anything too bad, just set up a few dates. He could keep his word to Joe and to Rose by making those times fun but nothing more. He would step back. No more kissing or flirting. He'd treat her like he would Raven or Kate. A friend: yeah, a friend.

Wrapping a towel round his hips, he gathered up his clothes and padded barefoot to his bedroom. 'Bathroom's free.'

'Damien, come here a moment.' Joe's tone alerted him to the approach of trouble. 'Kieran's sent us a new message and I think you'll want to see it.'

Rose woke up to a silent house. She had to train herself to stop expecting her father to return but still she was hoping that she'd fed the beast enough to persuade it to throw her dad back to her. She lay for a moment just letting the new day settle on her. A weak grey dawn tinged the white and gold curtains. Rain pattered on the sill.

Think of something good.

I have a boyfriend. As of last night, I am dating a vampire.

The thought made her smile. She wasn't stupid; she knew it was just a vacation romance for Damien while he was visiting but, still, he was gorgeous and genuinely seemed to like her. It made her feel twice as tall to know that she could attract a boy of his calibre and it would give her some kudos at school. No one expected geeky Rose to date. She jumped out of bed to do a little waltz with her reflection in the dressing table mirror.

Not such a weirdo after all, Rose Knight, she told her reflection. *Except for your unfortunate case of bed hair.* Grabbing her brush, she raked it through her tangles, putting it to rights.

Stuffing her feet into a soft pair of bootee slippers, she wrapped herself in her favourite candy-pink dressing gown. Ryan had always told her that it was an unfortunate colour combo with her hair, but what the heck: who was going to see her? If you fretted about being a fashion disaster in your own home, there was something seriously wrong with your priorities. Bounding down the stairs to the kitchen, Rose put on the coffee maker, deciding to treat herself to hot frothy milk, cocoa powder dusting, the works, as she couldn't be bothered to go out to a cafe today. From the look of the weather, it was exactly the right kind of morning to drink home-made cappuccino, do homework then read novels, all without getting dressed.

As she set the timer on the microwave, a prickle at the nape of her neck edged her mood back into the unease with which she had woken. Hating herself for giving in to the urge to look, she went into the hallway.

Another letter lay on the mat.

Oh no, no, no. She had no money left—she'd told them. Sweeping it up from the floor, she ripped open the envelope. No picture: just text.

One million dollars by Friday.

Made with what? she wanted to wail.

The microwave pinged. Abandoning her plans for her morning's treat, she went upstairs to her bedroom and switched on her laptop. She'd have to see about an overdraft but that would be incredibly difficult to organize without her dad to speak to the bank manager.

What? She stared hard at the screen, unable to take in what she was reading. Their account wasn't down to a few hundred dollars as she had left it after transferring the last ransom; it was now showing a balance of two hundred thousand, paid in late yesterday evening. She checked the payee—a string of numbers from an unfamiliar account.

That wasn't good. She didn't believe in fairy godmothers— not ones that planted seed corn money in a stranger's bank account. She couldn't touch it—should report it—not that she could do the latter as she had no desire to bring the authorities into this.

But there was no doubt she needed a sizeable sum to invest. To stay on the right side of the law, she would have to get her start-up money somewhere else. Desperate, not even thinking of the time zone issues, she reached for her phone and rang a number she'd only ever used twice in the past year.

'Who is this?' Fortunately the woman on the other end didn't sound as if she had been asleep. Soft music tinkled in the background.

'Mom, sorry if I woke you.'

Belle Knight laughed, voice husky. 'Honey, I haven't got to bed yet. What are you doing calling me at . . . well, I guess it's nine over there, isn't it?'

'Mom, I've got a problem.'

'Rose, you know the deal I made with your dad.' Belle had promised Don not to disrupt her daughter's life. She'd interpreted that as keeping out of the way and seeing Rose once a year during the summer, usually at some beach resort where Belle flirted with guys and Rose read her books on a recliner by the pool. Both had given up on getting much out of the mom-and-daughter bonding sessions as their interests had not proved compatible. Her odd duck, Belle called Rose.

'But, Mom, Dad's not here. He's in trouble.'

'He's always in trouble, hon. That's why I, and his other two wives before me, divorced him.'

'Not with a woman or anything. I meant he's . . . well, I've got to raise some money to pay one of his debts urgently.'

'Or what? They'll shoot him in the knee? Girl, your father hasn't changed.'

'So you see why I need a little money to make some money. I'll pay you back. With interest.'

Rose could hear her mom speak to someone else in the room, telling him she was just coming. 'How much?'

'A hundred thousand dollars?'

Belle starting laughing, then stopped abruptly when Rose didn't retract the figure. 'You're serious?'

'Yes. Or fifty thousand even would be useful.'

'Aw, hon, I don't have that kind of money. Even if I wanted to help, I couldn't, and to be honest, your dad has to stop expecting us to rescue him. He'll have to come to his own arrangements with these guys.' Rose could hear the impatience in her mom's voice. 'Look, hon, I've got to go, but why don't you come stay with me for Thanksgiving—have a break from your dad, hey?'

Rose felt the tears burn the back of her throat. 'I won't have money for the ticket.'

'Oh. What about Christmas then? I might be able to buy you the ticket as your present. You can book yourself onto a flight to Vegas and we'll have a little quality girl time together.'

'A spa weekend isn't going to solve this one, Mom.'

'But you'll feel better and that's all I care about.'

Wrong, all Belle cared about was Belle. She was probably doing the concerned mom act for the benefit of whoever she was with in that room.

'So that's a "no" to help then?'

'Yes, precious, it is. It'll all work out, just you see. Your dad always had a gift for drama—you have to stop rushing to rescue him. Give me a call in a week or so and let me know when you're coming. Love you.'

'You too.' Rose ended the call, head resting on hands. It had been a long shot but she had hoped her mom might at least sympathize. Steeling herself, she made the next call to Ryan.

'The house better be burning down or why on earth are you calling me at this time?' he asked grumpily.

'No quite burning but, Ryan, I need help.'

'What's up?' He sounded tired rather than interested.

'Dad's in trouble. I need some money to work up a . . . debt repayment . . . I need about a hundred thousand.'

Ryan gave a choked laugh. 'You're coming to me for that kind of money? Geez, Mop, don't you know I've just landed in debt myself to about twice that amount?'

'Can't you borrow it for me?'

'You have to have a decent credit history to get your hands on that kind of sum legitimately—something to mortgage.'

That was what she feared but she'd hoped he'd at least share the problem. 'So you can't?'

'No I can't. Tell Dad to cut a deal. Given enough time you'll be able to make that kind of profit on our stocks and shares, won't you?'

'I've already used those up.'

There was a shocked pause. 'And left nothing to work with? Have you gone crazy? I thought you were clever!' Now finally Ryan was awake.

'I had to—there were other demands.'

'Then you're up the creek without a paddle.'

'Thanks for the sympathy, Ryan.'

'So will you make rent? Will we lose the house?'

She pinched the bridge of her nose. 'I've got a few weeks until the next payment.'

'But you'll manage—you always do.'

'I'm not so sure I can this time.'

'You've got to. My life is already in the can. I can't lose the one place I have to call home. I'm counting on you.'

It would be nice to be able to count on someone in her family for once. 'I'll do my best, Rye.'

'Your best is phenomenal so I know I needn't worry.' And he ended the call.

'My family is really crud, you know that?' she told her reflection in the computer screen.

The cursor beat like a tiny heart. There was two hundred thousand just sitting in the account. What should she do?

'I'm still not sure about this,' Damien pulled Joe aside into the hallway, leaving Stevens and a female colleague talking to Carol and Patrick Masters over a stack of bacon and pancakes.

Joe rolled his shoulders. 'You agreed when I put in the call last night.'

'But I've had time to think it through some more. If Rose sees the FBI on her doorstep she's going to panic. It's her dad's safety we're risking. We should've kept it in our own hands for a while longer.' And Damien didn't like losing control of the investigation. Joe's instinct was always to appeal to the authorities earlier than Damien would by choice.

'There's no reason to think anyone's watching the house.' Joe rubbed the back of his neck. 'Look, I don't like this any more than you but Kieran's message was clear: she's got a heap of funny money turned up in her account. The other stuff she used before—well, that looked OK, nothing obviously wrong with it—but this new sum has bounced around the world from one tax haven to another.'

'I read the email. I know Kieran thinks it came from sanction-busting sales in Russia. But what if they're more interested in nailing this Roman Melescanu guy than helping Rose and her dad?'

'Which is why we need to be there—to remind Stevens of our deal. And if we act swiftly, before Rose has a chance to touch it, she won't have committed any offence under money laundering legislation.'

'Yeah.' That had been the clinching argument last night. 'But she's not going to like this.' Damien had wanted to be the one to solve her problems, both to help her and impress the Feds. It would have helped salve his conscience for maybe going too far with her the night before.

Joe grimaced. 'I know. You've only known her a few days but I've known her since she was little—it's one heck of a betrayal on my part—or at least that's what she'll think.'

Damien squeezed his friend's shoulder, the duty of reassurance swinging his way. 'But she'll understand eventually that you're doing it for her. You've got to hang tough on this one.'

Joe sighed. 'Maybe. But I think the damage might be irreparable. Can't blame her—I'm more or less serving her up to the FBI on a plate.'

'Hey, Joe, it's time to do this,' called Stevens from the kitchen, wiping his mouth on the serviette.

'Now you bring her here, you promise?' said Mrs Masters removing the dishes from the table. 'Don't leave the girl alone.'

'We wouldn't allow a minor to remain home alone, ma'am,' said the female colleague who had introduced herself as Joanne Jameson, the official in charge of the Melescanu investigation. An early thirties blonde, hair cut in a no-nonsense bob, she radiated efficiency rather than warmth. Like Stevens, she was dressed in a dark grey suit and white shirt, almost as if they were wearing a uniform, though she had added two-inch heels to her outfit and left off the tie.

'But you'll bring her here, right?' pressed Mr Masters, hearing the evasion.

'We'll have to consider what's best for her safety—and there'll be questions.' Jameson checked her gun holster. 'OK, Stevens, let's go.'

'But you can't just march in on her with no warning,' protested Mr Masters.

'Dad, it's OK, I've got this,' said Joe. 'Damien and I will stay with her.'

Damien followed Joe out of the house and walked behind the two FBI agents the short stretch to Rose's front door. Stevens turned round.

'You knock, Joe.'

Joe stiffened. The FBI were making him do the whole Judas routine, delivering his childhood friend into their hands.

'It's better it comes from you,' added Jameson. 'She'll be wary of us.'

That didn't make it any easier. Deciding to take the fall for Joe, Damien stepped forward. 'I'll do it.' He rapped loudly then called out.

'Hey, Rose, can you come to the door a moment?'

There was a short pause then the sound of a chain being drawn back. Rose opened the door part way, greeting him with a warm smile. 'Hey you. I'm sorry but I'm not dressed yet, Damien.'

That explained why she was hiding behind the door. 'It's OK—doesn't matter. We just need to talk.'

Her eyes went to the three people standing with him. 'Joe? Who . . . who are these?' Damien could see the moment when the penny dropped, face shuttering behind a blank expression. 'Oh, I'm afraid I can't let anyone in right now. You'll have to come back later.'

'Miss Knight?' Jameson handed her a piece of paper through the gap. 'I'm Agent Joanne Jameson and this is Agent Stevens, whom I believe you met last week. We both work for the FBI and we have a warrant to search these premises and remove any computers or other digital devices. You really do have to let us in.'

Stevens pushed a little harder. 'We understand you are under eighteen so it is within your rights to have an adult present. Is your father here?'

Rose was still stuck back at the warrant moment. 'No,' she whispered. She looked devastated. Damien felt an almost irrepressible urge to hug her but guessed he was the last person she wanted touching her right now.

'We can wait until an adult family member arrives—or you can call someone you trust,' continued Stevens.

'Damien and I will be with you,' said Joe softly. 'Let us in, Rosie.'

With a trembling hand, she pushed back the door to let them past her. Turning in the passageway, Damien saw she had been speaking the truth when she said she wasn't dressed. It would have been hard to find her looking more vulnerable than in a pink dressing gown and woollen slippers.

'Now, let's just take this slowly, Rose—can I call you Rose?' asked Agent Jameson.

Rose didn't reply. Her knuckles were white as she gripped her elbows.

'OK, let's just go through to your lounge and talk about what's going to happen.'

Joe tried to take Rose's arm but she pulled away from him. Saying nothing, she led them into the cold family room. The curtains were still closed. Damien took it upon himself to open the drapes but the grey light of an overcast day did little to cheer the atmosphere. Rose sat at one end of the sofa, hands clasped in her lap, head lowered. On the table beside her, a glass pyramid caught the light and cast faint rainbows on the beige carpet. One multi-coloured band fell across her cream bootee slipper and thin ankle like a manacle.

'Miss Knight, we need to ask a few questions, is that OK?' said Jameson.

Rose nodded. Damien circled to stand behind her, hands resting close to where her hair touched the back of the seat, but he had seen her reaction to Joe so didn't close the distance. It killed him to keep away but he'd lost the right the moment he'd knocked on the door. He'd really messed up this time—so had Joe.

'You're not in trouble, Rose,' said Joe, crouching beside her, his brown eyes full of sincerity. 'Just tell the truth. We're here to help you.'

Her chin dipped as she hunched into herself. 'I want to get dressed.'

'In a moment,' said Jameson. 'Do you know why we're here?'

Rose said nothing.

'I'm guessing you do because normally people would be demanding by now what the FBI was doing in their house. We know your father is in trouble with Roman Melescanu.'

'He is?' Rose raised her gaze to the agent's face. 'That's who's behind it?'

'You didn't know?'

Rose shrugged and went back to saying nothing.

'Our sources,' Stevens picked up where his colleague left off, 'have noticed that you have been paying large sums out to Melescanu and have recently received a large sum of money from the same individual.'

Rose gripped her hands more tightly together. 'And did you have a warrant for your electronic snooping, Agent Stevens?'

Damien gave her a silent round of applause. His girl had come up from the knock down swinging a punch.

'It wasn't the FBI,' said Stevens. 'The information came to us from an anonymous source outside our jurisdiction.'

Joe turned away, not liking the lies. Rose must have picked up on his awkwardness. 'Joe, why are you and Damien here?'

'Miss Knight, I think you don't quite understand how an FBI interrogation works. I get to ask the questions.' Jameson made it sound like a joke but they all knew she was serious.

'We asked them to keep an eye on you,' added Stevens. 'They called us in when they thought things had gone too far for you to cope alone.'

Rose squeezed her elbows. 'Then if this is an interrogation maybe I need a lawyer.'

'You're not a suspect. You're a witness,' said Jameson.

'To what?'

'To kidnap, extortion, and money laundering.'

'And if I said my dad was just away on business?'

'Then we'd all know you were lying and that you'd be perjuring yourself if you said the same thing before a judge.'

Stevens leaned forward. 'Perjuring means when you . . .'

'I know what perjuring means, thank you. I'm really quite intelligent, you know.' Rose ran a hand through her hair, her brain clearly whirling fast. 'Look, if I'm going to answer any questions, I at least want to get dressed.'

'I'll escort you to your room,' said Jameson, standing. 'You can select some clothes and use a bathroom to change as long as I check it first.'

Nodding once, Rose quit the room. Since smiling at him on the doorstep, she hadn't looked at him, Damien realized. She'd looked at everyone else but not him, which told him just how furious she was that he had joined in this little betrayal party.

Joe took a seat on the sofa. 'We're so screwed.'

'Only fair, as that's what she thinks we've done to her.'

Stevens tapped his knees impatiently. 'You're doing her a favour, guys. She can't handle Melescanu on her own.'

'What will you do with her?' asked Joe.

'Take her with us and arrange protective custody until this situation with her father is resolved.'

'And how will you resolve it?'

Stevens shook his head. Damien didn't know if that meant he had no idea or he was not allowed to share.

'He'll be OK?' pressed Joe.

'Don Knight mixes with the wrong crowd, Joe. Any risks he runs are ones he entered into with his eyes open.'

'I get that he's not your favourite person but he's Rose's dad.'

'We'll do everything we can to make sure no one gets hurt.'

The vague promise wasn't nearly enough to satisfy either Damien or Joe but it didn't look like the Feds were going to offer any more than that.

A door upstairs closed and Jameson came down the stairs. 'She's in the bathroom. Let's make a start in her bedroom— there's a laptop and paperwork on her desk. It looks like she runs things from there.'

'I'll be right with you. Good work by the way, boys.' Stevens clapped a hand on Damien's shoulder in passing. 'We couldn't have done this without your hacker friend in the UK. I'll let the boss know that I think an American branch of the YDA is a good idea.'

Chapter 8

Rose pressed her ear to the bathroom door.

Good work by the way, boys. We couldn't have done this without your hacker friend in the UK. The man's voice carried up the stairs confirming what she had suspected since Damien knocked on her door. The boys had sold her out, invaded her privacy in the most unforgivable way. Damien hadn't fancied her; he'd been using her. They had risked her dad's life and her months of work raising ransoms just to please the Feds with whom they were interning with this week.

Buttoning up her shirt and then zipping up a fleece, she stared numbly in the mirror. She'd grabbed warm clothes knowing what she would be forced to do. Fortunately the female agent had been too interested in the box file on her desk to notice that Rose had taken canvas baseball boots and her purse with her to the bathroom. She laced up the footwear, not daring to examine her feelings too closely. She wouldn't think about Damien and what she had begun to imagine between them, more fool her, nor Joe and the years of friendship that had just been ruined. The lace snapped after a violent pull. Rose had to make do with a knot to reconnect it. The boots should have enough grip. Dumping the contents of her purse on the counter, she grabbed her bill fold and keys, slipping it into a pocket of her jeans.

'You OK in there?' called the female agent, tapping on the door.

Rose lowered the toilet lid and pulled the flush. 'I'll be out in a minute.' She wasn't the least bit OK. She was just adjusting to the fact that once again she was completely on her own, let down by two boys that she had begun to trust. That was not an experiment that needed repeating. She'd do this on her own from now on.

Using the cover noise of the refilling cistern, she released the window lock and eased it open. It was going to be a tight fit but she could drop from here onto the flat roof of the kitchen extension, then from there she could jump to the backyard and get out over the neighbour's wall. Plans beyond that point were sketchy but she knew that the last thing she wanted was to be taken out of circulation by the FBI. She would have no hope of negotiating her father's release if they had hidden her away.

Rose climbed on to the toilet and hooked leg over the sill. It looked much higher from here.

Just do it, inner Lara scolded her.

Swivelling her hips round she got her other knee on the sill then lowered herself out, gripping with both hands to control her descent. Her feet ended up dangling about four feet above the kitchen roof. She let go, dropped to the rough tarred surface and brushed off her hands, imagining her internal guides, Lara and Nancy, giving her an approving whoop-de-whoop. A drainpipe took the runoff to ground level at the far corner. Walking as softly as she could over the gritty roof, she tested the pipe. It seemed firm and she didn't weigh much. Turning round, she gripped the gutter and eased over the edge on her stomach. With a crack, part of the gutter gave way, dousing her legs in dank cold water. Inner Nancy shrieked with alarm but Lara ordered her to hold it together. Rose almost lost her grip but managed to anchor herself on the downpipe which was more securely bolted to the outside wall. She swung for a moment one-handed like a monkey from a vine, heart racing.

'Hey, no!' Damien was at the bathroom window. 'Rose, wait!'

Not him—he was the last person for whom she would wait. Rose let go, falling the last few feet to the ground, landing cushioned by the purple-flowering hebe she had planted last year. Picking herself up, she ran for the wall and scrambled over using the back of a garden bench to boost up. She landed in Mr Masters' tiny pumpkin patch. The back door was open as Mrs Masters was taking peelings out to compost.

'Rose!' Joe's mom had no time to say any more as Rose barged past her. Rose ignored Mr Masters sitting at his computer and bolted out of the front door. She took a sharp right, running an erratic route until she had no more puff. Finding she wasn't far from her usual subway stop with her pass in her pocket, she clattered down the stairs and jumped on the first train. When she caught her breath, she realized that they were heading up the line to Penn Station, one of New York's big termini. The Feds would monitor major transport routes so she'd have to get away from something so easy to track. They could pin her down when they realized her route. Closing her eyes, she called on her guides. Her Lara was quiet now she had escaped immediate danger but her chipper Nancy Drew was full of suggestions. Losing herself in the crowds at the station then going on foot seemed her best option. Maybe she could even make it look like she continued her journey on one of the other lines, an intercity Amtrak train maybe? With this is mind, Rose got out and slowed her steps to blend with the other travellers. She paused in the polished glare of the station lobby with its oppressively low roof and pretended indecision as she gazed up at the huge announcement board.

Too obvious? Joe might not buy it but the Feds and Damien didn't know her, did they?

With a mental shrug to Nancy, whose idea this was, Rose

headed towards the entrance for tracks thirteen and fourteen before diverting to take the stairs to the surface. Following signs for Madison Square Garden and Seventh Avenue, she slotted herself into the flocks of Saturday shoppers and tourists.

After zigzagging in and out of shops and taking side streets, Rose arrived in New York's heart: Times Square. The looming skyscrapers made it feel as she was at the bottom of a ravine with little daylight reaching her. The flashing, pulsing advertisements mocked her, whisking garish images of success and beauty past tired and dispirited eyes. The roar of traffic and choking fumes from fleets of yellow cabs added to her sense of exhaustion as her adrenaline levels crashed. She couldn't let her energy dip, even though the immediate need to flee had passed. She needed to regroup, plan her next move. Spotting a burger bar, she bought herself a soda and took a seat out of the way towards the back of the store, pretending interest in a sheaf of tourist brochures she had grabbed from the display in the entrance. What now? Her pulse was still thrumming, cold sweat making her shirt stick to her spine, her hair flopping in her eyes. She rested her forehead on her hands, and stared down at the flyer for Broadway shows, ignoring the droplets falling onto the grinning picture of the stars of the latest blockbuster musical. She wasn't crying. Her eyes were just watering because it was so warm in here compared to the street. Using a handful of serviettes she scrubbed her face angrily.

OK, girl, suck it up. You can't go home and you can't go to friends as your best ones have just sold you out and the others will be watched. Damien was just a mirage—a boyfriend illusion hiding someone investigating you. You should've known better, seeing where Joe met him. Young *Detective* Agency—duh! Of course, he wasn't going to like a geeky girl like you. Get real.

But it wasn't all bad news. At least now, thanks to the Feds, she knew who her dad's captor was, something that she hadn't been sure about earlier. That had to be a step forward. If only she could reach out to this Melescanu person and explain her temporary difficulty raising money, then maybe he'd let her have some more time?

Or maybe she could find where he was holding her father and go rescue him herself? They could then get out of New York, relocate to Vegas for a few months while they figured out what to do next.

That meant kissing goodbye to her chance at graduating and attending college.

Rubbing her aching temples, Rose made herself face up to the reality that she would never get to spend a blissful three years studying in some quiet Ivy League cloister where the only crisis was failing to get an essay in on time. Her family had managed to kill off all hope of this happening. That future had been buried in a sarcophagus, carried into a hidden chamber, then walled off for ever under tonnes of rock.

Taking a sip of her drink, she winced as the iced liquid hit her sensitive teeth. She didn't know why she'd bought it: she didn't like the stuff but it had seemed something normal to pick rather than the weak black tea she would have preferred. She had to be unmemorable from now on.

Catching a girl in the next booth eying her wild hair, Rose self-consciously brushed it behind her ears. A baseball cap was the next thing she would purchase. Except in the St Patrick's Day parade, auburn wasn't that common even in central Manhattan. Anyone looking at CCTV would use it as a flag.

OK, the plan was beginning to form. Get a hat. Then drag Ryan from wherever he ended up last night before the Feds thought to locate him. That meant tracing his whereabouts by his cell. All she needed for that was a friendly owner of an iPhone.

Noticing the handset the girl opposite her had on the table, Rose patted her pockets, making out she had lost something.

'Shoot! I must have dropped my phone,' she said aloud. Sliding out from her booth she approached the girl with a friendly smile. 'Would you do me a huge favour and let me use the Find My Phone app?'

The girl sized her up a moment then decided she wasn't going to take the phone and make a run for it. 'Sure, take a seat.'

Rose slid in next to her and chatted inanely about how she must have left it when she bought her subway ticket, or maybe when she was browsing in Macy's. Thanking her brain for its ability to remember strings of numbers, she typed in her brother's contact details and waited for the app to do its magic. Brooklyn—over the river; that would mean more travelling and she really wanted to keep out of monitored areas such as the choke points of bridges or stations. She would have to risk texting him, hoping the FBI were still chasing her rather than putting a tail on her brother.

'Yep, looks like I'm headed back to Macy's.' She deleted the search. 'Would you mind if I sent a message to my friends to tell them I'll be late meeting up?'

'No problem. I've got an unlimited texts contract.'

'Oh, who's that with?' She pretended interest in the answer as she sent a quick SOS to Ryan. *I really need you. Borrowed a phone so don't reply just meet me by my favourite statue, Central Park, in an hour. Please. Mop.* 'Thanks—you're a lifesaver.' Returning the phone after deleting her message once she saw it had been delivered, she picked up her soda and headed back out into the crowds of the neon bright square.

It took her just under half an hour to walk to the park and then about the same again to reach the monument as she took a few wrong turns. She remembered the King Jagiello statue from when she was little but hadn't visited the spot for years. It was about halfway up the huge park that provided a green lung to the top end of central Manhattan. Jagiello had always been a favourite, reminding her of the elf Legolas from *The Lord of the Rings* but with a bad haircut. He held exuberant crossed swords above his head, and had a youthful face with flyaway wisps of hair peeking out from under his crown. She'd made up stories about him when she was younger, casting him as the hero and guardian angel of her adventure tales, leaping from his plinth to rescue her—or she rescued him: the honours always being equal. The benches around the old equestrian statue were occupied by a mixture of tourists consulting guide books or phone screens and old men reading the Sunday newspapers muffled in coats and scarfs. No one showed any interest in her. No sign of Ryan. Still, it was only just an hour after she had sent the text. He might have difficulty getting here so quickly from Brooklyn, even on his motorbike. Rose took a seat on one of the benches and dug her hands into her fleece, chin lowered to her chest. Her newly purchased NYU baseball cap obscured most of her features. Exhausted, she let her eyes close a second, ignoring the pigeons pecking hopefully around her feet.

'Hey, Mop, why all the cloak-and-dagger drama?' Ryan dropped his black bike helmet on the bench beside her. 'That's not like you.'

Rose sprang to her feet and hugged him. 'Oh, Ryan, thank you so much for coming!'

He grimaced then gave in to her frantic embrace and put his arms around her. 'You didn't leave me much choice. I couldn't phone you back to ask what you were playing at.'

'I'm not playing.' She swallowed against the lump in her throat. 'It's the FBI—they were at our house this morning asking about Dad and Roman Melescanu. I've run away.'

Ryan groaned and pushed her to sit down. 'Tell me what happened.' He sat next to her and put his arm around her shoulders.

Rose quickly ran through what had happened since she woke up and the truth about the last few weeks. He made no comment only hissing his disapproval when she described climbing out of the window.

'So I need to find out what you know about Melescanu,' Rose said in conclusion. 'All I can think to do now is bust Dad out myself—or both of us if you'll join me.' One look at his stony expression told her that idea was not going to be embraced with great joy and delight.

'Rose, did it not occur to you that you might've done better to stay at home?' He rubbed his chin, unshaven chin rasping. 'Let the Feds find Dad.'

She shook her head. 'They aren't interested in helping him, just catching this Melescanu guy.'

'But it's not your responsibility—it's theirs. You don't have a hope negotiating anything with Melescanu. At least the FBI would look after you.'

Rose curled up inside herself, wishing she could retreat like a hedgehog. She had thought Ryan would understand her choices. 'So you think I'm wrong to try? I've been managing to meet the ransom now for weeks—a million dollars each time. It's not easy but I've done it. Don't you think that would persuade them I have an ability worth a bargain?'

'And they've fed you another two hundred thousand to start up all over again?' Ryan crossed his ankles, buckles on his biker boots flashing in the weak light. 'Look, Rosie, I've got a better idea. Leave Dad to the FBI. You don't know him as well as me: he'll have figured the angles, have a way of surviving all this. He's a cat with nine lives and will land on his feet.' He shifted his body towards her, voice dropping to a familiar cajoling tone. 'What if you give me that money? It'll clear my debts here and then we can start over free and easy somewhere else. Dad can come join us when he's wriggled out of his fix—and he will, I promise. He's the ultimate comeback kid.'

Rose wasn't really surprised Ryan had worked out his own angle to benefit from this situation. He was very like her father in that respect. 'But it's not my money to give you. If I touch it I'll be committing a felony under money laundering legislation—and the FBI will know.'

'We'll draw it in cash before they freeze the account. You're sixteen—no one will prosecute you if you play dumb. How were you to know?'

She folded her arms mutinously across her chest. 'No, Ryan, I'm not doing that. And I don't play dumb. Ever.'

'But you'll get nowhere with Melescanu, trust me!' Ryan's temper was fraying, more because he was denied what he wanted than through concern for their father, thought Rose sourly. 'There's a reason the FBI haven't been able to arrest him—he looks legit, a respectable businessman. He covers his tracks. He knows the right people, contributes to politicians' fighting funds. I'd bet that the Feds won't be able to pinpoint the source of that money. And if you do go to him, you won't even get into see him.'

She hunched lower, stubbornly refusing to concede he had a point.

'Get real, Rose. His headquarters is a fortress on one of the Hudson river piers, all corporate headquarters not some seedy dive. He employs legions of lawyers to keep the FBI away and security teams to keep the rest of us at a distance.'

'But he wants something from me or he wouldn't have given me that money.'

'You don't want a man like him to want anything from you.' Ryan heaved a sigh. 'Look, sis, let's just get away from

Manhattan for a while. Come with me on the back of my bike. I've got a place to stay over in Brooklyn—at least I think Shelby will be fine with you crashing there for a few days.' He wrinkled his brow, evidently not sure at all.

'I don't have a few days to waste—I have until Friday.'

'But you can't meet the demand because you've already told me you're not going to touch that money.'

'I'll think of something.'

'You're not a miracle worker.'

'I've got to be.'

'I can't let you go running blind into danger. You've got to come with me—or I'll call the Feds myself and ask them to pick you up.' He took out his phone.

'You wouldn't!'

'Cupcake, you've no idea what I'd do to stop my kid sister acting like an idiot.' He took her hand in his. 'Come on: let's go back to Shelby's. She's nice and not a bad cook—you'll like her.'

Rose was torn. Part of her wanted to go with Ryan but she knew that if she had traced him so easily so could the FBI. In a way, she was surprised they hadn't found them yet—she couldn't stay here with him any longer. Gently she disengaged his fingers.

'Thanks, Ryan, but I'll manage. Shelby won't want me hanging around her apartment, especially not if I bring the authorities to her door—I doubt you'd like that either. And you're right: I need to give this more thought—not rush off to take on someone like Melescanu. What was I thinking? Sorry: I just lost my head a moment.'

Ryan frowned, realizing that she was right to believe she had trouble riding hot on her trail. He was beginning to work out the disadvantages of sticking by her for his own questionable dealings. 'But where will you stay? I don't just want to abandon my kid sister here.'

'With friends—Lindy will let me crash at hers. I'll wait until the Feds have searched there and then ask her if I can stay a night or two—I can trust her to keep a secret. I've not done anything illegal so they can't arrest me—I'll just keep dodging them and they'll soon lose interest. I'll call you later in the week.'

Ryan was still suspicious, as well he might be as she had no intention of dragging Lindy into this. 'And you promise you'll not try to free Dad yourself?'

Rose had spotted a park patrol walking towards them up the leaf-strewn path. She got up. 'I promise I won't do anything stupid.' Desperate maybe, but not stupid.

'OK then.' Rising, Ryan gave her a swift hug. 'Keep away from Melescanu. And if you change your mind about that money . . .'

'I won't.'

He gave a wry smile. 'You're too law-abiding for your own good.'

'Is that possible?'

'I'd say so, seeing the fix you're in.' He tucked his helmet under his arm. 'You've got no phone?'

'I left it behind. It's too easy to trace.'

He dug in his pocket and pulled out a fifty dollar bill. 'Get yourself a cheap burner.'

'Burner?'

'One you can throw away when it has served its purpose. If the thing with Lindy doesn't work out and you need help, send a message saying come fetch you.'

She pocketed the money. 'Will do.'

He tugged the peak of her cap down. 'Love you, Mop. Dad should be shot for putting you through this.'

'Not funny.'

'I wasn't making a joke.' With a wave of his hand, he

sauntered off towards his bike. Rose headed in the opposite direction, an instinct making her decide that she needed to keep her distance from that beacon in her brother's pocket. Everyone went about tagged these days, bleeping out their position to the silent watchers in the communications masts on top of the buildings. Carrying nothing but cash, she had the fanciful thought that she was like a stealth submarine, slipping out of sight under the surface of the city. If she could keep out of the range of CCTV, she should be able to evade capture for as long as it took to think her way out of this bind.

Having picked the lock to the bathroom when he got no answer, Damien stood frozen at the window, heart in his mouth, as he saw Rose drop from the roof to the flowerbed. She got back up and jumped the fence like the Thompson's gazelle that used to invade his parents' garden in Uganda. He found himself wishing she'd at least turned an ankle.

'Joe, she's escaped—heading over the wall for your house!' Damien shouted as he followed her out of the window and across the flowerbeds.

Joe was already on the street by the time Damien had made it through the garden.

'Which way?' Damien asked, scanning the parked cars trying to spot the distinctive redhead in the gaps.

'Damned if I know.' Joe kicked a wheelie bin in frustration.

Joe's parents joined them on the pavement.

'Where's Rose?' asked Mr Masters. 'She ran through our house without so much as a word to either of us.'

'Did those people scare her?' Mrs Masters pressed her hand to her chest. 'The poor dear.'

'We were just trying to help her.' Joe's tone was bitter. 'But I don't think she saw it that way.'

Stevens arrived at Damien's shoulder. 'I've alerted my

colleagues that she's fled. We'll ask the local precinct to make a search, but where do you think she's likely to go? Friends? Family?'

Joe rubbed his forehead with his fist. 'There aren't that many candidates. Her brother Ryan is closest—her mom's too far away to be any help. I can't see her going to the kids from school—Lindy maybe, but no one else I can think of.'

'Let's take this back inside. Mrs Masters, Mr Masters, don't worry: we'll look after her.' Stevens returned to Rose's house, clearly not that interested in the drama on the street outside.

'Joe, we've got to find her.' Mr Masters dug his hands in his pockets. 'I'll make a start by walking the local area. You go with the FBI—see what they can do.'

'OK, Dad. I'm sorry I let her get past us.'

'Your mom said she came over the fence. You weren't to know she was going to pull a stunt like that.'

Joe quirked a sour smile. 'No, it's not like her.'

Damien was eager to get searching too but he had already worked out that Rose would be wanting to put as big a distance as she could between her and her house. He doubted Mr Masters' search would turn up anything. The FBI were able to tap into the CCTV. His gut told him that they should check the subway. Not waiting for Joe to finish talking to his parents, he headed back into the house and found the two agents examining a sheaf of papers in Rose's bedroom.

'This is what the kid's been dealing with,' said Jameson, spreading out the photos of Don Knight shackled to a pipe holding a variety of newspapers giving proof of life. 'She should've come to us months ago.'

Damien didn't think a girl raised in the Knight household would consider the FBI her first port of call in a storm but held his tongue. 'Have you checked the CCTV at the local subway stop?'

'Got someone at the office on it now. They should be in touch any moment,' confirmed Stevens. 'If they pick her up there, they'll trace her along her route. We've got facial recognition software that should speed up the process.'

Damien had seen that when he visited the offices earlier in the week. As much as he wanted to get out there with Mr Masters combing the streets, he knew he was better off waiting for the breadcrumb trail to be spotted. Rose was a novice—she knew nothing about evading capture. Surely it wouldn't take long to find her?

'What about triangulating her position with her phone?'

Joanne Jameson held up a slim white handset. 'She dumped this in the bathroom.'

Not so much a novice then.

Joe came in. 'Any news?'

Damien shook his head.

'Then I guess we have to wait.' Joe glanced at the ransom pictures, mouth turning down in a grim expression. 'What has Don Knight got himself into now?'

After what seemed like ages but was really only a few minutes, Stevens' phone pinged. 'Ah, got her at Penn Station. Look, here's a little bit of footage recorded off the live feed seconds ago.' He turned the screen so they could see her standing in front of a large departures board. Damien thought there was something off about her motionless stance as she mouthed the track numbers of her chosen destination then headed out of shot. Stevens was satisfied, however, by what he saw. 'Seems as though she's making for the Amtrak trains. We'll check if any of the platforms have her getting aboard a service.'

Joe shook his head. 'Hold up: I'd check the CCTV around the station first. Rose was always a terrible actress and that must the worst performance of "girl fleeing FBI" yet. She knows she's being watched. She's throwing out as many red herrings as she can.'

Stevens reran the clip. 'Ma'am, what do you think?'

Jameson bent over the screen. 'I have to agree with Joe. That looks fake to me. The girl should be scuttling through public areas, not standing to mouth clues to camera.'

Damien shifted to the window, gazing out on the street view that would be so familiar to Rose, golden sphinx gleaming faintly against the white net. 'This way though she's always going to be one step ahead of us. Can't we make an intelligent guess what she's going to do next?'

'Lie low I expect,' said Jameson, gathering up the papers. 'Stevens, can you manage the computer? I'll get the phone and the files.'

'What are you doing?' asked Joe.

'Taking this back to our office to get our digital guys on it. To be honest with you, locating Rose isn't our priority right now, not with this new evidence to analyse. There might be enough here to get Melescanu on kidnapping charges if we can track it back to him. That's a hell of a lot better than charging him with tax evasion, which was our other possibility.'

'What do you mean she's not your priority?' Icy foreboding crawled up Damien's spine.

'The girl is in no immediate danger but Don Knight is and we'll have to work out a way of getting him free without putting him at any more risk. That's going to take careful planning. The daughter is old enough to look after herself. Once she's had a chance to cool down, she'll probably return of her own accord. We'll finish up here, then put a uniform on the door so we know if she comes back.'

'She's not going to come back if there's a cop on her doorstep,' said Joe.

'But the house has to be secured until we are sure we've

got everything.' Agent Jameson had clearly already moved on to the next stage of the operation in her mind. 'She's a loose end, but how about if you boys see to tying that one off while we get on with business? Stevens can supply you with any and all information we pick up.'

Stevens tapped his forehead in acknowledgement before closing the lid on the crate he had brought in to transport the computer. 'Will do.'

Jameson put her hands on her hips as she surveyed the bookshelf next to the desk. 'What about these files?'

'Come on: enough's enough. That's Rose's schoolwork,' said Joe, moving in front of it.

Jameson pulled one off the shelf and flipped through the pages. 'Tiny writing—it'll take hours to read.'

'But it's not relevant to your investigation.' Joe pointed at the carefully set out page she had alighted upon. 'Look: that's about the Middle Kingdom—Ancient Egypt.'

'But she might've hidden some details about the financial transactions among this material. I'll make sure it gets back to her ASAP—get an intern on it today.' Jameson handed the files over to Stevens to go in a second crate.

Damien felt like he was watching the sack of some beautiful old city by barbarian hordes as Rose's schoolwork got pulled off the shelves and placed haphazardly in the crate.

'I can't stand this,' he muttered to Joe. The guilt was killing him.

'Me neither. Let's make a start on following her. I'll check her friends—see if I can reach out to Ryan. You trace her route in case she doubles back or stops somewhere.' Joe raised his voice. 'Agent Stevens, sir, we're going to begin searching for her. Will you text us if you come across any further traces?'

'Yep—I'll copy you both in.' Stevens hauled a box into the hallway then took out his phone. 'Let me just check I've got your correct numbers. Ah, new message: she's been caught on camera passing by Madison Square Garden, still on the move.'

'When?' asked Damien.

'Ten minutes ago.'

'I'd better get going then.'

Joe followed him out. 'I'm going to call Marco—see if he can put me in touch with Ryan. My guess is that Rose is heading her brother's way as he's her only available family. I might be able to get in front of her. I'll catch up with you later, OK, if that proves a bust? Keep me posted as to where you are.'

'It's a huge long shot heading off on her trail.' Damien rolled his shoulders, trying to ease the tension that had settled in his body since knocking on Rose's door.

'But next time we get a clue as to where she is you'll be closer—might even be able to get to her before she moves on.'

'True.'

Dipping inside the Masters' house, Damien grabbed his jacket and wallet. Joe chucked him a map.

'Don't get lost. I don't want to come looking for you as well.'

'Thanks, you have such faith in me.'

Without hesitation, Damien headed for the nearest subway, tucking the map in an inside pocket without looking at it. One thing he was good at was navigation—he was famous at the YDA for his ability. He'd already studied the map of New York and had gained his bearings quickly.

A new text arrived from Stevens.

Times Square on foot heading north.

Damien took the steps down into the subway, finding some satisfaction that after a disastrous morning he was finally taking action.

Chapter 9

Damien had followed his breadcrumb trail of CCTV glimpses as far as Central Park and now stood gazing at the long paths through the open area feeling the hopelessness of finding Rose inside. Hemmed in by tall buildings the park gave the illusion of being an enclosed, searchable area but really, though there were a few cameras at strategic points, there were also so many more blank spots. He had to admire her thinking. She had known to go on foot and chosen one of the places in the much monitored Manhattan that would foil a close watch. There were just too many options, gates at all points of the compass. There was even a zoo to hide in with its crowds of Saturday visitors.

But a zoo didn't seem a Rose kind of thing. He couldn't see her getting all enthusiastic about *Madagascar* creatures.

His phone rang. 'Yes, Joe?'

'Marco's brother had Ryan's cell phone and we've got him on traffic cams leaving your patch of Manhattan on his bike and heading over the river to Brooklyn. No passenger.'

'Coincidence or has he already met up with Rose?'

'That's what the intelligent money is on.'

'So he met his little sister in the park for a Saturday stroll? Not buying it.'

'My guess is she asked him for help but Ryan, being the weasel he is, has left her to deal with it on her own.'

'OK, let's concentrate on what leads that gives us. Are you going after Ryan?'

'Yeah, I'm going to see if he'll talk to me. Not too hopeful about that but I'll try change his mind. The FBI are now getting permission to access his phone records to see what Rose has told him so far about Don.'

'So what do you want me to do?'

'Keep looking. Try get inside her head and think where she'd go now.'

'OK.'

Damien's path had taken him past the zoo and he had now reached a ridiculous statue of a military guy waving swords over his head while riding a horse. In that pose, a sniper would take him out in one shot, easy. Damien took a seat on one of the benches and consulted his map, eyes skimming the spots picked out by the tourist information centre. He was near several museums and art galleries and there were scores of attractions in the park itself. If it were him, he'd head for the Strawberry Fields memorial to John Lennon but Rose didn't strike him as a classic rock and pop fan. She was more an Academy of Ancient Music girl.

A light went on in his brain. Ancient stuff: the girl loved history, the older the better. If she was looking for somewhere that she felt at home it would be with the things she understood, and he happened to be not very far from one of the world's best collections in the Metropolitan Museum of Art. The museum was big enough to hide in, had facilities and places for a teenager to sit without attracting the wrong kind of attention. In one word, she would see it as safe.

Acting on his hunch, he headed out the eastern side of the park.

Damien found Rose sitting on a padded bench in one of the galleries, contemplating a granite statue of a kneeling pharaoh with one of those cobra-hood-shaped headdresses. He paused out of her eye line, just letting himself process the maelstrom of feelings—hunter's exhilaration that he'd found her, concern for her situation, but overwhelmingly, relief that his instinct was right. He had a rock solid belief that she'd be OK as long as she stayed with him. Thinking of her abroad in New York was like imagining Red Riding Hood heading out heedless of wolves to Granny's cottage. She wouldn't like it but he was applying to be her woodcutter.

Damien quietly took a seat beside her. He knew when she sensed he was there by the stiffening of her spine and stony expression on her face.

'Hatshepsut,' said Damien reading the label. 'Was he a good guy?'

'Actually he is a she. The beard is a false one—a symbol of power like a crown.' Her voice snipped away at him, taut with anger.

'Oh yeah. I see now she has breasts. Sounds a riot.'

'She's the first female pharaoh about whom anything is known. Quite successful—lots of trade and building. May have ruled fifteen years which wasn't bad in those days—longer than most.'

'Cool.' A spiky silence fell. Damien tried to think what he should say next but his usual confidence has deserted him. He decided to go with honesty. 'I'm sorry.'

She squeezed her palms together between her knees, arms held straight before her hunched shoulders like she was preparing for a tumble dive. 'Sorry for what?'

'For springing the FBI on you. We both are—Joe and me. In our defence, we did it because we wanted to stop you before you committed a crime.'

Her eyes flicked to his face. 'What crime?'

'Touching that money.'

She stood up and started walking away. He hurried to

follow. 'I wasn't going to touch that money. I don't know what you really think about me but I'm not stupid. I can spot a trap.'

'Yeah, I know you're not stupid but we thought you might be . . . you know . . .?'

'Desperate?'

'Yeah, that. Come on, sit down again. I've chased you halfway across New York—I need a breather.'

He coaxed her to take a seat on the next free bench. She sat stiffly beside him, gazing at a stone frieze. She could probably read the hieroglyphs but to him it was as incomprehensible as the girl beside him. What was she really feeling?

'Rose, were we right that desperation might've pushed you that far?'

'No, but wouldn't you feel desperate if your dad was being ransomed by some boss in the criminal underworld?'

He leaned back, hands resting behind him on the bench. 'Obviously, but in my case I worry about terrorists.'

As he'd hoped, that threw her. She turned to look at him properly for the first time since he'd arrived. 'What?'

'My parents—they work in an unsafe part of northern Uganda. I worry they'll be abducted one day when they go to the clinic in one of the outlying villages. It happened to one of their colleagues eighteen months ago.'

'Oh.'

He shrugged. 'It's their choice. Uncle Julian says they've got a martyr complex.'

'Or maybe they are just very brave people seeing to a need that no one else will treat.'

'That too. I guess they're both.'

Rose relaxed her rigid posture a fraction. 'Who's Uncle Julian?'

'My guardian in the UK. Dad's brother. He's in finance but at heart he's a twitcher.'

'He's a birdwatcher?'

'Uh-huh. If you stick by me, you'll find I'm amazingly knowledgeable about all the different species. I've absorbed it despite my best efforts to remain ignorant.'

She unbent a little more at the description, venturing a faint smile. 'I think you really like it.'

He shifted closer so his arm rested against hers. 'Maybe I do. He's a cool guy and he'd love you.'

She moved away. 'Me?' She touched her chest.

'Yeah. He'd think you were a very classy chick—that's how he'd phrase it, smiling ironically as he said it.'

She laughed as he'd hoped but it seemed a sad noise. 'You sound so British when you talk like that.'

'Seriously, he'd like you. I'd love you to meet him.'

Shaking her head, she wrinkled her nose sceptically. 'That doesn't seem very likely, does it? Just now I thought you were going to say sorry for stringing me along last night. All that talk about dating, and the k . . . kissing—I realize you were doing it to gain my trust—so you could investigate me. That was stupid of me. I know I'm odd. I shouldn't have thought you . . . It doesn't matter now. Have you come to bring me in?'

He'd really burned his bridges with her, hadn't he? She'd never trust him again. He felt a complete louse. 'Only if you want to go. I'm really here to make sure you're safe. Is it OK if I tell Joe I've found you and that we're going to talk? He's also out looking for you—so's his dad. It's not fair to leave them wandering the streets of New York.'

She sighed, then nodded. 'But only Joe and Mr Masters, OK? Not those two agents.'

'Deal.' Damien sent a quick text. 'Shall I ask Joe to join us?'

'If he wants.' She sounded too tired to care either way.

'It'll take him a while to reach us: he's halfway to Brooklyn as he's gone to find your brother.'

She didn't comment on this but Damien could see that she was piecing together how close they had been on her trail.

'Do you want to get some lunch in one of the cafes here?' he asked, wanting an excuse to prolong their time together.

'OK.' She stood up and rolled her shoulders. 'I only managed a few hours being a stealth submarine.'

'What's that?'

'I thought I was cruising under the surface, doing all the right things to evade capture.'

'You were, Rose. It's just that I know a little about you and made a lucky guess.'

'I'll bear that in mind next time I go on the run: act out of character.'

Following her lead, he let her pick the museum cafe and then bought her some vastly overpriced sandwiches and a black tea while he settled for crisps and fizzy water. She was still furious and hurt but not wanting to make a scene in a public place. He felt a long way from his comfort zone: he knew that if he was serious about looking after her he would have to encourage her to talk about her feelings. On missions, he normally left that kind of thing to one of the girls or Joe but he didn't want anyone else getting in between him and Rose. He would just have to make his best effort.

He took a deep breath. 'So, do you want to tell me about it?'

'About what?' She dunked the teabag on its string in and out of the glass of hot water, both of them watching the spread of colour from pale gold to a darker hue.

'The last few months—how you've managed?'

Discarding the teabag, she cradled the cup in her hands. 'Not really.'

He'd finally met a girl who didn't want to discuss feelings: he should be overjoyed. Instead, he was worried. She was still so closed in on herself and he wanted to be on the inside of her problems, not a stranger to them.

'How did it start?'

'Is this an interrogation?'

'No! Rose, I know you're angry with me . . .'

'Angry—yes, some; but it's more that I'm just . . .' She twirled a hand expressively in the air. 'Disappointed.'

He caught it and squeezed her fingers tenderly before letting go. 'Of course you're angry, but I guess you aren't allowed to say that to most people around you. I'm fine with your anger—my shoulders are big enough to bear it so you don't need to hold back. Tell me I'm a pillock. And I'm sorry I upset you.'

'All right then. You're a dumbass. So's Joe.'

'Good, keep it coming.' He brushed the back of her hand. 'Don't you think it's better you tell me what you've had to put up with? I want to help you and I want to understand.'

After a few moments considering his plea, she shrugged. 'If you're interested, I don't suppose there's much point keeping it a secret now. Dad just didn't come home one day.'

'You must have been scared.' He snapped open his packet of crisps and offered her one but she shook her head.

'Not really, not at first. He doesn't keep regular hours. I only worried after I got the first demand. Since then I suppose I've been too busy to get really desperate.'

'But you can see it'll never end as long as you keep on coming up with the money?'

She poked the dead teabag on the table with a stirring stick.

'But, of course, you realized that because you're not stupid, but you couldn't think of an alternative.'

She sipped her tea.

'Rose, you're amazing, you know that?' He met her eyes

141

through the curl of steam. 'I don't mean your very attractive brain and ability to make money, though that's very hot too.'

She gave him an insincere smile for that compliment. She clearly had no clue he really did like those things about her, and that was entirely his fault.

'I mean your loyalty to your dad. He sounds as though he has given you plenty of reasons to give up on him over the years but still you've put everything into saving him.'

'Wouldn't you?' Her face said she really thought her choices were obvious.

Would he? Damien's mind briefly turned to the semi-strangers who were his parents labouring in clinics half a world away, inoculating children, delivering babies, turning their hand to any medical emergency that came through their door. 'It's complicated for me. I love my parents but I also hugely resent them.' He'd never admitted it aloud before, he realized, not so bluntly. 'And that makes me feel terrible because they are clearly both saints doing a brilliant job for local people who have nothing else in the way of health care. It makes me super-selfish to resent that.'

'But you already said you'd worry if they were abducted.'

Damien rubbed his jaw. 'Yeah, I did.'

'So I think you're not much different to me because I'm also really, really angry with my dad. It might even be worse for you because my dad is clearly in the wrong whereas you are conflicted because maybe their choices are right?'

He couldn't help himself, couldn't sit there and not touch her. Damien reached across the table and took her hand, thumb caressing her knuckles. He didn't have a huge hand but her slim fingers were engulfed by his. He liked that. 'I think my parents had no business having a kid, but I suppose I have to be grateful they did—otherwise I wouldn't be here. And I'm glad you're angry with your dad.'

She glanced down at where their hands were touching but gently pulled away. 'Don't make the mistake of thinking I'm a doormat that welcomes being trampled.'

'You are the furthest thing from a doormat.' No, to him she was glorious—funny, clever, stubborn in the right way, gorgeous. She made him feel things he'd never felt towards a girl before, including an especially strong urge to defend her. She didn't know it yet but she needed him in her life right now to stop those who exploited her.

'But you and Joe treated me like one this morning, taking over, thinking you knew best,' she countered.

Ah, that was tricky because he too had his opinions on that. 'And I said we're sorry. We handled it unbelievably badly. We're normally more tactful—at least Joe is. The jury's out on me. But I won't apologize for involving the FBI. As much as you distrust them, I still think they are your best bet for extracting your dad from this situation.'

'I can see how you might reach that conclusion,' she said carefully, 'but I don't agree.'

Joe appeared in the doorway of the cafe before Damien could try to persuade her further. Joe waved when he saw them before joining the queue to grab some lunch.

'Look, before Joe gets here, can we talk about us?' asked Damien quickly.

'Us? You still think there's an "us"?' Her expression was incredulous.

Damien ran a finger down the back of her hand, pleased to cause a little shiver. 'Well done. Don't give me an easy time. I absolutely do not deserve it.'

'Why not?' She seemed genuinely puzzled by this confession.

'Raven and Kate would say you are evening the score for your gender.'

'You've been that bad, have you?'

'Terrible.' He lifted her hand to his lips and kissed the knuckles. 'They always said the tables would be turned and I'd be the one having to do the pleading.' He rubbed her fingers against his cheek. 'The abject begging.' He smiled at her. 'The going down on my knees to ask forgiveness.'

He wondered what she'd say to that but once again she surprised him. Pulling her hand free, she gave him her Hatshepsut smile. 'Abject begging? I have something to look forward to then, don't I?'

'I'd give anything not to have an audience right now,' he muttered, tamping down the rush of attraction her proud response stirred up in him.

Joe placed his tray on the table. 'Rose, you OK?'

'I'm all right.' She sipped her tea, acting as if the sparks had not just been flying between them.

'No, she's not. She's pissed off with us and who can blame her?' said Damien.

Joe gave him a searching look. 'I take it you apologized?'

'Yeah.'

'You need help, Rose. You were getting in over your head.' Joe was coming over all big brotherly again, the role he had always taken with her but Damien guessed that wasn't an approach Rose welcomed right now.

'Joe, back off a little. Why not let Rose tell us what she wants?'

Joe levered the tab on his can so it gave a little hiss. 'OK, fire away, Rose. How can we help?'

'By keeping the Feds off my back, but oh, too late for that, isn't it?' she said sarcastically.

Joe wasn't used to this new attitude but Damien smiled. 'That's it, Rose, put us in our place. We can both take a few punches.'

'This isn't a joke, Damien,' said Joe.

'I know, but Rose is cross with us and wants to scratch out our eyes, so let her get in a few insults first, hey?'

'I don't want to scratch out your eyes,' she muttered.

'She does—she just hasn't evolved yet to the stage where she'd admit it,' said Damien cheerfully.

'I'd say that, if I felt like that, it would be more a sign of devolution to your level,' she slipped in.

Damien laughed. 'That's it, keep it up.'

'Stop teasing me!'

'I'm not teasing you; I'm appreciating you.' He tweaked her baseball cap.

Joe looked between the two of them, waking up to the fact that Damien was still flirting with his neighbour despite numerous warnings and a full out betrayal that should have put Rose off him for good.

'I think I need the restroom.' Rose got up.

'You're not running again?' asked Joe, looking regretfully at his half-eaten lunch.

'No. Damien will only hunt me down again. It seems I'm too predictable to make a success of fleeing the scene. Don't worry, Joe, you'll be able to see me—the restroom's just over there.' She headed off, a slight figure among the crowds of tourists thronging the hallway. They both kept their eyes on her as she pushed through the door to the Ladies.

Joe nudged Damien's foot. 'What's going on between you two?'

Damien's expression turned sober. 'The Feds think Rose is no longer a priority, right? So she's no longer their mission? We're not working for them if we look after her?'

Joe nodded. 'Yeah, I guess.'

'That means she's no longer out of bounds?'

'I dunno about that.'

'Joe, I like her.'

'You said that already. That's not enough to mess her about.'

'I'm not messing. You know me and my rules about mates before dates?'

'You've told me often enough.'

'She's moved over to the mate category—but the kind I . . .' He didn't have a mate of that kind—the sort he felt all kind of protective and soft about. 'Kind I'd like to get close to, you know?'

Joe scrunched up his can. 'I don't think I want to know. I think of her like a little sister, remember. But you and her—it can't go anywhere.'

'Why not?'

'Do I really have to spell it out?'

'That's just geography. That's not what matters.'

'It's character too. You're the tough man; she's the fragile flower.'

'Oh yeah? So who was it climbing out the window this morning and giving the Feds the slip? Who was it who has been dealing with extortion for weeks on her own without cracking? She's not so fragile.' And Damien knew he wasn't so tough either. Not that he wanted anyone to guess that.

The door to the Ladies swung open and Rose appeared, hat now in her pocket. 'She's coming back. I dunno what to say. Just . . . just don't hurt her.' Joe gave his friend a shrewd look. 'Or yourself.'

Rose had taken the few minutes in the restroom to compose herself. She understood the boys' motivation. She recognized that had she been in their shoes she might well have made the same choices for a friend. That helped ease the knot of anger in her chest. And Damien, he did seem sincere about caring for her, as much as a tough guy like him could be. He was hardly the first person to muddle up motives when asking a girl out. He might have taken a different tack if he had felt nothing for her, let Joe take the lead rather than make so much of her at the party. She should take his interest as a compliment and not build it up to the betrayal of the century. But when push came to shove, they didn't share the same priorities. The Feds—and by extension the boys—were after Melescanu; she was intent on saving her father. She was on her own. Her idea that she should try reaching out to the man holding Don was the only runner in her list of limited options.

But she couldn't do that with the boys in tow.

She took her seat. 'So, what do you want to do now?'

'Come home with us,' urged Joe. 'Mom and Dad are worried about you. They'll be more than happy to offer you a place to stay.'

'But I only live next door.'

'You shouldn't be on your own right now. The Feds have been through the place and that will be unsettling until they return your stuff.'

'My stuff?'

'They took your notes and schoolwork,' explained Damien. 'I'm sorry—we tried to stop them but they have to be thorough.'

It felt horrible to know all her things had been taken but Rose admitted privately she hadn't helped by refusing cooperation. If she had stayed she might've been able to persuade them she'd disclosed everything she had on the ransom demands when she handed over the letters and the computer files. No point crying over spilled milk. 'It's OK. I don't blame you.'

'So you'll come back with us?'

That would be the best way to disarm them. With this close watch they were keeping on her she would never be able to slip away. 'OK.'

Damien looked suspicious. 'You sure?'

'Yes. My options aren't stellar: staying at Ryan's girlfriend's—I've never met her—or coming back with you. Better the devil I know.'

Joe arched a brow at Damien. 'She just called us devils.'

'Wicked.' Damien winked at her.

Up in the Masters' spare bedroom, Rose stretched out on the quilt. She guessed she had ousted Damien as he would now have to sleep on the floor in Joe's room. Turning, she sniffed the pillow but the sheets had been changed—no trace of him remained except perhaps the merest hint of his aftershave pervading the air.

She thumped her forehead. 'You are pathetic,' she berated herself. Her attraction to Damien was stupid and badly timed. They were on different sides, she had to remind herself. She couldn't worry about what he would think of her plans. She'd made her mind up, hadn't she?

'Rose, sweetheart, the cookies are coming out of the oven!' called Mrs Masters.

Rose swung her legs over the side of the bed. 'On my way!'

Mrs Masters had been clucking over her since she arrived mid-afternoon with the boys. They'd gone out to catch up with the FBI people and see if they could retrieve her school files, leaving her to rest.

'I've made those ginger chocolate ones you liked so much,' said Mrs Masters as she deftly slipped them off the baking sheet and onto the cooling rack.

'Thank you. That's so kind of you.'

Rose sat down at the kitchen table. It was a homely place. She had a good view of the grandchildren's pictures on the fridge—the offspring of Joe's older married sister, Laney, who lived in Boston. One of them had drawn Mr and Mrs Masters as big circles with hands sticking out like twigs. At least they had got the smiles right. She'd never made pictures like that, going straight into precociously accurate depictions of the human body, according to her dad. It struck her now that she might've missed something important by jumping a stage.

Mr Masters patted her back in passing and took his place for his own share of his wife's cooking.

'You mustn't worry. Now the FBI are involved, I'm sure they'll get your father out.' Mrs Masters placed a plate in front of her and a glass of milk.

'I'd prefer black tea if that's OK?'

'Of course it is. We want you to feel completely at home.' Mrs Masters put the milk in front of her husband and filled the kettle.

Rose nibbled a cookie. It was still too hot to bite into. 'Delicious. I was wondering . . .'

'Yes?'

'Could I borrow your computer, Mr Masters? I've got schoolwork to do and the Feds have mine.'

'I've never known such a conscientious student,' said Mr Masters, which after a whole career teaching was quite a compliment. 'Be my guest.'

'Dinner will be at seven. Pot roast.' Mrs Masters sat down next to her husband, looked regretfully at the rack of cookies and chose the smallest one for herself. 'So don't spoil your appetite.'

'Carol, did you stop to think about that before you got baking?' teased her husband. 'It's five already.'

'I just thought she needed a little treat. Something to cheer her up.'

Rose felt close to tears. The Masters were so lovely to her and she was plotting something she knew that they would strongly disapprove of. 'I did, thanks,' she said hoarsely.

Mr Masters drained his glass. 'I'll just set up the computer for you and then we'll leave you in peace.'

149

With Mrs Masters busy at the kitchen sink and Mr Masters pottering round the dining room, Rose had the computer to herself. The first thing she did when she was sure she wasn't being watched was check her bank account. The money still sat there. She cleared the search history. Then she summoned up Google Earth pictures of Melescanu's riverside headquarters. It wasn't that far from the West Village. She could certainly walk there. Was that what she was going to do? Just knock on the door and ask to see the big man himself?

Was there another way of doing this?

Not that she could think of.

Rose opened up her cloud account that held most of her recent schoolwork. At least the Feds hadn't removed this. Maybe it hadn't occurred to them that anyone with the least computer know-how would not have only hard-drive copies of files. Finishing an assignment for history, she printed it out.

'That's done. I just need to get a textbook from home to check a reference,' she announced.

Mrs Masters had her hands full of potatoes and peelings. 'Do you want me to come with you?'

'No need. It shouldn't take me long.' Rose put the essay on the table, pledge of her good faith that she would return.

'OK, sweetie.'

Rose let herself out the front door and stood for a moment. There was a police officer outside her house, leaning on his car and sipping a take-out coffee. He wasn't paying attention to her, but was watching some boys skateboarding further up the street. This was the moment when she had to decide. She could still carry out her task, go into her house and fetch the book she needed; or she could head off on probably a hopeless errand to save her father.

Lara? Nancy? Her inner guides were in agreement. Rose turned towards the river.

Chapter 10

Colosseum Investments. Rose hesitated in front of the entry phone at the gates. Melescanu was clearly running an Ancient Rome theme in the names he gave his various companies. He must consider himself some latter-day Caesar presiding over an empire. The office and warehouse complex was at the far end of a pier, unapproachable on foot on three sides, one narrow entry point from land. Maybe he considered this his fort? His Chester or Castor—if you went for the Latin root. She wondered if he actually spoke the language. It would give them some common ground if she needed to charm him. Unfortunately, persuading people to like her had never been in her skill set.

Pressing the button, she waited.

'Can I help you?' crackled a female voice.

'Hello. My name's Rose Knight. I'm here to see Mr Melescanu.'

'Do you have an appointment?'

At least the woman hadn't said he wasn't there. It was late on a Saturday so Rose had half-expected the office to be closed. 'No, but I think he will want to talk to me. It's about my father, Don Knight.'

Rose hunched against the stiff breeze coming off the river as they kept her hanging on for an answer. When it came it was not via the speaker: the gate slid back, inviting her inside.

Damien and Joe were going to kill her for doing this. Rose

accepted the invitation by crossing the staff parking lot and entering the lobby of the glittering glass office block. It looked like the rear of a cruise ship, built so that the upper stories jutted out over the river. From the ground, the effect was oppressive, like the building was going to fall on her head.

'Miss Knight, take a seat. Someone will be along to fetch you.' The smart receptionist dressed in a cream suit was packing up for the day. She wrapped a floaty scarf around her neck and surrendered her seat to a security man.

Rose sat down on the white sofa by the coffee table covered with company brochures. Not knowing what to do with herself and the nerves biting away at her confidence, she flicked through, looking at photos of shipping, road building and other infrastructure projects in Eastern Europe. It all looked very legitimate. She wondered if the receptionist had any idea about the true nature of her employer. Like those oligarchs with their sports clubs and mansions living in London, Melescanu seemed too big for anyone to take down, even the Feds.

Wishing the security man a good weekend, the woman walked out to her car. The guard locked the double glass doors, leaving entry and exit only by a smaller side door. Rocking on his toes at the entrance, gazing out across the concrete to the skyline of the financial district, he seemed not to be paying any attention to Rose. She checked her watch: fifteen minutes had passed since she sat down. How long should she wait before asking if she'd been forgotten?

Another assistant emerged from the elevator, this one a young man, smart suited and dark haired. He looked anaemic, like he'd been sucked dry by a vampire. 'Miss Knight? Follow me please?' He held the door to the car for her.

She stepped inside, quickly noting the number of floors. The building wasn't high-rise, only five storeys, but they were heading for the top. The doors opened onto a carpeted corridor done in imperial purples and whites, eagle motifs and laurel-leaved borders. *The Pines of Rome* by Respighi played on the sound system, musical echoes of lost legions. It had as much authenticity as a Vegas themed casino. All he needed were a couple of butch actors dressed as gladiators and he'd have all the clichés, thought Rose.

'This way. Mr Melescanu is in the executive boardroom,' said her guide.

'Not the imperial box,' murmured Rose.

'What's that?'

'Nothing.' Nerves were making her tendency to mock more acute. She needed to get a leash on it if she wanted to charm the man into cooperating with her. She knew nothing about manipulating others. She should've paid more attention to Damien and Joe: they were both masters of the art, as she knew to her cost.

The man opened a door at the far end of the corridor. 'Go on in.'

Hugging her elbows, Rose did as he instructed and walked into the board room. The first thing that took her attention was the huge window overlooking the smooth-flowing river. In front of it stretched a mahogany table surrounded by twenty empty chairs. Where was he? Looking to her left she saw that the room continued around the curve of the building to a sofa and bar area. A man was sitting in a large leather armchair watching her, his meaty hands cradling a delicate tumbler of amber liquid. Grey haired and built like a bear, that had to be Mr Melescanu. His navy suit looked wrong on him; he seemed the type to be more comfortable in fishing gear or lumberjack shirts. He beckoned her to approach. Ignoring the shivery feeling in her stomach, Rose made her way towards him, trying to remember all the clever bargains she had thought up.

As more of the room came into view, she realized he wasn't alone. She could see another man sitting on a sofa with his back to her, leg crossed over his knee, phone pressed to his ear.

It couldn't be.

'Dad!' Her head swam with the shock of seeing him there.

'Hey, Rose.' He put the phone away and came to give her a hug. 'You certainly surprised us turning up here out of the blue.'

'You're OK? You're really OK?' She wanted to weep. She kept her arms wrapped across her chest, not returning his hug. She felt like she was going to fall to pieces and had to hold herself together.

He patted her back. 'Sure I am. But you shouldn't be here.'

'I . . . I ran out of money. I wanted to talk to Mr Melescanu—explain.'

Don tugged her down beside him. 'This is my little Rose, Roman.'

'Pleased to meet you, Miss Knight.' The man in the armchair raised his glass to her. 'Fetch your girl a drink, Don. She looks a little pale.'

Don squeezed her knee. 'Stay right there, sweetheart.' He walked over to the bar and found her a bottle of water with the ease of someone who knew his way around its stock. Rose's brain was shaking off its surprise and beginning to put the clues together.

'They've released you?' she whispered, looking at her hands. They were shaking so she clenched them together in her lap. Maybe she was wrong about her suspicions.

Don put a glass into her grasp. 'I'm so proud of you. I told Roman you were a genius and you proved yourself again and again.'

'I must say, Miss Knight, you did far better than my own financial adviser. I'd like you to teach him some of your secrets.'

154

Melescanu watched her with faint amusement. Everyone was waiting for her to admit to the game.

Rose closed her eyes. Her dad was not chained to a pipe; he was sitting as a guest in Melescanu's penthouse. They were on first-name terms. Had he ever been in danger?

'How are you, Rose? Managed OK without me?'

'Yes.' She sipped the drink then put it aside. If she didn't get out of here she would scream or—or beat his chest with her fists. 'I just came to check on you and say that I can't touch the money that came into the account. Now I see you're OK, I'll go.' She wished she had a handkerchief but made do with the back of her hand across her eyes. 'I might not make rent this month so . . .' She shrugged. 'Anyway, glad you're not dead.' That was about all she could manage. She still wasn't sure if she wouldn't kill him herself for doing this to her. So cruel. She stood up.

Her dad grabbed her hand. From his inability to meet her eyes, she felt his guilt but he would never to admit to it. Don Knight didn't do mistakes; he only did opportunities. 'Sit down. You can't go now.'

Melescanu's smile chilled her to the bone. 'Your father's right. Now you're here, you have to stay. We know about the FBI visiting your house. You'd better let us know what they took.'

'Everything I had,' she said bleakly.

'Still, that's not too hard to pass off as a prank, Roman. I don't think there's any danger there. You didn't report the notes did you, Rose?' asked her dad.

'No, Dad, I know the rules. But they've got them now.'

He nodded appreciably. 'Knights don't go to the authorities. We get ourselves out of our own difficulties.'

She revised the motto in her head to 'Knights make their own difficulties'.

'You'll tell them it was a little role play thing we were doing, won't you? A game.'

'That would be perjury.' She felt so tired. Her shoulders slumped forward.

'Not really, as you now know it was a . . . a little challenge. Not real.'

'Why, Dad?'

Don shot a worried look at Melescanu. 'Let's talk about that later, OK?'

So numb, Rose could only nod. She knew the answer. There had been no ransom. Her father had set her a test to prove to his dangerous ally that his daughter was as good as he boasted. She had lived in terror for months but all as part of some perverse game Don had cooked up. Melescanu wouldn't have known to involve her unless her father had said something.

'For now you can stay with me in my suite downstairs. Is that OK, Roman?'

'No problem. I trust you to make sure your golden goose is comfortable.' Melescanu got up and put his empty glass on a side table. 'I've got a dinner with the deputy mayor. I'll see you tomorrow. She'll be ready by then?'

Don settled a hand on her shoulder. 'Of course. She's just adjusting at the moment. But she knows where her loyalties lie.'

Melescanu came to stand in front of her. 'As I said, nice to meet you at last, Miss Knight. In case he doesn't remember to tell you, your father still owes me ten million dollars. After that debt is cleared, I'd say there are plenty of openings for someone with your skills in my organization. I'll make sure you're treated well for your trouble.' His knees clicked arthritically as he turned to go. 'Have a good evening.'

Rose waited until the door closed behind their host before getting up. 'I'm going home, Dad.'

Don stood to block her exit, arms spread like a basketball

player in defence. 'Sorry, but he knows where we live. You've got to stay here.'

'I'll go somewhere else then—hide.'

'If I let you go, he really will kill me. You wouldn't do that to me, would you?'

Rose shuddered. 'Don't you dare use that one again. All those ransom demands—you were never in danger.'

'I was! At least I would've been if I hadn't come up with the idea of making the situation seem like a kidnapping. I knew you'd never send the money to him if you didn't think my life was threatened.'

'So you sold me out. You said, hey Mr Melescanu, don't worry about the debt. I've got a daughter who will ruin her life, worry herself sick, while she makes the money for me?'

He tried to hug her again but she backed away. 'Don't be like that, darling. You don't know what these guys are like. I had to offer them something.'

'But it was me you offered—your own daughter—you get that, don't you? He's not going to let me go willingly, is he?'

Don slicked back his hair. It really did need a trim: the photos hadn't lied about that. His silence was more telling than any amount of excuses.

'I bet you had a real laugh posing those ransom shots. How can I make Rose worry? The handcuffs were a nice touch. Gaunt look and newspaper—a classic. I can't believe you've done this to me.' Oh but she could. Everyone had warned her—Ryan, Mom, they all knew what Don was really like—only she had thought he would make an exception for his daughter. His love came with conditions, top one being that you looked after him before your own interests.

Don as ever was quick with his self-justification. 'But I thought you wouldn't worry too much because you knew you would make the ransom.'

'It wasn't a ransom.'

'But you're my little genius. I knew you wouldn't fail.'

Rose crumpled onto the sofa. 'You have no idea how difficult it is, do you? You think I perform some kind of magic and effortlessly settle bills and stump up cash. It's my fault. I made it too easy for you and Ryan to think that.'

'Look, I know you're upset now . . .' Don began to pace.

'You think? I'm not upset; I'm furious.'

'I'll show you where you can sleep and we'll send out for a pizza. Roman's got cable.'

'Oh, zippedy-doo-dah. A prison with all the channels.'

Don slammed a hand on the bar. 'Don't take that tone with me, young lady.'

'What tone do you want, Dad? The one belonging to the girl delighted to be exploited by her father and happy to be given no say about where she stays?'

'Don't you sass me. You're my responsibility. I say where we stay. Don't talk nonsense about prisons.'

Rose wanted to say the obvious retort to the claim of responsibility but a thick grey cloud of depression was weighing on her. She didn't have the energy. 'Fine, it doesn't matter anyway. Show me my room.'

'Good. That's my Rose.' Relieved that she had stopped fighting him, he did as promised and showed her to a guest room on the floor below next to his. 'Have a lie down while I sort out something to eat and some clothes for tomorrow. What do you want?'

'I'm not hungry—and my clothes are all at home.' Rose stretched out on the bed, remembering that she was expected for pot roast at Mrs Masters. 'You should let the neighbours know I won't be there for supper. They'll worry.'

'I'll get a message to them. I'm afraid you won't be able to fetch anything from home for the moment so I'll make a guess at your sizes. Here—this is the remote.' He put the controller beside her, a kind of peace offering. When had he ever known her to watch television to relax? Maybe he just had never noticed? 'I won't be long.'

Rose curled up. She felt so utterly alone, like an astronaut in a malfunctioning capsule losing orbit, knowing there was no way back. She was spinning off into the darkness, bombarded by radiation and sapped by cold. Her family—each member only caused her pain and disappointment. Her oldest friend— he handed her over the FBI. Damien—pretended to be attracted to her to get a job done. It felt too much effort to care any more.

Half an hour of silence passed as the numbness lodged a little deeper. She rolled over and must have hit the remote because the huge wall-mounted TV came on with a blare of cheery music. A yellow square cartoon creature bobbed across the screen. Rose sat up and hugged her knees, remembering Damien's explanation at Lindy's party.

'I don't understand anything,' she whispered, letting tears fall. 'It all hurts too much. I want out.' But there was no one there to hear.

Damien and Joe came back triumphant. They had managed to persuade Joanne Jameson that the files really were innocuous and should be returned to their owner. Backing into the kitchen with his crate, Damien called out.

'Hey Rose, we did it!'

Mrs Masters rushed over. 'Oh Joe, Damien, I'm so glad you're back. Rose went home to get a book a couple of hours ago but hasn't come back. Will you fetch her? Supper's been ready for half an hour now and will be getting dry.'

Damien was instantly suspicious. 'You let her go on her own, Mrs Masters?'

'Of course. She's not a prisoner here. There's a nice young officer on the door so no harm can come to her.'

Damien and Joe exchanged a look and returned to the street.

'Excuse me, sir, but has Rose gone into the house?' Joe asked the police officer, who had moved into his patrol car after standing on the step for a few hours.

The cop crumpled up a take-out coffee cup. He looked supremely bored by his watch. 'No. No one in or out.'

'You've been here the whole time.'

'Since four. But I'm the last when my shift ends at eight. The FBI has said we can stand down and not waste manpower on this. We'll do regular drive-bys.'

'Thanks,' said Joe.

'We should've anticipated she'd run again.' Damien wanted to punch the wall. Rose had been too subdued. They'd thought she was tired but she'd really been plotting her next move. 'What do you think she's doing?'

'Let's ask my parents.'

Back in the kitchen, Joe broke the bad news that Rose had gone missing again. 'Dad, do you have any idea where she might be?'

'She asked to use my computer. Here—see if you can see what she was looking at.' Mr Masters relinquished his seat. Joe checked back through the search history but saw that Rose had deleted it. That at least confirmed that she was up to something and didn't want them to know.

'I don't suppose you noticed what she was looking at?' Damien asked.

Mr Masters rubbed his jaw thoughtfully. 'I think I saw Google Earth open.'

'Try that, Joe. It might reopen where she left it.'

Joe selected the option and a view of Manhattan came up

on the screen. Joe zoomed in on the address she had searched. 'Colosseum Investments. She's gone after her dad.'

While they were processing that unwelcome piece of news, the phone rang. Joe's mum reached it first.

'Hello. Who's calling?' asked Mrs Masters. 'Oh, Ryan. What's that? She won't? Oh. OK. Is she all right? Yes, I see. Thanks for letting me know.' She put the phone back in the cradle. 'That was Rose's brother. He says she's staying with family and won't be back for supper or to stay with us.'

'So she didn't go after her father—or thought better of it? She went to Ryan?' wondered Joe.

'Is she with him though? He didn't say that. Did he mention where we could contact her?' asked Damien.

'No. He didn't offer any details,' admitted Mrs Masters. 'You know what he's like, Joe. More slippery than a bucket of eels.'

'Yeah, and getting any information from him is impossible. So that's it? We can't do any more for her if she won't let us.'

Mrs Masters banged some plates on the stove to serve the meal. 'I don't like it.'

I don't believe it, added Damien silently.

But she's not your responsibility. If she's taking stupid risks, that's on her. His tough inner voice sounded a lot like his mentor back at the YDA. He told his recruits that they always had to know when to cut their losses and move on. You couldn't save everyone.

Yeah, but she's a mate now. Aren't you going to live up to what that means? Another voice piped up in his head, one he thought might well be his conscience. He'd let Rose down by bringing in the Feds; he couldn't make the same mistake twice.

'Joe, we've got to do something,' he said under the cover of the rattling pots and pans.

'Yeah, but what? She's not left us with many options.'

'We locate her and yank her little butt out of danger.'

'How exactly are we going to do that, short of roasting Ryan's toes over the fire until he blurts out where she is?'

'Tempting, but I think we've got the clue. She went after her dad. Find him and we'll find her. I think there's more to this kidnapping scenario than meets the eye. For a start, if she did reach him and is now banged up with him, captors don't usually send messages saying people won't make pot roast night. They sent threats and menaces.'

'Maybe Ryan's covering?'

'Oh yeah, I have him pegged as the sort who would bother with social niceties. No, Rose will have asked that your parents are told so they don't worry.'

'You want to pay a call on Colosseum Investments?'

'I was thinking our Sunday morning run might head that way, yeah.'

'OK. I guess she's safe for tonight.'

'I think so, but I was imagining we might want an early run. A really early run.'

Joe cottoned on. 'Right. I'll get out some blacks for us.'

'Climbing ropes might be necessary.'

'What are you two whispering about?' asked Mrs Masters, putting a plate down in front of Damien.

'Just plans for another trip out for Damien,' said Joe, not quite lying. 'OK if I take the boat out for some early morning fishing?'

Mr Masters was less easy to placate. 'You two be careful now. Don't do anything foolish.'

'Have you ever known me to do that?' asked Joe.

'Humph. I've known you take risks but so far you've not been caught. There's always a first time.'

'We'll be careful, sir,' promised Damien.

162

Mr Masters cast a glance at his wife, indicating he'd prefer her not to know and be spared the anxiety.

'Understood.' Damien took a mouthful. 'This is fantastic, Mrs Masters.'

'Yeah, Mom, great. Good fuel for fishing,' Joe added in an undertone.

Three in the morning. Even at this time of night, New York was not asleep. Cars whirred by on the damp roads. A fall of rain earlier had created puddles in the gutters where leaves blocked the drains. Dressed in black and carrying lightweight backpacks, Damien and Joe ran to the marina one pier upstream from Colosseum Investments where Joe's family kept a little boat for fishing trips. Gaining entry through the key-pad-guarded gate, Joe made short work of taking the vessel out of its berth.

'Done this before at night?' asked Damien, impressed.

'Best fishing times are dawn and dusk. In retirement, Dad's become a serious sailor and angler.' Joe set the powerful outboard motor chugging. 'I'll cut this when we get closer and take us in on momentum.'

Out on the river, Damien used Joe's binoculars to scan Melescanu's building at the end of the pier. Lights were on in the corridors and a couple of offices. He could see a cleaning crew making its way through the top floor.

'Do we have any more intel on this place?' he asked.

Joe pulled up his hood against the mist of rain. 'Kieran hacked the fire department database for me and sent the architectural plans over.'

'Thank God for the Owls.'

Joe flashed him a grin. 'Yeah.' He passed Damien his phone so he could scroll through the images. 'Five storeys. Top floor belongs to the boss man. There are guest quarters on the fourth as well as a library and public reception areas. Floors below are offices. IT and data centre are on the ground floor. No basement with the river just below.'

'So if Rose is staying there—or being kept there—she's likely to be on one of the upper floors.' Damien pieced it together. 'Not the top because the cleaning crew is up there and Melescanu is hardly going to invite them in and see his ransom victims. Where does he live?'

'Penthouse near Central Park.'

'Could he have Rose there?'

'Unlikely. He doesn't control the whole building so would have to bring her in past witnesses. Plus that's his home turf; I imagine Rose and Don are in the business category in his mind.'

Damien nodded. Cats like Joe were good at getting into the heads of their targets so he trusted his instinct on this. 'OK, so back to our first thought that she's here somewhere.' He turned the binoculars back on the building, trying to think through where he would stash a guest he wouldn't want to leave. They'd swung out so he could now see the river-facing side of the building. 'There's a balcony on the fourth overlooking the water and the windows appear to have curtains rather than blinds.'

'Seems our best guess. Can you get up there?'

Damien trained his binoculars on the balcony. 'Yeah, I think so. There's a nice strong steel rail. If I can shoot a line over it we should be able to fix the rope.'

Joe squinted at the building edge. 'Man, that's never going to work. And I'm not catching you if you fall.'

Damien pulled out a spring-loaded grappling iron. 'A little gift from Nat. You know him and his thing for free climbing? Well, he got me this for my holiday with you, thinking we'd like the new tech when we went upstate for some mountaineering.

164

Glad I packed it now.' He pressed the end and the legs of the grapple sprung out like a spider. 'This should catch on the rail.'

'Or fall back on our heads and brain us.'

'Yeah, there is that. I suggest you stand clear.'

'This is either monumentally stupid or a stroke of genius.'

'That's sums up my life quite well.'

'Here goes nothing,' muttered Joe, but understanding Damien was intent on trying this, he moved the boat into position, cutting the engine so they could drift in on the current. The boat bumped up against the pier immediately below the balcony. Damien stood at the prow and began swinging the rope in vertical loops, attempting to get a feel for the weight of his grapple and the speed needed to launch it from river level up four storeys. His first two attempts fell back into the river without gaining sufficient height. Joe refrained from making any sarcastic comments—he was doubtless saving them for when they reached safety. As the rope left his hand on the third go, Damien knew it was going to fall just where he wanted. Sweet. The grapple fell with a clatter on the concrete floor of the balcony and Damien gently tugged until the hooks caught on the railing.

'OK, sure you want to do this?' asked Joe, steadying the bottom of the rope.

Climb five storeys up a building belonging to a hostile? Oh yeah, did he ever. Damien gave Joe a thumbs up. 'Just keep the meter running, mate. There's a big tip if you're still here when I come back.'

'Package in tow?'

'We'll cross that bridge if it comes to it. I can't see Rose liking the idea of shinning down a rope, can you?'

'I've given up on trying to understand her. She never does what I expect.'

'First rule of Rose then: expect the unexpected.' Damien

put on his gloves to help him grip and began his climb, thanking all those hours put in at the YDA gym for giving him the muscle power to make the ascent. Halfway up he risked a quick glimpse down. As the boat was running without lights and was now hidden in the darkness at the base of the pier, he couldn't see Joe. Good. Hopefully any CCTV cameras would have equal difficulty seeing the night visitors. He climbed the remaining distance, relieved to reach the railing and throw his leg over. Whoa: he was lucky to make it. One glance showed him that the hook of the grapple was barely fixed on the rail, lying at an awkward angle. He took a moment to reposition the grapple in a firmer spot looped round a post, pleased Joe hadn't witnessed that his throw hadn't been as secure as he had planned.

'OK, find the maiden and save the day.' Damien grinned manically at his reflection in the glass doors. Sometimes he loved his job.

Chapter 11

Rose woke up certain that she wasn't alone. 'Dad?'

A cold hand smelling of steel and river water covered her mouth. Her scream died when she recognized Damien's voice.

'Ssh, Rose, it's just me. You missed a great pot roast.' He gently lifted his hand away and sat on the side of her bed.

'What are you doing here?' She scooted up, back cushioned by a mound of pillows on top-quality cotton sheets. Wanting to see him, she reached out to hit the touch sensitive bedside light but Damien caught her wrist.

'Can we do this in the dark, please? I'm not exactly an invited guest and it's best whatever security system they have doesn't see that I'm here.'

Rose put her slowness down to her having been roused from sleep. Only now could she deduce the means by which he had come to sit on her quilt. 'You . . . you climbed in?' She now saw that the sliding door to the balcony was a little open, the white curtains lifting in the breeze. 'From the river?'

'Yes.'

She couldn't make out his expression as he was dressed in black with a beanie covering his blond hair, face in shadow. It all felt close to a dream. 'Why?'

'Because you missed dinner.'

She shook her head. 'You shouldn't be here.'

'Neither should you.'

She dropped her head back on the soft mound behind her and gave it two thumps. 'I know. I was so gullible.'

Damien laced his fingers with hers. 'Come on then. Get some clothes on suitable for climbing out of here and we'll slip away.'

If only it were so simple. She wiggled her fingers free. 'You don't understand. I've got to stay now.'

'Uh-uh, no, you don't. The only thing you've got to do is listen to me and I've come to tell you that I think now is the perfect time for you to have your first lesson in abseiling.'

She almost smiled. 'How do you know I don't already abseil?' If she truly were Lara Croft, she'd have that down, no problem. How she wished she were Lara, not the pathetic mess she really was.

'Rose, you are many things but an action hero isn't one of them. I've been in your bedroom, remember: not a bit of sports kit anywhere. But abseiling is easy—all you have to do is fall in a controlled fashion.'

'I should be good at that.' She tried to tug the duvet a little higher to cover the childish nightdress her father had got her—dancing polar bears were so not her thing, certainly not something she wanted Damien to see her in. 'But I really can't leave. Dad's here.'

Damien took her hand again, seeming to need to touch her. 'Then we'll get him too. Do you know where he's held?'

She gave a hollow laugh. 'That's the point: he's here willingly. It was all a set-up to force me to make the money to pay off his debt. The hostage thing was a fake. But Dad's problem with Melescanu is real. He still owes him ten million.'

'And how is that your problem?' Damien's tone turned cold. He clearly thought her father not worth the worry.

She saw how that might be the conclusion of an outsider

but she couldn't shake off the fact that Don was her dad. 'I think I hate my father right now, but I still love him.'

Damien swore under his breath—funny English words that sounded charming rather than rude in his accent. She wished he would hug her—she badly needed a hug—but was too shy to ask. Besides, she had decided her way forward and it was going to take them further apart than ever.

'I know you don't like it but I'm going to play this out. Get Dad free of the debt he owes and then that's it.'

'That's not how it works: your dad's addicted to the hustle. He'll keep on dumping you in it if you help him now.'

'You're probably right, but I can't be anything other than what I am. I can't suddenly become hard-hearted because I know he's so wrong about what he's doing to me. I've promised myself I'll do this one thing then I'm going to take that scholarship I was offered at MIT and leave home immediately. They said the door would be open for a while. If I'm not here, Dad won't think to use me—at least I'll make it very difficult for him.'

'And you think Melescanu will let you go? I don't know much about the guy but nothing I've learned says that to me. Considering his background, I'd guess there's a few bodies buried in his past—I don't mean that as a metaphor. He could be a real threat to you.'

That was the weak part of the plan. She hadn't felt in physical danger from Melescanu as yet, but neither had she wanted to cross him. There was something cold and predatory about his gaze.

'Anyway, Rose, you don't want to study at MIT. You want to dig up pots and zap mummies with MRI machines.'

'I like the zapping part the most, rather than the fieldwork, but that was always a bit of daydream. No one wants another forensic archaeologist.'

Damien raised her hand to his cheek and rubbed it against his warm skin. 'I do. I think you'd make a great one. You can't let your dad steal your dream like that.'

'Sometimes you don't get your druthers, Damien.'

'Druthers? What does that mean?'

He was making her feel so much better just being there. Even if he was only here because she was a mission, she still liked him. 'It means, British boy, that you don't always get what you would rather have.'

Damien nibbled her fingertips. 'Don't I know it. But I'm being good here and have come to rescue you so please don't spoil my moment by opting to stay with the dragon.'

She sighed. 'It's not a dragon, it's just a very greedy businessman with an emperor complex.' Rose blinked away tears. 'I'd like to see a dragon—wouldn't life be so much better if that was what we had to fight? If I did, you would absolutely be the first person I'd call and you could swing into action and save me.'

'If you become the archaeologist you are supposed to be, you might dig one up. Wouldn't that be fun?'

'That's palaeontology, silly.' She had to let Damien go before anyone woke up to the fact there was a perimeter breach. He was part of that dream, the road she wasn't going to take. 'Thank you for coming for me. As you can see, I'm OK. They're treating me well. Dad won't let anything happen to me.'

'I don't trust your dad to protect you any further than I could throw him.'

Rose caught his hands against his chest, held hers over them for a moment and then released them. 'Yeah, well, he's a loser dad, but he's my loser dad so I'm going to do what I do best and get him out of this.'

'But I'm only interested in you—I want to get you out of this.'

'You've done enough.'

'Babe, I haven't even got started yet. '

Her skin tingled at the promise his words contained. 'I'm not so selfish as to drag you into my trouble.'

He hitched himself a little closer to her. 'Rose, you don't get it, do you? I blew my best chance in gaining your trust so I doubt you'll believe me, but I've done some serious rethinking over the last few hours, getting my priorities sorted. I really need to help you. It's totally selfish on my part as I've decided you are necessary to me. That means you have to be safe and well. So me getting neck deep in your trouble is the way it has to be. You can send me back out there but I'm not giving up.'

She didn't understand. Why would he bother when even her own father and brother would barely cross the road to help? 'You should walk away.'

'Nope. I need a prickly genius in my life and I've decided you fit the bill.' He put his hand to his chin, mocking thinking pose. 'I guess I could look around for another but I fear you are unique and it'd be a wasted effort. No, I'm more the type to lock on to my target and go all out to acquire, not mess around trying to find a poor substitute.'

'So I'm just a mission to you.'

'You are *the* mission, Rosebud. You'd better get used to it.' He dipped forward and gave her a quick kiss. 'There's more of that when we get you safe. You do what you feel you have to do, but don't forget, same goes for me.' He padded silently to the open door. Rose scrambled out of bed to follow him.

'You want me to smuggle you out the front way?' she asked, quickly running through the interference she would have to upload to the security cameras. She knew the theory and was pretty certain she could get him out a safer route.

'I'll be fine. Just throw down the rope when I'm done.' He

cupped the back of her neck and rested his forehead against hers. 'Stay out of trouble.'

'I'll try.' Her heart stuttered as she watched him put on a pair of gloves, swing his leg over the balcony, then shoot down the rope with a soft whirring sound of leather on nylon. A little shake of the line told her he was down. She untied the grapple and dropped it over the edge. From the clunk and the swearing below she guessed she should've whispered a warning.

'Sorry!' she called.

The boat pushed away from the pier and let the current drag them clear. Once far enough out into the main channel, Joe started the engine. Back lit by the lights of the far shore, she saw him wave to her. Damien was busy coiling the rope, back bent. He stood up as the boat surged into a U-turn and held up his hand. She didn't know if they could see her but she waved anyway, then turned to go inside. It was only then that she noticed her father was standing at his door that also connected to the balcony.

'Should I worry that you're entertaining boys in your bedroom in the middle of the night?'

Rose didn't feel she owed her dad anything, not even an explanation. 'I wasn't entertaining him. He came to see I was OK.'

'Friend of yours?' He lit a cigarette, hand shaking a little as he cupped the flame.

She folded her arms across her chest. 'Yes, Dad, a friend.'

'I recognized Joe in the boat but who's the other?'

'A boy from London.'

'Will they make trouble for us?'

Maybe. 'They just wanted to check up on me.'

'Pretty extreme to climb a five storey building.'

'They are pretty extreme about friendship.' She got that now. 'And no, I don't think they'll make trouble. I told them I was staying until I got you out of your fix, but you know I'm done after that, don't you?'

He nodded and threw the half-smoked cigarette over the edge.

'You'll back me up on this, because I got the idea your associate isn't so keen on letting me go.'

'Sure, Rose. Now go back to sleep.' Don returned to his bedroom, sliding the door closed behind him.

And she put as much faith in that promise as she did a bull promising not to break anything as he charged into a china shop.

Ropes stowed in his backpack, Damien joined Joe at the stern.

'Cool exit,' Joe remarked, nodding back to the building behind them.

Yeah, and Damien's hands were feeling the glow even now from the slide. He'd gone faster than normal to impress his audience. 'You know me: I like to make an impression.'

'I'm surprised you left her there. I was expecting you to carry her out in a fireman's lift.'

'If I had my druthers, I would.'

Joe chuckled at the old-fashioned phrase and made a course correction. 'So, go on, spill. What happened?'

'Short version: her dad set her up. There's no hostage situation just Don Knight getting his girl to make money for him under pressure so he can settle his debt. His chestnuts are in the fire but not in the way we thought. She's decided to stay to sort it out for him but quite how she's going to do that without breaking the law is anyone's guess. I think she'll have to get her hands dirty if he's not to have his legs broken by Melescanu's heavies.'

'Well, isn't that just perfect.' The marina light marking the entrance to the moorings appeared to starboard. 'The Feds aren't going to be pleased.'

'How do you mean?'

'Remember how excited they got that they could get Melescanu on kidnap charges?'

'Oh yeah.' Damien could just imagine Stevens' sour face when he realized the Knights had messed up yet another attempt to nail Melescanu.

'So even if it felt like a kidnap to Rose, the one they would have to charge is Don Knight—and that would be for mental cruelty. I can't see her pressing charges, can you?'

'And she's being set up to commit a crime to save that waste of space. She's going to have to use dirty money to do it.'

'The Feds aren't going to be forgiving.'

Damien scrubbed his hands over his face, trying to clear his thoughts. 'I think we should go to Isaac's contact, Agent Hammond, about this. She seemed genuinely interested in people, otherwise why get into training the next generation? Those other two agents—Jameson and Stevens—are too close to the investigation to care about Rose. If we make the case to Hammond that the best candidate for an Owl is about to get swallowed up by Melescanu's outfit, then she might rein in her guys when they take him down and cut a deal for Rose.'

Joe killed the engine and jumped ashore to tie up the boat in its berth. 'But Rose doesn't want to join the YDA. She wants to study old pots.'

'Yeah, I know. But we might be her best bet now that her father's just trashed her future. Isaac and Agent Hammond would at least understand the complexities of her situation.'

'Does she realize that most universities won't take students facing criminal charges?'

'My thinking is somewhere inside she does but she's just doing what she feels she has to. If she were a bit nastier, she'd walk away, but she's too nice to do so.'

'There's a time when nice has to stop.'

'Says Joe—the nicest guy at the YDA. That's your new motto then. I just wish it were hers.'

The glow of light off the water woke Rose. Ripple patterns fluttered across the white ceiling reminding her of her night visitor. Rose brushed her fingers over the place he had sat. Damien. It had been really sweet and very, very Indiana of him to climb up to see her. And that exit! Her heart was still going pitter-pat from that bit of showmanship. OK, she knew that she should be too sensible to fall for such stunts but secretly she was a romantic, and there was nothing like a little wild man act to get her fantasies going.

That didn't make her situation any better though. It wasn't that particular male in her life that was her problem: that title went to the man in the next-door room. He was one huge road block to her happiness.

As if listening for his cue, there came a knock on the adjoining door and her dad entered with a breakfast tray.

'Arise and shine, sleepyhead,' he said blithely, putting the tray down on the circular table by the window. 'You didn't eat last night so I ordered us both a big breakfast—pancakes, bacon, maple syrup, the works.'

Rose threw back the covers. 'Thanks, but I'm still not hungry. I'll just take the juice and toast.' She dipped into the bathroom and splashed cold water on her face. *Keep a hold on your temper*, she told her reflection. When she blamed him, her dad always managed to turn it on her. She couldn't stomach another argument.

Her dad was making inroads on his plate by the time she emerged, a folded newspaper on the table beside him. This was all so surreal. He was acting as if they were on vacation in a superior hotel, not held under menaces in a creditor's gilded cage.

175

'What's the plan for today?' Rose asked quietly, taking a seat across from him. The river light threw his worry lines into relief—he should've had more of them but somehow he shrugged off so much that he did not want to think about. His pallor wasn't great though—a little grey from spending so much time inside. How had she possibly come from this man? Where had he learned in his life that exploiting his family was OK? For that matter, where had she learned that it wasn't, seeing how she was the only one in her home not to have that view? By upbringing, he should have been an ordinary dad. His parents had been small-town storekeepers with no criminal connections, but they hadn't been part of his life for years, not since the first stint in jail in his early twenties and his decision to move away and cut ties. Clearly their probity hadn't rubbed off on their hustler son. She wished now she had known them; they had died before they could be part of her life.

'Roman is expecting us for dinner at his penthouse.' Don topped up his coffee. 'He realizes there isn't much you can do on a Sunday with all the markets being closed but he'll like to hear your investment strategy. He takes an interest in that kind of thing.'

'So I'll have time to do my schoolwork?' She watched his face closely for any sign of prevarication.

'I guess so but I was thinking we might want to spend some time together, considering how we've not seen each other for weeks.' He wasn't meeting her eyes.

That was an odd way of describing his decision to let her think he had been kidnapped. Rose could feel her temper rising like a cake with too much baking soda bursting out of the tin. Mentally she let it rise then sink back to a stodgy mess—that was exactly what her emotions felt like.

'So I will be allowed to go to school tomorrow?' She gave herself a mental pat on the back for keeping her tone level.

'I'll have to talk to Roman.'

'It'll raise more questions if I don't.' She bit into her toast and realized she was hungry after all.

'I'll make that point to him. I guess it will be all right if his driver takes and collects and you don't talk to anyone about any of this.' He slathered maple syrup on a triangle of pancake. 'How much did you tell that boy?'

So that was the real reason he had brought her breakfast: to grill her about her visitor. 'Enough so that the Feds know they don't have a hostage case against Mr Melescanu.'

Don nodded. 'Roman will enjoy their disappointment. I won't tell him that your friend came calling; he wouldn't like that so much. Make sure it doesn't happen again.'

Rose swirled her orange juice in its tall glass, reviewing his last few comments. 'How long since you threw your fortunes in with him, Dad? You sound as if you're playing on his team now, not for yourself.'

He refolded the paper to check the sports news. 'It's hard to be an independent with him controlling so much of the business in this part of the city.'

So that was a yes then: her dad had more than sold her out, he'd also sold his soul to his new boss.

'And what kind of business is it exactly?'

'Import, export, all sorts of things.'

Her disappointment with her father bloomed into huge great flower of woe which rapidly shed petals like her favourite illustration in *Blake's Songs of Innocence and Experience*. 'I see. And you think it's a good idea for me to advise this guy on investments?'

'It's not illegal.'

'But where does the money come from, Dad?'

'You don't need to know about that.'

'But under the law of this country, I have to ask. And in

case you've forgotten, the Feds are looking at all of us very hard right now. The first slip we make, then we're all arrested for money laundering.' Not to mention, she wanted no part of that ugly business.

'Then we won't make a slip. His people are very good at clean up.' So he was admitting that the money was dodgy.

'This isn't the way I want to spend my life, Dad.'

He stood up abruptly. 'I had some clothes delivered last night. I'll bring them through.'

That wasn't going to make it any better. 'Can I use a computer?'

'For what?'

'Schoolwork.'

'I'm afraid you can't go online, not until Roman clears it.'

'But all my stuff is in the cloud.'

'Sorry, but it will have to stay there. I don't have clearance either.'

'So theoretically I can do my homework but you're not giving me the tools that will let me do it?' Temper reappeared. Deep breaths. Count to ten.

'I'll send a note with you to school tomorrow if you need to be excused.' Her dad reached the connecting door. 'I'll get you those clothes. I've got you something pretty to wear for dinner. The other guests are always well turned out.'

She folded her arms. 'You know me: that's my speciality. Fashion icon.'

The door banged closed.

'Yeah, Dad, run.' She picked up a bread roll to throw at his retreating back but he had been too quick. Instead, she opened the sliding door and chucked it as hard as she could over the balcony. A seagull plucked it mid-flight. She picked up the rest of the bread and tossed handfuls into the air, letting out little grunts of fury as she put her back into it. Soon a flock of birds mobbed her, making sure not a single crumb fell to the river. It felt cathartic, like she was throwing her anger away with it. By the time gull breakfast was over, she was calmer, more focused. A plan had begun to form in her mind, risky, possibly very dangerous, but potentially very satisfying. Flopping back on the bed, she began to scheme.

Damien left Joe to take on the task of putting in an early morning call to Agent Hammond while he got online to Kieran. It took a while for his friend to answer and when he did Damien immediately noticed a marked improvement in his appearance.

'Raven back?' Damien asked.

Kieran grinned. 'Your detective skills are coming along. Come say "hi" to Damien, Raven.'

His girlfriend came into frame, long spiralling hair spilling over her shoulders, dark eyes smiling. 'Hi.'

'Hello, Raven. All go well with the mission?' Damien had a very soft spot for the sharp-witted American girl. She'd done wonders for their friend over the last few months.

'It was only surveillance and, yeah, it was fine. We're now all back at HQ. Kate and Nat say "hi" too.'

'You got Kieran to clear up?'

Raven rolled her eyes. 'Of course. I refused to come anywhere near him until he sorted it out. Major health hazard.'

Kieran pulled her onto his knee and gave her a look that could only be called adoring. 'You see the cruelty I have to put up with, Damien?'

'Yeah, you look really miserable.'

Raven patted Kieran's cheek. 'Ace, you were in danger of brewing some new pathogen in here.'

Kieran's eyes brightened. 'You think? That would be so cool.'

'Not if it wiped out humanity or turned us into zombies or something.'

'I don't know—still cool, if inadvisable.'

Raven got now that Kieran was teasing her so punched him lightly in the ribs. 'Why are you Skyping so early, Damien? Joe OK?'

'We're good, thanks. I'm calling about that neighbour of his. There've been developments.' Damien quickly filled them in on the events of the last two days.

'That girl sounds an idiot. She should leave that father of hers to sort out his own mess,' remarked Raven.

Damien might have thought something similar once but, loyalties having done a one-eighty, he now felt he had to defend her choices. 'Rose is very far from an idiot. She knows he's a lost cause but she told me she can't suddenly be someone else. She's used to looking after that disaster of a family of hers.'

'I can kinda understand the loyalty.' Raven toyed with the cord on Kieran's YDA hoodie. 'So she's sacrificing herself for them?'

'Yes. But I want to save her from herself. She deserves better.'

Raven chuckled. 'Wow, Damien, what happened to Mr Tough Guy? You sound like you really care.'

Damien stiffened. 'She's a friend now. I stand by my friends.'

'Yes, you do. Sorry, I didn't mean to make it into a joke.' Raven tapped Kieran on the chest. 'Stud Muffin, have you got a plan?'

'Stud Muffin?' Damien pretended to gag.

'I'm trying out new terms of endearment.' Raven grinned at Kieran's embarrassed frown. 'So far this is the one he hates most.'

'Pest,' muttered Kieran. His eyes had drifted to another

part of the screen, his fingers flying over the keyboard. 'Just looking up a few things.'

Joe came back into the room behind Damien and waved to Raven. She blew him a kiss.

'I was going to ask Key if he could watch what she does online but, of course, the Feds have her equipment,' said Damien.

Kieran waved that away. 'No matter. She'll be using the systems Colosseum Enterprises have in place and if I can get in at the back door I should be able to keep an eye on that. I know her digital habits now—they're like a fingerprint to me. I've already got a programme monitoring her bank account. The money's still sitting there, by the way, but I think Melescanu will want his two hundred thousand back, don't you?'

Raven rested her head against Kieran's chest, eyes following his activity on the screen. She sighed. 'Looks like you two have just ruined our Sunday. He's gone into deep processing mode.'

Damien grimaced. 'Sorry, but she's worth it, I promise.'

'Then you must try to bring Rose back with you so we can meet her.'

'I'll see what I can do.' That's if she wasn't under arrest and facing charges by then.

Joe leaned over Damien's shoulder. 'Raven, tell Key to text us if there's any activity from Rose today, but I'm guessing she'll wait until tomorrow with most markets being closed.'

'You could talk to me. I'm still here,' muttered Kieran, not breaking concentration.

'He's not really,' said Raven. 'His brain is in Kieranland. I'll make sure he lets you know. Oh, by the way, what are you going to do for Damien's eighteenth? It's in a couple of days, isn't it?'

'We were going climbing upstate but this business has

taken over.' Joe squeezed Damien's shoulder. 'What do you want to do, Damien: still take the trip or stay to sort this out?'

'Stay,' Damien said quickly.

Joe and Raven exchanged smiles. 'Yep, this is one special girl,' concluded Raven. 'See you guys later.'

As Raven closed the call, Joe perched on the desk next to Damien. 'So what happened to no commitments and "sampling widely"? I swear I heard a speech on those lines but a few days ago.'

'Yeah well.' Damien pushed away from the screen, stood up, and stretched. 'The thing is about samples, the clever guy is the one who stops when he's found the right match to his colour scheme.'

'Must be bad if you start talking like an interior designer. Are you really that sure? I don't see it, you and her. She's not like anyone you've liked before.'

'That's no bad thing. I promise you it works for me.'

Joe shook his head. 'I guess I'll just have to get used to it. But I appreciate what you're trying to do for her.'

'Thanks.' Damien felt easier now Joe was coming round to seeing he was set on this course.

Joe folded his arms. 'But if you hurt her, I'll kick your butt from here to London.'

'Fair enough.' Damien's phone broke into a snatch of birdsong. 'Hey, Uncle Julian, how're you?'

'Damien, my boy!' bellowed his uncle, his rounded tones hardly compressed by the journey up to the satellite and back. 'What would you say to a few visitors in the Big Apple for your eighteenth?'

'I'd say "great!"' Damien couldn't bring himself to dampen his uncle's enthusiasm even if the visit was appallingly timed.

'Good, because it's too late to stop us in any case. I've booked us a suite at the Waldorf Astoria.'

'Who's "we"?'

'Your parents, of course. They sent you a letter but it will take an age thanks to back-country post in Uganda and will probably arrive after the event. They had a last minute invitation to attend a UN conference in New York on enslaved children or some such topic, thanks to a couple of other doctors having to drop out. They had been hoping to see you as they broke their journey in London, but I told them you were already over the pond. So we decided to kill two birds with one stone and all descend on you. Not that I approve of killing birds but you get my drift.'

'My parents are coming here?'

Joe's eyebrows winged up at that surprising statement. He'd never met Damien's parents and knew how distant the relationship had become.

'They wouldn't miss your coming of age for the world.'

No, Uncle Julian wouldn't miss it; his parents were just multitasking as usual. 'Well that's great. When do you arrive?'

'Tomorrow. I'll let you know when we've checked in and then you and Joe can come out with us. We'll paint the town red.'

'My parents—I can't imagine that.'

'Ah, my boy, just because they've been living in that five goat village of theirs doesn't mean they aren't the party animals when they get back to the city lights.'

'I'm not sure I'm ready to see this.'

'We'll have a wonderful time. Just you wait. Signing off now. Goodbye!' Uncle Julian ended the call.

'Well, there you go.' Damien put his phone down on the table in a state of shock. 'Uncle Julian has just invited you and me to paint the town red with him and my parents.'

'Meaning?' Joe smiled. All of Damien's friends had a soft

spot for Uncle Julian, larger than life and a staunch friend of the YDA students.

'We're to have a wild night of partying apparently. Geez, my saintly parents with their stethoscopes, Uncle Julian in his corduroys and flannel shirts: I can just see it.'

Joe bit his lip to stop himself laughing. 'Looks like your eighteenth is going to be a blast.'

'At least the people who witness it will mainly be in New York. If this were London, I'd never live it down.'

'And what about Rose?'

'The timing couldn't be worse, but let's see what we can come up with in the next two days. She might even be free of this mess by then to celebrate my birthday with us.'

'Yeah, maybe.' Joe gave him a sympathetic look. 'Let's warn my mom that your parents are heading our way. She'll want to start baking immediately.'

Chapter 12

With mounting awe, Rose unpacked her new wardrobe from the array of designer bags on the bed. Her dad must have employed a personal shopper because she couldn't believe that he would come up with these outfits—his taste was almost as bad as hers. The dress picked out for dinner was an above-the-knee gold tunic with a black belt, accessorized with matching shoes that had four-inch heels. She'd never worn high heels before. Standing in them in front of the mirror, she felt distinctly unsteady but she had to admit the whole look suited her. For school there was a dress made from a Native American eagle print fabric, collarless cream coat, large fishnet nylons and thigh-length brown boots. She would have students falling out of their seats in shock.

What happened to jeans and sweaters? There wasn't anything normal in the bags at all. Every purchase seemed to have sauntered straight off the catwalk.

'Focus,' she told her reflection. 'What you wear isn't important right now. Life crisis, remember?'

Her double stared back at her wide-eyed, not quite able to get with the programme.

'Geez, Rose, you are as ditzy as every other girl when faced with totally cool shoes,' she told herself in disgust, angling her feet so she could take a better look.

There came a knock at the door between her father's room and hers.

'You can come in.'

Her dad entered, looking very smart in a charcoal grey suit. During the afternoon he had found time to get a haircut and a barber shave so he looked very presentable, not at all like the guy chained to the wall in the photos. Oh yeah, but that had all been an act. Rose's temper flared back into life. Maybe she should be asking if he were nuts to go to such extremes to get her cooperation? Sane parents didn't do that kind of thing, did they?

'Rosie, you look lovely. Are you pleased with the clothes?' her father asked.

Oh. She suddenly realized the agenda: she was being bribed. The gold material now clung to her like the shirt of Nessus, poisoning the wearer. She wished she could rip it off but she had walked into this trap without a change of clothes. 'They're OK.'

He frowned at her cool response. 'The car's here. Are you ready?'

'I suppose.'

'Good. We mustn't keep Roman waiting.' He fiddled with the knot of his tie.

Rose picked up the little gold clutch bag she had been given. It was only big enough to hold a lipstick, phone, and a tissue—the exact opposite to the large tote she hefted around school stuffed with books and files. 'No, we wouldn't want to do that, would we?'

Melescanu's apartment overlooked Central Park on the west side, the primest of prime real estate. The elegant stone building had a uniformed concierge who tapped the brim of his top hat as he held the door for them, a marble foyer in creams and browns, and a mirrored lift that swished up to the top floor with barely a sound. The good taste ended as the doors opened. Rose stepped into another of Melescanu's Roman Empire fantasies: too much mosaic, purple, and gilt. Marble statues lined the hallway. They may well have been genuine but in this setting they screamed 'fake!' like a jewel in a plastic setting. You could get away with it in Italy maybe, but in Manhattan it just seemed trashy. She might have appalling taste herself, but she recognized a fellow sufferer of the same affliction. They hadn't progressed very far when they were met by a maid in a spotless black dress and white apron. She appeared to only speak Romanian but it was clear that she intended to conduct them into the presence of their august host, leading them to the far end of the broad passageway.

'Amazing, isn't it?' said Don in a low voice.

'Amazing that money can't buy everything? Yes, it is.'

'What do you mean?'

Rose flicked her hands at the decor. 'This. It's awful.'

'How can you say that? It's clear he spent a lot of money on this.' Don paused to admire a fragment of a male torso and head, part of a statue of Mercury that would have stood eight feet tall, she estimated. Something about the turn of the head and cheekbones reminded her of Damien.

'He should sue the interior designer who let him do this— Roman nightmare by way of Las Vegas,' she said acerbically, annoyed she was bringing Damien into this even in thought.

Their squabble had to end as they had reached the dining room. The maid opened the door and ushered them through. Melescanu was already seated at the head of the table. All the chairs were occupied apart from two either side of him. So tonight they were to be the guests of honour, were they?

'Don, Rose, so pleased you could make it.' The businessman stood up and shook hands with her father.

Like they had had a choice. Rose kept her hands behind

her back but that only gave Melescanu an excuse to kiss her cheek as if she were a favoured niece.

'Sit down, sit down. Don, you know most of my top team, don't you? Rose, these guys are the ones who keep Colosseum Investments ticking over.' Melescanu rapidly introduced the men and women at the table, mentioning various departments, such as finance and logistics. Rose couldn't bring herself to care. Normally she would remember names but inside she was floundering in a grey sea of depression. 'This is Don's girl, people—the one with the golden touch. Rose, I've put you next to my investment manager. You can brief him on your strategy while we eat.'

Rose glanced at the thirty-something man beside her. He didn't seem that pleased to meet her, which was most likely because she had outshone him in recent weeks.

'Now let's eat.' Melescanu tapped a gong on the sideboard and took his place at the head again. With the efficiency of a well-oiled operation, the door at the far end of the room opened and two waiters entered with the first course.

Rose picked at her meal, mainly spending her time sipping water from a crystal glass. She answered the investment guy's questions with yes and no, refusing to expand on her 'strategy'. He must have thought she was guarding her professional secrets; really she was struggling with fury at her predicament, glaring at her father across the table from her. It was clear from the casual conversation around the table—talk Don appeared to be lapping up—that if her father got any deeper into the organization, he would not be cutting the corners of the law but driving a truck through it. But what could she do when the person she still loved didn't want to be saved? She got it—she wasn't stupid: Melescanu's superficial air of success was like an addiction to Don; her father wanted to turn junkie, just like the idiots in school who hung out with the bad guys because they

188

seemed cool. They ended up making all the wrong choices, on the streets, in rehab if lucky, prison if not; lives ruined.

Melescanu realized after a while that Rose was not participating in the meal. 'The steak not to your taste, Rose?'

'It's lovely. I'm just not hungry.' She put her knife and fork down, only a tiny piece of the meat eaten.

His bearlike face sank deeper into brooding disapproval, eyes sunken in puffy lines. 'Your father says you want to go to school tomorrow.'

'I think it's best that I carry on as normal—less questions that way.'

'But you'll keep your side of the deal?' He cut at his fillet, utensils absurdly small in his big hands.

What deal? Oh, the threats and menaces that if she didn't pay her father's debt, they'd both regret it: that deal. But she didn't say that. 'I'll do my best.'

'Have you told Curtis how you are going to go about it?'

She glanced at the scowling manager. 'No.'

Melescanu gave a grunt of laughter and raised a toast to her. 'Knowledge is power, is that it? I like a girl who knows when to keep her mouth shut.'

'My Rose is very discreet. She knows where her loyalties lie,' her dad interjected quickly, showing that he had been paying more attention to her than it appeared on the surface.

Stop toadying up to him, Dad. 'I work by intuition,' Rose lied. 'Like a composer. I can't explain where the decisions come from; I'm just following an internal tune that seems to make sense.'

'Ah, she's an artist.' Melescanu nodded to his investment guy. 'You hear that, Curtis, you with all your spreadsheets and market analysis outmatched by a natural money-maker. We must put you head-to-head one day with a hundred grand each and see who comes out top. I know which horse I'd back.'

Rose prayed that this interminable meal would end. 'I'll start tomorrow after school. I'll have to have access to the internet but I suppose that's OK?'

'Anything you need, Rose. Anything. Just ask Curtis here if you want any more people. You needn't do all the heavy lifting yourself.'

'It's OK. I work best alone.'

He patted the back of her hand in what was supposed to be an avuncular gesture but came over as more of a threat. 'But if you go to school, you say nothing to anyone, OK? I'll have people watching and anyone you talk to will get a visit from one of my guys to check you've kept quiet.'

She twisted the stem of the wine glass, letting the light refract off the different facets. 'I can't be completely silent. That'd be weird.'

'Sure you can talk boys and music with your girlfriends—whatever you teenagers talk about. I meant that we would be watching for any approach by the authorities—an overly concerned teacher or one of those FBI people camped out at your house—your neighbours.'

'Neighbours?'

'Yeah, those guys next-door to you are far too interested in your business. Don told me that the woman is always interfering. Wasn't the son the one who called in the FBI? He's been seen with them this week according to my sources.'

Rose thought it best neither to confirm nor deny, though it was alarming he had sources inside the FBI. Another reason not to trust the Feds. 'Joe doesn't go to my school.'

'OK, so it won't be a problem. If the Feds do ask to speak to you, refuse. Plead the fifth. You can't be made to talk. You understand?'

'Yes, I understand.'

Satisfied that she was on side, Melescanu turned the

conversation to a delayed shipment on board a container vessel called the *Southern Star*, expected in from Albania. It didn't take Rose long to read between the lines that the consignment included illegal immigrants from Africa and the Middle East, hidden below decks and among the crew. Melescanu did not care for their welfare; his concern was reserved for the increased costs brought by the extension of the voyage. She felt sickened by the callous way the whole thing was discussed. How could her father possibly want any part in this?

She asked Don that question during the ride home in the cab.

'People trafficking isn't a sin, Rose,' her father argued, looking out the windows at the passing lights of the shops and restaurants. 'You have to understand the terrible situations these people are fleeing from. We're giving them a fresh start—a chance at a new life.'

'But it's illegal.' Her heart sank at his use of 'we'—he was already involved, then.

'And that's why we can make money doing it. We're providing a risky service. Haven't you got any compassion for the people trying to escape wars and persecution?'

'Of course I have. But don't tell me Melescanu does. I've heard stories about traffickers like him—they don't care what condition the people are in when they arrive and they abandon them at the first sign of trouble. It's like the slave ships in the eighteenth century all over again. They used to chuck their so-called "cargo" over the side if the captives were sick or something went wrong.'

'Nonsense: there's no comparison at all. These people are making a free choice.'

'And they'll all be free when they get here, will they? There are no women and children being trafficked into the sex trade, no workers signed up for exploitative jobs where they can't escape because they're not here with the right permits? Just because I'm sixteen doesn't mean I haven't read the press stories about all this.'

Don undid his tie and top button.

'See, Dad, I think you are the one who's lacking compassion. Just because you don't want to look too hard at what's going on, doesn't make it right. If you try to make out that man's doing this out of the kindness of his heart, then I'll leave you to his mercy.'

He grimaced at that. 'You wouldn't.'

'Just make sure you have a Plan B, Dad, because I'm not sure you can rely on me this time.' That had to be warning enough. As Ryan and her mom had said, one day Don would have to work his own way out of his difficulties. That day was just going to come a lot quicker than he was anticipating, because after what she heard tonight she wasn't going to pay Melescanu another cent to be put into this trade in human misery. The challenge was not getting them both killed for her decision.

A chauffeur-driven black limo was waiting outside Colosseum Investments the next morning to take her the short distance to school. Rose welcomed the sunglasses that had come as part of her outfit as it hid her wide-eyed stare as she took in the driver and car. The stocky chauffeur with matt black hair and walrus moustache rushed to open the rear door as she stepped out into the sunshine.

'Ready to go, Miss Knight?'

'Yes, but . . . er?'

'I'm Peters, miss.'

'But it's really not necessary.'

'I don't think you understand: I'm your designated driver for the day. Mr Melescanu said to take you anywhere you want if you get bored of school. You have access to our onboard computer if you wish to begin your work.'

'That's fine but I don't think I'll want to cut class.'

Peters gave her a thin smile, clearly doubting any teenager would resist the temptation to cruise Manhattan in a town car. 'Let's just see how your day goes. I'll be waiting out front.'

'You don't have to do that.' She slid onto the back seat, buttery yellow leather kissing the back of her legs.

'I really do.'

Oh, so he was part of the team keeping her under a close watch. She had to remember he was not there for her but his boss.

'Can you let me out here?' Rose asked as they turned into the street where the main building of the school was located.

'I've been told to take you door to door.' Peters drove up and parked on the yellow kerb 'keep clear' lines outside the school to let her out. The students clustering through the gates stopped to gawp at the spectacle, just what Rose had been trying to avoid. She reached to open the door but it did not release until Peters opened it for her from the outside. 'I'll be just across the street,' he told her, handing her a powder-blue leather satchel stocked with fresh supplies of paper and a pencil case.

This was ridiculous. 'I hope you've got a good book with you. It's going to be a long wait.'

'I have plenty to do, I assure you, miss.'

Squaring her shoulders to run the gauntlet, Rose strode through the crowds of spectators. Usually no one made way for her as she scurried from class to class and she had to squeeze her way through the crowds, but something about thigh boots and a limo caused the students to step back.

'Is that Rose?' she heard them whisper.

She was too embarrassed to take off her sunglasses. The

only way to carry this off was to pretend she'd meant to arrive like this. Coat flapping in the light breeze, she walked across the schoolyard. Once in her form room, she heaved a sigh of relief. The first to arrive, she quickly stashed the shades in their glasses case and checked the contents of the new bag. She had no schedule but fortunately her excellent memory meant she could recall the day's classes and rooms.

What am I doing? Momentarily coming up for air from the tide of events that had swept her away, she felt a twist of panic. *I can't do this—pretend to be this cool girl who can make millions.* People kept presenting her with parts to play and shoving her on stage without allowing her time to learn her lines. She wished she could just halt the show, return to her plans of studying and research.

But no one wanted another archaeologist. They wanted a financial wizard—a loyal daughter—a sister who held the home together.

I do. I think you'd make a great one. You can't let your dad steal your dream like that.

The snatch of the conversation with Damien two nights ago came back to her. There had been one person who liked her for what she was, not what she could do for them. What had Damien meant about doing what was necessary to save her? So wrapped up in her own plans, Rose had forgotten that she wasn't the only one mixed up in this drama. He wasn't going to bring the Feds back into the situation, was he? That would be a disaster, a nine on the Richter scale. He was far too trusting of the authorities in a way she could never be with her father and brother on the wrong side of the law. If she had a chance, she'd have to tell Damien to back off. She had it in hand—or more accurately had plans to catch the tiger by the tail. If she ran fast enough, she might, just might, escape the snap of its jaws.

194

Her classmates filtered into the room. Everyone did a double-take to see her with her new look. Lindy gave her a delighted grin and hurried over, doubtless intending to grill her on her wardrobe, answers she would fail miserably to give, but before Lindy could take her usual seat, Marco slid into it.

'Morning, Ginger.' He kissed Rose's cheek.

Rose was too shocked to correct his use of the nickname. 'You're sitting in Lindy's seat.' She looked up to find her friend gazing at them with puzzlement that rapidly turned to hurt. 'Get out.'

Marco stretched and dropped his arm on the back of her chair. 'Can't. Been told to keep you close.'

Lindy turned away with a devastated expression. She sank into a chair among some sympathetic girlfriends who immediately started hissing sympathetic words, interspersed with shooting Rose and Marco poisonous looks.

'Move. Now. You go apologize to Lindy.' Rose shoved, hoping to dislodge him from the chair.

He caught her hands and playful kissed the tips, making out like they were indulging in a little flirting. 'Can't, Ginge, or he'll skin me alive.'

It finally got through to Rose what Marco was talking about. 'You're doing this for Mr Melescanu?' She should have guessed. Marco's family was very like her own, skirting on the edge of trouble.

Marco put his hand to her lips to quieten her. 'Not so loud, Ginge. Do you want the whole school to know you're his latest project?'

Snatching her bag from the desk, she stood up and crossed to the door, fully intending to storm out. Her exit was spoiled by the teacher arriving with coffee cup in hand. Rose's cream coat narrowly avoided a baptism in latte.

'Rose, something the matter?' asked Mrs Fallon.

'Excuse me. Feel sick.' Rose rushed past her and headed for the nearest bathroom.

'Lindy, check on Rose for me, please,' she heard Mrs Fallon say.

No, no, no, she couldn't deal with Lindy right now. Rose carried on running, habit more than any clear thought taking her into the library. There was a corner out of view of the librarian's desk near the rarely visited Ancient Civilisations shelf. It had been her bolt-hole numerous times before. Rose leant her head against Tolkien's edition of *Beowulf* and took deep breaths, reciting the opening lines to calm herself.

'You OK, Rose?'

Just her rotten luck. Lindy had found her in any case. Her question was asked in a flattened tone, not the usual Lindy with her enthusiasm for meddling in everyone's lives.

Rose carried on running the poem, reaching line thirty.

'I can get you a trash can but maybe if you feel sick you'd better go to the nurse.' Lindy waited. 'I'm not angry, you know—about Marco. If he likes you then that's fine. Plenty more fish. Not your fault. Maybe our relationship had, you know, run its course.'

'I hate him,' Rose whispered, not sure if she meant Marco, her father, or Melescanu for that matter.

'Oh, that's a bit harsh. He's sweet. Really thoughtful when you get him on his own—not like the image he projects at school.' Lindy really was too nice for him, trying to be fair to a guy who had just kissed another girl in front of her.

Rose should have guessed that even a jerk like Marco would have hidden depths or else why would Lindy bother with him? 'He's not interested in me, Lindy.'

'He should be. You look great today—well, apart from the deathly white face and the "I'm gonna barf on your shoes" expression.'

Rose gave a soft huff of laughter. Lindy rested a hand between her shoulder blades. 'If he's not after you why was he making a clear move on you in registration?'

Rose shrugged.

'I noticed when he saw you with Damien at my party he got all riled like he thought you were his to kiss. We argued about it later after you went home. We kinda broke up already over it.'

Could life get any more bizarre? This was not how she imagined her day would go. 'Lindy.' Rose straightened and realigned the spines of the books she had pushed backwards with her forehead—Anglo Saxon riddles, *The Battle of Maldon*, Seamus Heaney's wonderful verse translation of *Beowulf*—her brain couldn't stop noticing the details others skimmed over. Sometimes she wished she could switch it off.

'Yes, Rose?'

'There is not, nor has there ever been, nor will there ever be anything between Marco and me except hostility. If he's a nice guy to you out of school then I'm pleased for you. Personally, I think him a blight on my life. Are we clear?'

Lindy smiled, her relief obvious. 'We're clear. Great boots by the way. Where did you get them?'

'They were a present.' Lindy would know she hadn't picked them out herself.

'You feel better now?'

No, but Lindy did so that was all that mattered. 'I'm good, thanks.' Rose then recalled what Melescanu had said about anyone she talked with getting a visit from his people. 'But if Marco asks what we were talking about, just say we were talking about boys, OK?'

'Sure. Because we were, right?'

'And if you see him hanging around me, don't assume the worst. He's just enjoying bugging me as usual.'

'I'll tell him to cut it out.'

'Don't bother. He'll get bored in a couple of days.'

'Still . . .' Linda shrugged, giving up the argument. 'Let's get to class.' She checked her shoulder bag. 'You did your calculus assignment?'

Rose damned Melescanu and his stupid greed to Hades and back. 'I think I might go lie down in the nurse's office for a while.'

Lindy's mouth rounded in a little 'o' of shock. 'Rose, you didn't forget again! What will Mr McGinty say?'

'You know what he'll say so that's why you'll cover for me.'

Lindy put her arm around Rose's shoulders. 'You do look a bit green.'

'I thought you said I looked pale.'

'Green, pale—the point is you look like someone who really needs to cut class.'

'We definitely can agree on that.'

Chapter 13

The boys were sitting in Joe's local Starbucks where they had gone to plot without Joe's parents accidentally overhearing. Damien reviewed their emails so far, pleased that their scheme was taking shape. They'd been working on an extraction strategy for Rose and her father. Joe had successfully appealed to Agent Hammond, the senior agent they had met at the school, to take an interest in the case and she had spent the weekend discussing with her bosses the idea of offering Don a place in their witness protection scheme if he'd turn against Melescanu. Agents Jameson and Stevens had reluctantly agreed when they heard from the boys that prosecution for abduction was a bust. Hammond's latest message was a promise that Don would get a new life somewhere far from New York if he agreed to testify. She warned, however, that they couldn't do this if Knight and Rose got their hands too dirty in the interim.

'Rose is at school,' announced Joe.

'How do you know?'

Joe angled the screen of his tablet so Damien could see the photos posted on Facebook. An auburn-haired beauty with sexy boots was striding across a sunlit playground.

'That's Rose?' Damien tugged the screen nearer. 'What have they done to her?' It had been less than forty-eight hours since he'd seen her in polar bear PJs. In the photo, she looked glamorous but all wrong. He preferred her with the purple polka dots and hair in a sock, her prettiness camouflaged so only he noticed.

Joe slapped him over the head. 'Damien, you're missing the point. She's at school. Accessible without climbing a five storey fortress, you follow?'

Damien stood up, abandoning his half-drunk coffee. 'Let's go.'

Joe grabbed his sleeve and jerked him back down. 'Slow down. We've got to work out what this means.'

'It means she's negotiated day release from her prison.'

'Yes. But what else?'

Damien forced himself to remember his training. Joe was right: the one lesson that they all had had drummed into them was that they should only ever go into a situation with all available data analyzed and a plan made. 'She's the one who would want to go to school so that means she has got her way somehow.'

'Yeah, Melescanu and her father need her cooperation. It's no longer a "chained to a wall" situation but some kind of deal.'

'She's agreed to work for Melescanu.' Damien could feel her getting further and further away from them, swept up into that man's whirlpool of crime. There would soon come a point when she would be too far in to be saved.

'Looks that way. We knew she'd do what she had to in order to rescue her dad, but to go as far as letting her out on her own means she had got their trust. To a certain point.'

'You think?'

'I suppose Melescanu still has her dad as a guest. He might feel that's enough to make her behave.'

'We have to tell her what the Feds can offer—she has to hold off doing anything criminal as long as possible so that plan has time to be put in place.'

'Melescanu will be watching her.'

200

'At school?'

Joe just raised a brow, reminding Damien that this was Melescanu's home turf. Of course he could watch a sixteen-year-old at school if he wanted. The caretakers, teachers, other students—so many of them would be vulnerable to the application of the right kind of pressure.

Damien quickly ran through their options in his mind. 'Then we need a plan to get her alone for a moment.'

'I can't think how.'

'Joe, don't you think you sometimes lack a rebel mindset that helps a guy like me in these situations?'

'I do?' Joe didn't know if he should look hurt or not so settled for a half smile.

'I bet you always coloured within the lines, too.'

'And you were what: kindergarten's Jackson Pollock?'

'Totally. Look, mate, the answer's obvious. I just need you to get me into that school again and locate Rose. We went there last Monday, right? She'll be in the science lab mid-morning?'

'I guess.'

Damien stood up. 'Come on then. What are you waiting for?'

Joe sweet-talked his way in past reception with the same ease as he had a week ago. His excuse this time was that he had to see Mr McGinty about an international maths competition he was thinking of entering. The receptionist was so chatty and interested that she didn't even stop to question why he felt he had to bring his British friend with him.

Damien led the way to the science corridor he remembered from the last visit, scanning for the necessary location from which to launch his plan. He could see the bent heads in each classroom and the murmur of teachers at whiteboards, punctuated by the occasional burst of laughter or mumble of student chatter. They paused outside Rose's classroom and caught a glimpse of her wearing plastic goggles, heating a test tube over a Bunsen burner. It was a hot look, Damien decided, auburn hair bundled up out of the way, white coat, and the hint of long brown boots flashing under the hem. Lindy hovered near her, making up for her silence with a continuous stream of talk.

Joe folded his arms. 'OK, what now?'

Damien nodded to the red fire alarm on the wall beside the lockers.

'You're joking?'

'Don't tell me, Joe, you've got all the way through school without once setting off the alarm?'

'Exactly. Most people do, you know, because most people learn the lesson of Cry Wolf.'

'How did you and I became friends, remind me?'

'Can't think.' Joe took a deep breath. He raised an elbow to the Perspex panel, then dropped it. 'Can't we just go in and ask to speak to her? Catch her during lesson changeover?'

'She's being watched, you said. We need the cover of confusion. Tell your conscience that it's a life or death situation—just not the fire kind.' Putting Joe out of his misery, Damien thumped the panel with the heel of his hand, letting the clear cover snap and spring out. Immediately the alarm began ringing throughout the building. 'I suggest we hide.' He pulled Joe away from the tell-tale fragments into the shelter of a gap between the lockers near the stairwell.

There was a pause as teachers assessed the likelihood that this was just a brief test, then came the universal order to evacuate. Doors opened and students filed out. None of the pupils showed any signs of alarm; in fact, most looked quite happy to have the interruption, chatting despite the teachers' shouted orders to leave swiftly and silently. Rose was one of the last to come out of the laboratory, arms folded defensively across her chest, head hung as if she didn't want to speak to anyone. That made her easy prey. She had barely passed them when Damien snagged her arm and drew her into their refuge.

'You're coming with us,' he said in low voice.

'But we've got to leave the building,' she said in bewilderment. 'There's a fire.'

'There's no fire.'

Damien pulled her into the classroom she'd just vacated. 'Joe, keep watch OK?'

With a nod, Joe stayed in the corridor.

'But they'll miss me on the register. I'll get in trouble.' Rose tried to escape but Damien didn't let go.

'Like that features high on the list of things you're in danger of getting in trouble for,' he said dryly. 'Rose, what's going on?' He gestured to her clothes. 'Have you sold out so quickly?'

'What?' She was so surprised by the accusation she forgot to keep pulling away. 'No!'

'You look a million dollars—or at least a few thousand—which means someone has been spending money on you.'

'It's not like that!'

'No? So you haven't wrapped Melescanu round your little finger so he showers you with sweeteners? We saw the limo outside.'

'I didn't ask for any of that.'

'No? But I bet you're enjoying it anyway—you wouldn't be human if you didn't. But Rose, you have to pay the piper if you start dancing to his tune.'

'What kind of analogy is that?'

'Do you prefer "there's no such thing as a free lunch"? Both apply. Melescanu will want something return for the princess treatment. If you get sucked in too far, we can't help you.'

'Sucked into what?'

Damien thought for a second that she might be genuinely confused but then he saw the hint of guilty knowledge in her brown eyes. 'Don't give me that. I know you, remember?'

She closed her eyes briefly, then opened them to give him a direct look. 'You do? So why are you doubting me?'

'Because you have a fatal soft spot for your family.' He brushed a thumb over her pink lips, distracted by how soft and pretty they were. They should be smiling but he had rarely seen her looking happy. Cut it out, Damien: concentrate. You've got something you want to tell her. 'Look, the FBI says—'

She shook her head, straining to escape his grip on her arms. 'Stop. I don't want to hear about them. They started all this.'

He gave a choked laugh. 'Yeah, they're the ones to blame for the drug-and gunrunning, the people trafficking. Will you be able to face yourself if you help that crook do his dirty work, Rose? I don't think you will.'

'This is my problem, Damien. Not yours.'

'I already told you: I'm making you my problem.'

'I don't want that.'

'You do—you just don't know it yet.'

'Stop telling me what I want!'

'Someone has to as you're not making the least bit of sense!'

'I'll be fine on my own. I'm handling it.'

'No, you're not.'

'I am! I don't need the FBI—or Joe—or even you to stick your nose into my business!'

'You are just the most infuriating girl in existence.' Not knowing what else to do to persuade her, he gathered her closer and gave her a hard, furious kiss which she surprised him by returning with the same leashed anger. They broke apart, feelings jagged, breath coming in gasps. He ran his fingers through her hair, cupping the back of her head, hairpins scattering as he loosened them. He wished he could control her thoughts as easily as he could hold her like this. He brushed his lips across hers gently, pleadingly. 'Why won't you let me help you, Rose?'

'I don't need . . .'

'You do. Joe and I—we've got a solution. We just need to talk to your dad. Can you arrange it?'

Her eyelashes swept down, resting on her cheeks to veil her expression. 'You need to talk to my dad, or the FBI does?'

'Both.'

'Then no. They'll put him in jail.'

'If you stay with Melescanu, they'll eventually put you all in jail—you along with the rest of them.' He removed his fingers, smoothing the hair he had dislodged. 'How would you like juvenile detention—no hope of a college place or any kind of decent career?'

She stiffened. Good, he was finally getting through to her. So far she hadn't been nearly scared enough.

'You know what they'll do with a marshmallow like you in juvie? It won't be pretty. You'll go from hero to zero in no time flat—top science student to last in the pecking order.'

'You have no idea . . .' she whispered.

'Oh I do. You're under unbearable pressure—divided loyalties. You're not doing this because you're greedy or bad but because you're sweet and just a little too innocent to survive in the kind of world your father lives in. Back out now, Rose. Be sensible. Get your dad to talk to us. The Feds have a deal for him. New life for you both if you testify.'

He took encouragement that she appeared to be really considering the offer.

'We disappear?' she asked.

'To a new place where you can pick things up again.'

She frowned, two lines appearing between her reddish-gold eyebrows. He wanted to smooth them away with the pad of his thumb but didn't dare break her concentration. 'Melescanu gets to employ his full panoply of lawyers so that it's our word against his?'

'I suppose so.'

She sighed and used her right hand to lift his fingers off her arm. 'And I'm the gullible one in this situation?' She stepped back. This time he let her go. 'Thank you, Damien, for trying to sort this out for us but my dad . . . my dad is not reliable. The Feds won't find him a good witness and I know next to nothing of value. We can't bring Melescanu down this way. All that would happen is we would lose our old lives and then live in fear that he would catch up with us to take revenge. Melescanu has sources everywhere, even in the FBI. It was kind of you to try, but no.'

'Don't do this.' Damien couldn't contain his fury at her logical dismissal of the plan he and Joe had spent so much time negotiating over the last few days. She might have a point about the risks but it was still by far the best of bad options. Besides, he had an extra plan to keep her safe. She hadn't even let him tell her about that. 'Rose, you'd be a fool to throw away your last chance!'

'Maybe.' She gave a shrug which tried to say she didn't care but didn't do a very good job.

'There's no helping you, is there? I thought you'd have some red lines you wouldn't cross even for your dad but it appears I was wrong. You help Melescanu and you're inflicting all kinds of misery on others, but you don't care about that, do you? They're faceless so they don't matter.'

She hugged her arms to herself.

'If you do this, you won't be able to be with me either, but you know that, don't you? I was going to ask that you could come to the UK—get you out of the US altogether for a really new start—but you won't even try it my way. You've given it—what?—three seconds' consideration but Miss Genius knows best.'

Rose curled her fists, shaking with anger or fear—he no longer knew. He realized he didn't really know her all that well, did he?

'Fine.' He threw his hands up in the air. 'I get the message. Nice knowing you, Rose. Good luck with the rest of your life. Just don't take any of your godawful jumpers to juvie—they'll eat you alive.' Exasperated by her silence, he stormed out of the lab. 'Come on, Joe. Let's go.'

'But . . .' said Joe, looking back at Rose.

'Not now. We're done here.'

Rose couldn't move from the spot where Damien had abandoned her. She was still absorbing the pain of his parting jabs. Among them all, she had heard that he had been very serious about her, thinking of moving her abroad to be with him. Little wonder he was angry. But she couldn't say anything—couldn't trust this plan. She'd only known him a few days—not enough to change beliefs formed over years. The Feds did not protect her sort; they used them: and that wasn't enough to bank her future on.

One of the school fire marshals, dressed in a fluorescent vest and holding a clipboard and checklist, stuck his head round the doorjamb. 'Miss Knight? What are you doing still inside?' His foot crunched on the Perspex laying on the floor outside the room, eyes taking in the broken alarm. 'Do you know anything about this?'

Rose couldn't think of the appropriate response and ended up giving the wrong one: a shrug.

The marshal's gaze swept the lab, noting the open cabinets

and Rose still in her white coat. 'Then I think you'd better come with me and explain yourself to the principal.'

Numb, Rose bent to pick up her bag.

'I'll take that.' The marshal opened the flaps, checking for contraband but found nothing. 'You in here—it doesn't make sense.' He appeared to be asking in the hope that she had a perfectly good explanation.

No, it didn't make sense.

'You're normally such an obedient student.'

'I haven't done anything.' Finally Rose found the right words.

'We'll let Mrs Chandler decide that. Did you not stop to think that you might've forced a firefighter to risk his life coming to get you out if this hadn't been a hoax? We have fire drills for a reason.' The marshal reported his find on his walkie-talkie, also giving the all-clear for the students to return to the building.

In a haze, Rose walked through the other pupils flooding into the building as if they weren't there. She'd never, ever been called to the principal's office for anything other than commendations. The head's study was quiet, a welcome break from the buzz of the corridors outside. Rose wanted to curl up in a corner and shut her eyes, sit in the patch of sunlight glancing off the Inter Schools Science Competition cup. She found she couldn't concentrate as the marshal gabbled his story of finding Rose on her own near the incriminating evidence of the fire alarm.

Mrs Chandler steepled her fingers, elbows resting on the arms of her leather swivel chair. 'Do you have anything to say, Miss Knight?'

Rose's inner Nancy Drew—her sorted, level-headed side—gave her a nudge. 'I didn't do anything, Mrs Chandler.'

'Why didn't you leave the building?'

She couldn't mention that she'd been cornered by Damien as she didn't know who was reporting on her in the school. 'I . . . I can't remember. I must've got caught up with something.'

Mrs Chandler turned back to the marshal. 'But there was nothing in her bag?'

He held it up. 'It's a brand new Mulberry satchel. These things retail for over a thousand dollars.'

'That's not a crime,' Rose murmured.

'But hardly appropriate to bring to school.' Mrs Chandler studied Rose's new outfit in more detail. 'Miss Knight, Rose, what is going on? There's a man in a car at my gates who refuses to move. He says he's your chauffeur. It's not your birthday or the school prom so I can't think why on earth you would want a town car to ferry you about. And your clothes—I don't think thigh boots are explicitly banned in the school uniform rules, but they should be. They are hardly compatible with usual student activities. I've never had any problem with you before. Why have you suddenly become . . .' she waved a hand at Rose, 'like this?'

Rose fell back on the only gesture she could summon up at short notice: a shrug.

'Sudden influx of expensive clothes and accessories—a driver who looks more like a thug: it doesn't take a genius to guess that these things are not honestly come by. If they are, please correct me.'

Rose didn't fill the pause.

'If you won't explain your presence in the building near the vandalized alarm, I will have to exclude you until you do. I can't have students disrupting lessons, disobeying fire regulations, and ordering a car to block the school entrance all on a whim. I'll phone your father and inform him of my decision. The exclusion lasts a week. I expect you and he to be in my office a week today with an apology and a decent explanation for all that has gone on here today. I can't begin to tell you how disappointed I am in you.'

'This isn't fair.' Rose addressed the remark to her fingertips as no one seemed to be taking her side.

'No, then explain why.' Mrs Chandler let the silence stretch. 'All right then. It is with great reluctance I must ask you to leave the school premises. And when you return, don't bring your personal chauffeur with you.'

Hurt beyond bearing, Rose walked out.

'Miss Knight, your bag!' called Mrs Chandler.

'Keep it. Raffle it off for the school development fund. I don't care.' Rose walked straight past the students milling about the entrance hall, not wanting to see anyone.

Peters threw aside his newspaper as she exited through the gates. 'Changed your mind, miss?' he asked with a knowing smile. 'Thought you would.'

'Take me away from here,' Rose ordered, sliding into the back.

'Where do you want to go? Shopping?'

'No, just drive until I say stop.' Folding in on herself, knees against her chest, she watched the streets of Manhattan pass by and for once didn't take in any of the details, her vision watery. Peters drove in a grid up and down Park Avenue and Lexington, probably hoping that the bright lights of the shops and hotels would tempt her to prove him right about her materialistic nature. A pause in the traffic stopped them at the lights outside the Waldorf Astoria. Her gaze was caught by an array of international flags and a banner welcoming delegates to the third UN conference on trafficked children. Posters showed the world-weary gaze of child soldiers and teenage slaves. Then to her astonishment she saw Damien running along the street. He must've just got off the subway. He threw himself into the arms of a heavyset man in a blazer and navy jeans. The bear hug was incredibly touching to watch as they rocked to and fro, slapping each other on the back and laughing.

Peters was about to pull away as the lights changed but Rose tapped his shoulder. 'Wait, please.'

Peters put on his hazard lights, ignoring the outraged hoots of the taxis and cars behind him.

Damien pulled away from the older man and then exchanged a more restrained greeting with a sun-bronzed couple standing a little awkwardly a few feet off. The petite lady with upswept blonde hair kissed his cheek and smiled sweetly up at him. The man, dressed in a battered jacket and pale cotton chinos, shook hands. He had a bead necklace high on his collarbone, the same colour as the band Damien wore on his wrist, along with a leather tie and a few favourite club and festival passes. His parents—had to be. The saintly doctors from Uganda. Rose glanced once more up at the conference banner and put two and two together, arriving at a very high probability explaining their sudden appearance so far from their remote clinic. The little party disappeared into the hotel, adding further weight to her theory.

'OK. Can you take me home please?'

'Home, Miss Knight? Where's that?'

Indeed, where was it now? 'Bank Street, West Village. I've got some things I need to collect from my house to do my work. Can we drop by a computer store on the way? I'd like to pick up a replacement laptop.'

Fortunately, Peters had no instructions not to humour her wishes so did as she requested, taking her to the nearest Apple store.

Hugging the white box of her new computer on her lap, Rose felt the last pieces of her plan fall into place. Almost perfect. The flaws were the things that lay beyond her control—too many of them—but at least she now saw clearly what her role should be. First step would be to make good use of Melescanu's seed-corn money sitting in her account.

Chapter 14

Uncle Julian's text that he and Damien's parents had just arrived came at a welcome moment for Damien. The interview with Rose self-destructing into a row, he'd not wanted to rehash the conversation with Joe and now he had been handed the perfect excuse to delay the autopsy. He was aware that he had lost patience, using his words to attack her before he'd even laid out the whole plan. He didn't normally lose his cool so quickly. He guessed it was close to the panicked anger that a friend feels when seeing a drunken mate stagger out in front of a car. He had wanted both to shake her and hug her until she came to her senses but instead he'd shouted at her and stormed out. Not his greatest moment.

'My boy!' bellowed Uncle Julian as they took seats in the hotel restaurant for lunch. 'It feels an age since I saw you. How's America treating you? Seen any interesting birds?' The twinkle in his eye told Damien the *double entendre* was entirely on purpose.

'I've not noticed that much in the way of wildlife.' Damien refused the invitation to reply with one of his own arch comments. What did Uncle Julian expect? Geez, his parents were sitting right there. 'Mum, Dad, how are you?'

'Fine, thanks. Work going well.' His dad adjusted the wooden beads at this throat. Damien tucked his own wristband under his shirt sleeve. His mum had given them both a matching set three Christmases ago, bought in a street

213

market in Kitgum. Damien had got into the habit of wearing his but now regretted the sentimentality that showed.

Damien's mother hadn't taken her eyes off her son. 'I hadn't realized.'

'Realized what, Mum?'

'Just how old you are getting. Where have the years gone, Lawrence?'

'No idea, Grace. It doesn't seem five minutes ago he was rambling in nothing but a T-shirt around our bungalow in Padibe. Do you remember the old place, Damien?'

'I remember the nest of poisonous centipedes I poked with a stick,' he said wryly. He still had nightmares about the huge black shiny insects squirming out around his bare feet.

His dad chuckled. 'Ah, yes. Thankfully, Jason was there to rescue you.'

'Jason?'

'Our cook and houseboy. His sister was one of the LRA abductees—terrible business. All our staff loved looking after you.'

'They say it takes a village.' Burying his resentment, Damien promised himself he wouldn't pick a fight with his parents. Walking out on one person was enough for one day.

'Very sensible,' agreed his mother. 'The children of Padibe have a wonderful upbringing as long as the LRA soldiers aren't around, aunties and uncles keeping an eye on them. They have far more freedom then their European equivalents. We wanted that for you.'

Was that how his parents saw it? They were right to a certain extent: his childhood had had its idyllic side. Long rambles with local boys in the fields, exploring, kicking his football about on a dirt pitch. When he got to England he had been genuinely upset to discover he had to wear shoes and that toughened soles were not the norm. 'Is Jason still working for you?'

His mother shook her head sadly. 'Died of pneumonia, underlying cause HIV picked up from his mother.' Her eyes then brightened. 'But we have got infection rates right down and maternal transmission has almost stopped thanks to our treatment plans. His sister is back though, part of our counselling service for ex-child soldiers.'

'I'm pleased.' Damien checked his inner voice, alert for his usual sneer, but he found he actually was pleased. 'I'm proud of you both.'

His mum's eyes glistened with tears. 'Oh Damien: that's the nicest thing you could have said to us. And we're so proud of you. I look at you and wonder what we did to deserve such a capable young man, striking out on his own path with this detective training. I know you feel like we weren't there enough for you—'

'We weren't,' said his dad.

'We meant to be but we're both so . . . so driven by what we do. The terrible need—it's hard to describe what that does to you. We thought you'd be fine—and no thanks to us, you are. And now you're about to be eighteen. We both want to close the gap that's opened up between us in the last few years since you lived in London.'

Few years? More like ten. Damien realized his parents had probably come all this way in part to make this speech, an offer of a more adult relationship with them. 'Uncle Julian has been fantastic.'

His father slapped his brother on the arm. 'He helped raise me so I knew he'd be a great guardian.'

'He did?'

'You'll remember us saying that our mum—your grandmother—died of cancer when I was little. Our dad retreated from family life and concentrated on earning enough to get us the education he thought we needed. Julian brought me up—a fifteen-year-old running around for a pesky six-year-old, if you can imagine.'

'I wouldn't say I brought you up—dragged you kicking and screaming,' rumbled Uncle Julian, colour high on his cheekbones at his brother's praise.

'Mum's death was why I became a doctor—did I never tell you that?'

Damien shook his head.

'You have to be tough to do the things we do—see on a daily basis the things we see. We constantly have to make life or death choices. It's not easy coming from a family like that. I think the children suffer the most—you suffered not quite neglect but you certainly didn't have our full attention, did you?'

'It's OK. It toughened me up too.'

His mum reached out and held his hand. 'But it isn't OK. Julian says you feel you have to be strong the whole time. None of us can be. Your father and I had each other in our weak moments. We want you to know that you have us—all of us.' She nodded to the other two at the table. 'You always will.'

Damien's throat clutched. He had a sudden flash of Rose admitting that her father wasn't reliable. She didn't have anything like this behind her. Imperfect though they all were, he had his family rooting for him. She had no one. 'Thanks, Mum.'

'Now enough of this maudlin stuff!' bellowed Uncle Julian breaking the mood before any of them did anything so crass as weep. 'Where's the bottle of fizz I ordered? I'm having the oysters. What about you, Damien?'

Relieved to be back on safer, less emotional ground, Damien took a quick scan of the menu. 'Buffalo burger and fries.'

After the waiter had taken their order, Uncle Julian sat back and admired his flute of champagne. 'So how are we going to celebrate the big day tomorrow?'

'There's the gala dinner opening the conference,' his mum reminded them all.

'Oh those things don't go on that late. We'll get Damien and Joe tickets—fine dining all in a good cause—then go out from there. How about a night helicopter tour of the Statue of Liberty and city lights?'

'Sounds great,' said Damien.

'Anyone else you want to invite?'

'No. No one.'

The first review of Rose's financial progress was set for mid-morning the day after her school suspension. Her father hadn't taken the news seriously when she told him part of what had happened in the science lab and Mrs Chandler's study, leaving out the conversation with Damien. She just implied she had been in the wrong place at the wrong time. As Ryan had spent more time out of school than in, practically taking up residence on the chair outside the principal's office, Don had no conception that this was a disaster for Rose. Her unblemished record had been scrawled over by the combined efforts of Don, Melescanu, and Damien. She burned with resentment, channelling her fury into her plan, working far into the night when she had the company systems all to herself.

'So, Miss Knight.' Melescanu sat at the head of the long conference table in his headquarters, Rose on his right with her dad next to her. Curtis, the financial guy, sat opposite, making notes with a sullen air. 'How's your strategy unfolding?'

'Excellent, thank you. I'm liquidating some of your low yield assets and reinvesting them in places where they will make a good return.' She pushed over a printout of the sums that she had been moving about—at least, the ones she had decided at three in the morning that she could let everyone see.

Curtis took the file and scanned the figures. 'What's this RTC fund?'

Rose took a sip of water. 'It's a new financial instrument I heard about recently. It's got some really inspired people behind it, promising quick high yields.'

'Not a Ponzi scheme, I hope?' asked Curtis.

'I know what one of them looks like, don't worry.' Rose found she was almost enjoying herself. 'This fund invests in some of the more difficult areas of the world. I agree there are risks but the few losses will be more than outweighed by the returns in other areas.' She was speaking the absolute truth. Rubbing her thighs nervously to remove the damp from her palms she moved on to the second phase of her plan. 'I've been thinking about your corporate image, Mr Melescanu.'

That caught the boss man's attention. 'I have a PR department for that.'

'Not the public one—your image with the Feds.'

He raised his thick black eyebrows, encouraging her to go on.

'Well, we know that they are suspicious of the money you put into my father's account so I decided that we should make use of it in a conspicuously sound way—stop them having any appetite for accusing you of money laundering.'

'And how can you make that money seem whiter than white?'

'I spent about half of it on tickets to the charity gala dinner at the Waldorf Astoria tonight—bought a whole table for you. I checked with your secretary first and she said you were free.'

'What charity?'

'I don't think it's one you normally support but the mayor of New York, senators, and the vice president are all going to be there.' A bead of sweat trickled down her spine. Was he going to take the bait? 'It's a UN event on child soldiers.'

Melescanu tapped his fingers on the empty blotter in front of him. 'Child soldiers.' He was working the angles, seeing how this would play in the company brochure. Him exchanging handshakes with some of the political elite against a backdrop of moving photos of victims. 'That's . . . an inspired thought. That money had turned toxic with the Feds watching it so I can't think of a better way to turn the tables on them. Well done.'

Her dad relaxed and gave her an approving nod. That wouldn't last long.

'So you're happy with what I've done so far?' she asked the room at large. 'I've got big plans for the rest of the money. I'll move it when the Feds aren't watching.'

'Yes, yes. Carry on. Curtis, give her anything she needs, OK? When do you expect the first results, Rose?'

She didn't want to be Rose to Melescanu. 'Very soon, sir. I'll let you know as soon as I've good news.'

'Excellent. You'll come to the dinner, of course.'

That definitely wasn't part of the plan. She had intended to use that event as a cover for her getaway. 'Oh, I couldn't.'

'No, no, I insist. This is your idea: I wouldn't want to go without you. Let's rub the Feds' noses in it together. Don, make sure you and your little girl are ready by six thirty. We'll have cocktails in the lounge beforehand. Is it black tie?'

Rose nodded.

'Send out for whatever you need. Curtis, ask my secretary to put together a briefing on the guests expected tonight. Let's see what useful contacts we can make.' Melescanu gestured to the door. 'Off you go, people. Good work, Rose.'

Damien was sitting with his parents, Uncle Julian, and Mr and Mrs Masters in Joe's kitchen trying to do justice to the cakes Carol had produced for her guests, including one shaped like

219

Manhattan in honour of his birthday. The older people were all getting on well, their shared ethic of public service and Uncle Julian's outrageous sense of humour making the conversation trip along lightly. Damien, however, couldn't concentrate. Joe had disappeared upstairs ten minutes ago. He wondered what was keeping his friend up in his room.

'Excuse me a moment.'

None of the adults noticed as he left the table. He found Joe talking to Kieran and Nathan on Skype. There was a rather guilty silence as he came in.

'Hi, everyone.' Damien leaned on the back of the chair behind Joe. 'Why the funeral faces?'

Kieran bit the end of his pen then threw it aside when he registered the bitter taste. 'Rose moved the money from her father's account, Damien. I'm sorry.'

The last chance to prevent her coming under criminal charges puffed out like the candles on his birthday cake. 'Where did she move it to?'

'About half went to a UN charity, which is kinda OK, I suppose. As for the rest, she appears to be consolidating vast sums in a fund called RTC—not sure who's behind that yet but I'm working on it. Looks very dodgy. My guess is she's laundering Melescanu's dosh, making that charitable donation to put us off the scent.' Kieran's fingers started flying over the keyboard again. 'I have to say—she's upped her game since I last looked. Makes me think she wasn't really trying to cover her tracks before.'

'Do we still want to know?' asked Joe softly. 'Do you want us to leave this to the Feds, Damien?'

This was the worst birthday present ever: to find the girl he'd fallen for—he didn't want to give the slushy emotion the dignity of being called 'love'—had taken an irretrievable step into crime. But he'd said she was a mate, and sometimes you had to help a mate by doing something hard, like handing them over to the authorities to arrest before their activities went any further. 'Yeah, Key, find out what's going on. Text us when you have an answer.'

'You got plans?' Nathan asked. 'Happy birthday, by the way.'

'Thanks. Party when I get back, OK?' Damien consoled himself with the prospect of celebrating with friends who didn't wear socks in their hair and make disastrous life choices.

'You're on. But what about tonight?'

'Penguin suits at a fancy dinner then a helicopter flight.'

'Awesome. Have fun.'

Damien swirled the sparkling water in his glass, impressed despite himself at the elegant surroundings. The white, gold, and red grand ballroom was packed with circular tables of philanthropists who had each paid at least fifty thousand dollars to be present at an event that boasted a VIP guest list—the money buying them a gilt-upholstered seat at a pristine white tablecloth, crystal glasses, and a tall cream flower arrangement holding four elegant candles. His parents had earned their place among such exalted company on the strength of their participation on the conference programme. They were looking fabulous: his dad was in a DJ but his mum was wearing a brightly-coloured Ugandan dress in swirling turquoise and yellows. It made the other ladies' safe black gowns fade into the background. He half expected her to break into the ululation, followed by the hand clapping dance that the mothers used to do at church on Sundays any time someone announced a favourite hymn. His father sported a matching cravat and cummerbund that somehow made black tie deconstruct into fun. They were outrageously out of place—and he loved it. A number of colleagues came over to greet them, all marked out by their lack of designer tuxedos and earnest conversation—the worker bees in a hive mainly populated by drones. Doing the maths, Damien concluded that he and Joe were there thanks to king bee Uncle Julian's generosity.

'How much do you get paid in the city?' Damien asked his uncle shrewdly.

'Too much, dear boy, too much. I'm not worth a fraction of your parents to humanity.' Uncle Julian tore his warm bread roll and slathered butter on half. 'But life isn't fair, as I'm sure you realize. Half these people are only here to shake hands with the vice president and put in a word for their company.' Julian eyed the swan ice sculpture. 'You know, I think that's a cob trumpeter—you can tell from the slightly blunted end of the beak.'

'I think it's that way because it's melting.'

Julian frowned. 'Perhaps it started out as a Tundra swan then.'

Damien didn't like to spoil his uncle's birdwatching, though he suspected that the sculptor had not had a specific breed in mind when they got hacking with their pick.

Joe nudged Damien. 'Table two from the front,' he said in a low voice.

While Damien had been contemplating swans with his uncle, a familiar party had walked in and taken a table in a prime position. The men were barely distinguishable from each other thanks to the DJs but Rose stood out like a beacon with her auburn hair and short green cotton dress. It was totally inappropriate for the gathering, the same one she'd worn at the barbecue. Another misfire of her fashion sense.

'Which one is Melescanu?'

'The big guy on her left. Her dad is the one on her right.'

Yeah, the bearlike man looked the right sort to hold a

criminal empire together, the kind of man in another era you could imagine wielding an axe as chief executioner. 'What are they doing here?'

Joe shrugged. 'No idea, but I do know that Melescanu takes every opportunity to rub shoulders with the politicians, so I guess this is the kind of social event you would expect to see him at.'

Rose must've felt their eyes on her as she started looking around the ballroom trying to locate the source of her disquiet. Finding their table, she kept her gaze fixed on Damien as she reached into her handbag. Coolly, she shook out a purple polka dot cardigan and slipped it on. He wanted to laugh at her blatant daring of him, instead he tipped his sparkling water to her in a silent toast.

'What does that mean?' asked Joe.

'Looks like she knew we were going to be here and she's telling us both to butt out—me especially. I guess she hacked the guest list to pre-empt any surprises.' Damien leaned back so a waiter could put his first course down in front of him. 'She's telling me that if she's going down, she's going down in her own style.'

'She's got guts—I hadn't realized that about her.'

'Yeah, your little neighbour is an iceberg—the stuff you can see says one thing, but there's a whole huge confusing other story going on under the water.'

The meal passed pleasantly with the chink of glass on glass and cutlery on china plates.

His mother frowned at the lamb cutlet placed before her. 'I could probably feed all the women in my maternity ward for a month on the cost of this one piece of meat,' she mused.

Lawrence cleared his throat. 'Birthday, remember?'

Grace smiled apologetically at her son. 'Sorry. Habit.'

Damien poked his cutlet with a fork. 'Don't blame you—

hardly anything on it but they charge a fortune. Good job I stocked up on pizza at lunch.'

'And cake this afternoon,' added Joe. 'I'm holding out hope for dessert.'

'Teenagers,' said Uncle Julian. 'I'm sure they only come and see me in Greenwich because I have a toaster and an inexhaustible supply of bread.'

The food was cleared away and coffee served in impossibly tiny cups. This was the signal for speeches and the guest of honour, the vice president, made his way to the podium. He made what Damien thought of as a beige speech—not memorable—about the work of NGOs dealing with child trafficking. Over at Rose's table, Melescanu's expression soured. He'd obviously failed to brief himself properly on the nature of the cause they were supporting. Damien thought his expression apt—he was like a wolf who had drifted by mistake into a convention of shepherds. Damien then wondered if Rose was also feeling uncomfortable now she'd thrown her lot in with such a bad person? Maybe something she heard tonight would change her mind? He could only hope it would.

The head of the UN programme dealing with the issue stepped up to the mic next.

'Ladies and gentlemen,' the deep-voiced South African official said, 'health professionals, counsellors, business leaders—those of you who work so hard to help the children who are the most vulnerable in today's world. I stand here to thank you for all you have done to help children trafficked across borders, into the terrible trade in human flesh, those trapped as child soldiers, forced to commit acts that no young person should have to do. It's a great honour to stand here before you and thank you on behalf of the international community.' There was a scattering of applause. Damien noticed his parents exchange wry looks. As workers at the sharp end in a community hit by abductions, repayment in a light round of applause in a Manhattan ballroom did seem ridiculous.

Damien's phone buzzed. Sliding it out of his pocket he saw a text from Kieran. *It's not what we thought*.

'Now it may seem invidious to select a single person from among you,' continued the speaker, 'but there is one person here tonight who has astounded us this week with his generosity. We have received an enormous contribution to our fund which has promised to support our work through many years to come.'

The crowd murmured; Lawrence winked at his wife. 'Not feeling so bad about the lamb now, love?'

The speaker held up his hand for silence. 'I know he is not expecting me to mention him by name, as the official company press release about his plans to step out of business and devote his life to the Greek Orthodox Monastic Community on Mount Athos has only just gone out to the press this evening, but I couldn't let this opportunity pass. I want to thank the founder of the Restitution for Trafficked Children Fund, or RTC, Mr Roman Melescanu. He has donated five hundred million dollars to get our appeal off to a flying start, an amazingly generous amount as I'm sure you will agree. So please join me in a round of applause for Mr Melescanu, and please, sir, do come up here and receive our thanks in person.'

The stunned looks at Melescanu's table said it all.

Rose, what have you done? wondered Damien. A day or two ago, he'd called it the first rule of Rose and then promptly forgotten it: expect the unexpected.

'Don't be shy, sir,' coaxed the speaker.

Melescanu heaved himself to his feet, grabbed Rose by the wrist, and took her with him to the podium.

'Joe, we have a situation,' said Damien.

'Clearly. What do we do?'

'Text the Feds. We mustn't let him take Rose out of our sight.'

Melescanu seized the microphone, giving the audience a chilling smile. 'Mr Vice President, ladies and gentlemen, this honour comes as a huge surprise to me. All I can say is that the announcement about my plans to join the brothers on Mount Athos is premature. I'm still fully in charge of my business and I detect someone playing a little joke on you all.' He glared at Rose who hung back, trying to shield herself behind his bulk. 'I'm delighted my contribution has helped your important work, though I fear there may be a mistake in the number of zeros at the end of that cheque. The inspiration for my generosity is my student intern, Rose Knight, so it's her you should thank, not me. Isn't that right, Rose?' He tugged her in front of the mic. 'And any errors in the specific amount donated will be hers too.'

Damien wanted to leap up and yank Rose away from him, but she was at least safe in front of all these witnesses who were watching the scene with bemusement.

Rose straightened her shoulders, proudly displaying her car crash of a fashion combination. 'Yes, that's right. I think there was a slight error in the name of the fund you mentioned, sir. It's really called the Revenge of Trafficked Children fund. If you search online for the recently posted private boardroom minutes of Colosseum Investments you'll see why.'

Melescanu actually growled. Pushing the mic stand over, he dragged her off stage, clicked his fingers at his party, and hurried out.

'Oh, erm, well thank you anyway,' said the host, picking up the microphone. 'And now, ladies and gentlemen, sit back and enjoy the Soweto choir who are about to perform for us from the balcony.'

Damien pushed back from the table, tipping his chair over on the way. 'Let's go.'

Chapter· 15

Rose couldn't quite believe this was happening. Something wild and reckless had bubbled up inside her, shouting down her inner guides that she had characterized as Lara and Nancy—calculated daring and sensible intelligence.

Oh no, I've become Indiana Jones. So far from the well-thought-out strategy she had begun with, she was now totally winging it, aware that her actions could well be fatal. She had known she would be destroying Melescanu in front of Damien and Joe. Back at the office this had seemed a sweet way of getting back at the pair of them; now their presence appeared more like her only lifeline.

Melescanu bundled her into the back of his limo. Her father scrambled in after her, as did two of Melescanu's bodyguards, the gladiators as he called them. Last to enter was Curtis. It was a ridiculous squeeze. Rose had a sudden, completely stupid, memory of the Ant Hill Mob in the Wacky Races cartoon, a favourite of Ryan's, when the characters all piled into their black bulletproof car.

Don't laugh, Rose. Don't lose it.

'Curtis, stop that cheque. Peters, drive to my yacht. We're leaving the US,' said Melescanu tersely. His shoulder hemmed her in on one side, a bulky bodyguard on the other; the gladiator was gazing stoically straight ahead.

Rose felt a completely inappropriate bubble of laughter—or was it hysteria? 'I'm afraid you can't do that. I sold your yacht this morning and the new owner's already taken possession.'

'What?' Melescanu grabbed a fistful of her hair, yanking her round to face him.

'Rose,' murmured her father desperately. He had looked ashen ever since the announcement in the ballroom. He had taken one of the jump seats opposite her; if he had been close enough he would have plastered his hand over her mouth.

Rose swallowed. 'It was one of the low yield assets I told you about. The Bronx youth club was surprised to get it so cheaply but they'll make good use of it.' Oh God, she had to have a death wish. Why was she telling him this?

'How cheaply?' Melescanu was so furious he was almost beyond words.

'A hundred dollars. I threw in the internal fixtures and fittings as a goodwill gesture.' Her voice rose into a squeak as Melescanu tightened his grip.

'You sold my two million dollar yacht to a youth club?'

'They . . . they help children from the most deprived parts of the city. It'll bring a really good return in the lives made better.'

Melescanu pushed her away so she jostled the guy on her far side. 'Take us to the GCT Bayonne terminal, Peters.'

'Right away, sir.'

She wondered if she should mention she had also sold his fleet of cars but decided against it. The limo that no longer belonged to him did a U-turn on Park Avenue and started heading north to the container terminal. Her father used the pause to start bargaining. He'd been silent while figuring the angles; Rose recognized the expression that came over his face as he played his best card.

'Roman, Mr Melescanu, sir, I can't tell you how sorry I am for my daughter's foolishness, but you'll need her to undo what she's done. If she promises to put everything back the way it was, can we call it quits?'

'Quits?' Melescanu laughed harshly. 'She's attacked my business—she attacked me—made me make a public statement that will be very hard to back away from without loss of face. She is about to find out the consequences.'

Don closed his eyes briefly. 'She's just sixteen. Idealistic. Headstrong. She can get the money back for you.'

'Sixteen is old enough to know better. She's going to pay with her life—it's just that the end won't come as quickly as she will wish. Rose is going to join my latest cargo. As she loves the fools who ask to be moved illegally across borders so much, she can become one of them.'

'Can't you just leave her here? Get yourself away until the mess is sorted out?'

'I can't afford for her body to turn up in Manhattan—the Feds are too interested in me as it is. Financial crimes are always too complicated to prosecute; killing not so much.'

That wasn't what her dad had meant, of course. Rose met her father's eyes. *Come on, Dad, stand by me*, she urged silently, but he hung his head, shoulders slumped.

Curtis cleared his throat. 'Sorry to interrupt, sir, but I can't stop the cheque. It appears that all our accounts are closed down.'

'And what Curtis isn't telling you, I'm afraid, is that you won't be able to make rent on your headquarters this month either—and your employees won't get paid.' Rose said it loudly, hoping the gladiators spoke enough English to understand the profound change to their boss's fortunes. They looked like mercenaries who would follow the money.

'If you wouldn't mind letting me out on the corner,' said Curtis, 'I'll go . . . see what I can do.'

The hesitation gave away the fact that the investment

manager intended to be the first of the rats to leave the sinking ship. He reached for the door, looking as if he were contemplating leaping from a moving vehicle.

Melescanu shoved him back down. 'You're going nowhere. How did she do it?'

'You said to give her everything she needed,' Curtis replied, looking grim-faced at the passing streets of north Manhattan. 'She said she needed access.'

'How can you not have noticed that she has sold my empire from under our noses?'

Rose knew there was little hope for her unless she could scare Melescanu into running before putting his plan for her into action. 'At this point,' she said softly, 'you might like to recall that you owe the Three Brothers cartel in Mexico City thirty million for that last consignment of drugs. I dug that little fact out of your secret files. I'm not sure they'll accept the excuse that you lost it all to a teenager with a few computer skills. That's why I thought the monks on Mount Athos in Greece might be your only viable option.'

'Shut your girl up or I'll do it!' bellowed Melescanu at her father, pushing her off the seat and onto the floor.

Don reached out and took her hands. 'Rose, don't say any more. Please.'

Rose bit her lip. She rested her head against her dad's knees, his hand heavy on her neck. The dreamlike euphoria that had sustained her so far ebbed, leaving only a dull sense of dread. She'd really done it this time. Revenge had been sweet for about ten minutes, now it was leaving a bitter aftertaste. Her biggest regret was that her dad was unlikely to come out of this unscathed. He'd pitched her over the cliff into this situation but she was now pulling him down with her. 'I'm sorry,' she whispered.

The car turned into the port area. It must have had the

right clearances for they were waved through the checkpoints onto the dockside with only a cursory inspection from the gate guards. The white cranes were still loading under the floodlights as the terminal worked twenty-four-seven. Peters took the car up to the end of one of the piers, next to a container ship registered in Liberia. The name of the huge rust-red vessel matched that discussed in the meeting on Sunday.

'Out!' barked Melescanu. The men piled out of the rear seats. Her dad made sure he got between her and Melescanu.

'Stay behind me,' Don said. 'We're going to have to run, you understand?'

Rose gulped, thanking her impulse to go for her normal footwear rather than the ridiculous heels she had been bought. She'd done that to show Damien that he was wrong about her, but now it could be the difference between life and death.

Damien. A faint flicker of hope kindled. He'd been watching her at the gala. Had he seen them leave? Could he do anything to help? For once in her life she really would not be sad to see the FBI arrive. She'd given them heaps of proof to take Melescanu down when she'd published the confidential company memos online that night. Maybe they could repay the favour?

Please God, let them repay the favour.

Rose and her father stood apart from the small gathering of Melescanu's most loyal men. Curtis had drifted further off towards the nearest stack of containers; he was looking for his chance to leave but feared to make the break. The other men arranged themselves in a semicircle hemming in the Knights. Rose felt she was facing a firing squad, an impression made concrete when handguns appeared in the hands of the two bodyguards.

'Mr Melescanu, please,' said Don, 'just consider what you're doing. If it's as bad as it sounds, Rose may be your only bargaining chip. Get rid of her and you lose any leverage with the Feds.' Her dad had to be desperate if he was suggesting cutting a deal with his old enemy.

'In this case, Knight, my honour is involved. She goes.' Melescanu jerked his head to the huge container ship. Crewmen had appeared at the side and were letting down a ramp to the dockside. 'That's non-negotiable. You can do my bargaining with the Feds instead.'

Melescanu took a gun from one of his henchmen. 'Peters, stay at my condo until you hear from me. Stefan, Alexandru, you're with me.' He jerked his head at the two guards.

Don took hold of Rose's hand, squeezing it as a warning to get ready. 'Where are you going?' he asked.

'Thanks to her, I can't stay here. You'll bargain my way out for me. I'll be on board with your precious back-stabbing daughter, and if you don't persuade the authorities to let me cross into international waters then she goes over the side. Say your goodbyes and hand her over.'

Don turned Rose to face him, his eyes shining with grim determination. 'Ready, love? Now!' As Melescanu checked the firearm with the ease of someone familiar with weapons, Don set off at a sprint for the nearest cover. Rose ran with him. A shot rang out and her father stumbled.

'Go on!' he urged, one leg useless.

She tried to drag him but he screamed at her to run. He collapsed face down on the concrete.

Sobbing, telling herself that Melescanu needed her father alive, Rose let go, ran the final hundred yards, and squeezed into the narrow gap between two stacks of containers. More shots were fired but they now hit the metal shipping boxes. Glancing back, Rose could see her father lying sprawled on the pier, blood pooling from his thigh. If he'd been hit in an artery he could bleed out. Oh God, what should she do? She'd chosen this hiding place as the men were too large to fit in the narrow gap, but if she didn't move they could still take pot-shots at her down the narrow alley. She had to lose them in the maze of boxes and hope that someone else came to her father's rescue. Taking a left then a right, then two more lefts and rights, Rose was now in the middle of the stack. Her intention had been to lose them but she was pretty much lost herself. She hunkered down at the bottom of a green container, hoping the shadows would hide her. Remembering the all too visible polka dots, she slipped off her cardigan and sat on it. Now it was waiting game. Would they spot her down one of the narrow lanes and start firing, or would the cavalry arrive in time?

Maybe she did need help after all, she admitted.

Damien reached the pavement outside the Waldorf Astoria just in time to see the limo pull away. He hailed a taxi and threw open the rear door. 'This isn't a hoax—follow that car— the black limousine.'

Joe jumped in beside him, close on his heels were Damien's parents and Uncle Julian.

'You got cash, pal?' asked the driver, looking at Damien doubtfully.

Uncle Julian held up a wad of fifties.

'OK. The black limo, you say?'

'We'll triple the fare if you keep up with it,' said Uncle Julian.

'Leave it to me, sir.'

The taxi pulled into the traffic and fell into the stream of cars eight down from the limo.

Damien's mother tapped his leg. 'Would you like to explain what is going on?'

'It has to do with that girl at the gala, doesn't it?' said his dad.

Joe looked up from his phone screen. 'I've sent the registration to Jameson. She's on the case, getting a team together.'

'But will she muster it in time?' Damien knew his question was unanswerable.

'Come on, old boy, blurt it out. There's some damsel in distress, I guess?' asked Uncle Julian.

Damien scrubbed his hand over his face, not quite sure how he had got himself in this position. 'You could say that.'

The driver surprised them all by taking a sudden U-turn. 'They've changed their minds. Now heading north. Still want me to follow?' he asked around the toothpick that he was chewing.

'Yeah. Stick with them,' said Joe. 'By the way, we're the good guys—they're the bad.'

The driver shrugged as if it didn't make much difference to him. 'I want to see some of that money now if I'm going to go north of Central Park.'

Uncle Julian stuffed a fifty through the little hatch in the partition. The taxi picked up speed, closing the gap that had opened up between them and the limo. 'You were saying, dear boy?'

'Rose—she's like Kieran, you know?' Damien began.

Uncle Julian nodded.

'Brainy,' he added for his parents' benefit. 'Her family are small-time crooks and she got swept up with them into the path of a very bad guy.'

'Mr Melescanu,' guessed his father, 'the man who didn't look as if he were a natural to join the monks at Mount Athos.'

'Yeah, he's the kind of guy that conference is out to shut down, but Rose got there first. She's sabotaged his whole operation in the last twenty-four hours and he'll be wanting revenge. Look, this might get very dangerous. We'll let you out at the next lights. Go back to the hotel. The FBI are handling it. We're meeting them wherever that car is going.'

234

His mother smiled sweetly. 'Damien, are you telling me that two doctors with twenty years' experience of a war zone are of no use in this situation? We should be the ones telling you to jump out at the next lights.'

'Rose is . . . is special. I'm not leaving.'

'Neither are we.'

'Nor me,' boomed Uncle Julian. 'I'm completely useless in a combat situation of course, but I do have the money to cover the fare. You need me.'

'I like your family.' Joe grinned at Damien. 'And Jameson says she's got eyes in the sky on the car. Melescanu appears to be heading towards the port area. She's not sure yet which terminal he's going for. She doesn't want to set up a road block as Rose and Knight are trapped inside—it could turn into a hostage situation. She'd prefer to take them out when they reach the port. So far Melescanu doesn't know anyone's following him so he won't be suspicious.'

'He's making a run for it,' said Damien.

'Only option left to him, thanks to Rose.'

'So what did this Rose of yours do, exactly? I didn't quite understand that speech at the gala,' asked his mother.

If Damien wasn't so scared for her, he would laugh. 'She gave all his money to his victims. I couldn't have been more wrong about her. I accused her yesterday of selling out and all the while she was selling Melescanu out, big time.'

'I think I like your Rose.'

'She's not mine—I blew my chance yesterday when I lost my cool.'

His mother squeezed his hand. 'If I had to list the number of times I've had to forgive your father for something then we'd be here all night.'

'It's true,' agreed his father. 'And then I'd take up the next day with my list the other way round.'

'You see, I love the silly old man despite that.'

'Hey, enough with the old!'

'If she loves you, forgiving you comes as part of the package.'

'Flowers help too. Though saving her from the villains might be more applicable in this situation.'

Damien realized his parents were chatting like this both to take his mind off the crisis and to reassure him. He'd never seen them working together during an emergency, always being kept far away from the trauma room, but it was probably how they got through the many dark moments they had faced. He was learning a lot about Grace and Lawrence Castle.

The taxi driver pulled over as the limo drove through the gates of the Bayonne terminal. 'Sorry, guys, can't go any further. That's a restricted zone. Two hundred dollars please.'

'How much to wait for us?' asked Uncle Julian peeling off some bills.

'No way, pal. I heard you talking about bad guys and combat. I'm strictly civilian.'

Damien was already out of the car, leaving Julian to try his powers of persuasion. 'How close are the Feds?'

Joe put through a quick call to Jameson. 'Ten—fifteen minutes.'

'I doubt Rose has that long.'

'We're going in?'

'Do you have to ask?'

'How exactly?'

'Distraction. Mum and Dad can ask nicely, start on the explanations.' His mother nodded and lifted her long skirt up a few centimetres, ready to march into the guard hut in all her vibrant finery. 'You and I, Joe, are going to jump the barrier and run.'

Joe eyed the fifty metre dash the other side of the gate before they could get out of sight. 'Sounds like a plan.'

Not much of one but it was all Damien had. 'Dad, you got a phone?'

'We've been using Julian's. Not much call for one where we live.' His dad loosened his cravat and stuffed it in his pocket.

'Fine—we've got his number already. Stick with him. We'll let you know what's going on when we know.' Damien looked down at his polished black shoes, wishing he wasn't dressed in a DJ for this rescue and wishing he had some proper comms gear for coordination.

Uncle Julian hurried over as the rear lights of the taxi disappeared back the way they had come. 'No backbone,' he said, panting a little. 'Most disappointing. Where do you want us?'

Damien couldn't get over how lucky he was to have his uncle and parents in his corner right now. 'Just follow Dad. Be careful—these guys let Melescanu's car in without so much as an inspection of the passengers so I'm guessing they're in his pay. Make as much fuss as you can but just don't get shot.'

Uncle Julian beamed. 'Oh, I do like the sound of that. Make a fuss: my vocation.'

The three adults barrelled into the guardroom and began their part in the plan. From the gesticulating hands of his uncle, Damien guessed the urgency of the situation was being rammed forcefully down the throats of the guards in the plumiest of plum tones. The hard-boiled New Yorkers would have trouble placing what kind of threat three smartly dressed Brits posed their operation.

'Ready?' asked Joe.

'Let's do this.' Damien started to run, feeling his shoes slipping a little on the tarmac but he kept his balance. Reaching the barrier, he vaulted over first, closely followed by Joe.

'Hey!' called the security man who had been watching the goings on in the guardroom. 'You can't go in there!'

Just watch us. Damien was thankful he and Joe had kept up the daily run; it felt good finally to be on the move. Behind them the security team would no doubt be heading for their vehicles to round up the intruders; they just had to make sure they reached Rose first.

Running between two long rows of stacked containers, Damien was surprised to see a guy in a tuxedo heading their way, sprinting full out.

'Let's get him!' said Damien, recognizing one of the men who had been sitting at Melescanu's table. As they changed course to intercept, the man realized the new threat and veered away down a junction between container stacks. Damien dug deep and pulled out a burst of speed. Coming within grabbing distance of the guy's coat-tails, he rugby tackled him to the ground. Joe quickly pinned his shoulders so he couldn't kick free.

'Where . . . are they?' panted Damien.

The man was sobbing, cheek pressed against the cold earth. 'It's nothing to do with me. I don't condone any of this.'

Joe frisked the guy's pockets and came away with the gala invitation. 'Robert Curtis, investment manager at Colosseum.' He chucked it aside in disgust. 'Answer my friend's question or I'll leave you to him. He's not as nice as me.'

'They're up at the end of the pier by the last ship. They're shooting. At least one down—I didn't hang around to see how many.'

Damien felt something inside him die at that news. Fingers shaking, he sent a quick text to Julian telling him there was a medical emergency.

'The girl got away though. She's hiding somewhere there.' Curtis awkwardly nodded to the maze of containers.

'What do we do with him?' asked Joe.

Hearing that Rose was still alive sharpened Damien's focus once more. 'Let him go. We haven't time for him. He's the FBI's problem.'

The boys rolled off their prisoner, who sprang up like a wildebeest fleeing lions and headed for the exit. He was passed by two motorbikes coming the other way, Damien's parents on one, Julian on the other.

'How on earth . . .?' asked Joe.

Julian slowed alongside them. 'Money talks. Get on. Where's this casualty?'

Damien opted to slide on behind his mother, thinking that Julian's bike wouldn't bear the strain of three. 'Down the far end. Be careful: they've guns.'

His dad revved the engine. 'We rather cottoned on to that fact when you reported a gunshot wound.' With expertise honed after decades negotiating potholed dirt roads, Lawrence sped forward, his wife holding on calmly.

'You got enough room?' Damien asked her, grabbing on to the bar behind him.

'Of course, darling. In Kitgum, we'd still have room for a crate of chickens and a cold box of vaccine supplies.'

God, his parents were cool, Damien decided.

The casualty wasn't difficult to find. Rose's dad had been left sprawled on the ground. Further off, the limo patrolled the long maze of containers, a shark hunting its next kill; Damien guessed that all the others had vanished within the tower blocks of containers, hunting her.

Lawrence brought his bike to a halt and Grace hopped off. Pulling on some surgical gloves that she had in her evening bag—Damien underlined the cool part of his assessment of his parents—she knelt beside the man.

'Not the femoral, thank God, but he's haemorrhaging

fast—too fast. Femur looks broken. We'll need a splint—and we have to transport him to hospital immediately. He can't wait for an ambulance.'

Lawrence pulled his cravat out of his pocket and wadded it up. 'Bow ties!'

Joe, Damien, and Julian ripped theirs off so he could secure the bandage.

Damien swung back on the bike. 'Joe, can you head off the car? I'll go after Rose. Dad, I'm taking the bike.'

Joe grabbed the second bike and screeched off in pursuit of the limo.

His father nodded, deep in triage mode. 'We can't risk moving him without a splint in case the broken bone does more damage. He'll need blood—an IV. Julian, give me your phone: I'm calling 911—we're going lose him.'

Julian patted him on the shoulder. 'Already done, Lawrence. Remember that helicopter I booked for the night flight? Well, it's coming here to fly your patient to the nearest hospital. You won't lose him.'

Lawrence flashed him a grin. 'Big brother, you might just have saved his life.'

Damien slipped the clutch and revved a few times to get the feel of the unfamiliar bike. Then, gripping the clutch control, he shot away, front tyre kicking up a little in a wheelie. He cruised down the aisles of the containers looking for the hunters. He'd reasoned that Rose would have gone to ground so they would be easier to find. But they had guns and he just had a bike. Spotting a plank lying at the foot of some wooden pallets he slowed and picked it up, tucking it under his arm. It could form a rough kind of shield or club if he got close enough. He found the first of his targets peering around the corner of a stack of blue containers, attention attracted by the engine noise. Melescanu's contingent had no idea that anyone had followed them from the gala, so the bodyguard didn't know what to make of the blond teenager bearing down on him. A second too late, he raised his gun but Damien had swiped him sideways with the plank. The gun flew up from his hands as he crashed against the metal sheeting behind. The plank snapped on impact.

Damn: he'd lost his best weapon. Damien cut the engine and hurried over the prone man. Knocked out cold. Last thing Damien needed was for this guy to come back into play. Using the plastic handcuffs the bodyguard had in his own pocket, Damien quickly secured the man's wrists behind him and then his ankles. Damien then looked round for the gun. It was nowhere to be seen. He checked the guy for other weapons but both his ankle and shoulder holsters were empty. The guard didn't have his second piece on him, which struck Damien as a little odd.

Damien then noticed the storage box under the rear seat of the bike. Lifting the lid, he hoped for a tyre iron but found a helmet. That would do: held by the straps it would serve as a club should he meet anyone in the maze, and a decoy to check he wasn't walking into an ambush. Holding it firmly in his fist, Damien entered the container city. He had to trust that Joe had at least succeeded in taking out the car driver, leaving him with the guys on the ground. It immediately became clear that he was too vulnerable searching these alleyways: too visible with no cover. Up it was, then.

Rose shivered. She'd moved position a couple of times, aiming to make her way to one of the edges of the maze, but she had caught glimpses of the men hunting her and realized that she might be better off remaining still. How was her dad doing? She couldn't bear thinking that he might be dying out there while she was crouched in here. She wanted to run back to him but instinct told her that would be suicidal.

241

'Come out, Rose,' taunted Melescanu in the distance. 'I won't hurt you if you give yourself up.'

She held her breath, curled up in a tiny gap between two containers.

'The longer you leave it, the angrier I will be.' He waited for her reply. She gave him nothing. 'Alexandru, any sign?' A pause. 'What do you mean you can't raise Stefan? . . . I see.'

Rose swallowed a whimper of relief. One of the bodyguards was out of the picture. That could mean someone else was there. Had Damien got a message to the FBI in time?

Melescanu continued his hunt, his voice getting nearer. 'Rose, your father needs medical attention. If you come to me, I'll make sure he gets it. I don't want him to die. Do you really want to kill your own father by holding out too long?'

She almost showed herself at that. Only her father's clear wish that she should run held her back. He'd found it in himself to make a sacrifice for her. She couldn't waste it.

'Ah, there you are. Finally.'

Rose turned her head to find Melescanu standing in the main aisle. She was out of reach in her narrow passageway and he was too big to follow her. Their eyes met.

'I have a gun.'

She began to shuffle further down her alley.

He put his cell phone to his ear again. 'Alexandru, can you see her? She's in the channel between the Maersk containers.' Melescanu put the handset back in his pocket. 'No escape that way. My gladiator is waiting for you in the next aisle. I'd really prefer not to shoot you in there—would be a hell of a job to retrieve the body. Besides if you come now, you could still save your father. You want to save him, don't you?'

Rose shuddered. What should she do? She was trapped. Giving herself up was the best of her bad choices.

'Rose, don't listen to him!' Damien's voice rang out, somewhere close. 'Above you. Climb up. I'll get you out.'

'Damien? Climb? How?' She desperately scanned the patch of sky above but couldn't see him.

'Shuffle up. Brace either side. You can work it out.'

A shot pinged off the boxes overhead as Melescanu tried to get a bead on Damien. Then came a grunt. Melescanu was on the tarmac holding his head, a motorbike helmet rolling on the ground beside him. Taking her chance, Rose began the climb. The corrugated edges of the containers gave her soles some purchase but she was terrified of slipping.

'That's right, baby. You can do this. You're doing great.'

'Have . . . have you watched *127 Hours*?' she asked shakily. 'That's my only exposure to mountaineering.'

'Great film, but you won't need to saw your arm off with a penknife, I promise.'

Her foot slipped and she shrieked, before catching herself on the roof ridge of the container below. She thought she could hear Damien's sharp intake of breath above before he began speaking again in the same calm tones. 'Well done. You handled that well. Now you're almost within reach. Edge up a few more metres and then reach up. I'll pull you the rest of the way.'

Obeying his instructions, Rose squirmed up a little higher, got a firm position for her feet, then slowly lifted her hands over her head. Warm fingers grasped hers, then moved down to grip her wrists. 'OK, I'm pulling you up now. Try to take some of the weight with your feet.'

Rose was lifted out of the maze and dragged on top of a container. Her knees were skinned, her elbows raw, but she was safe—for the moment.

'Damien?' she began sobbing.

He knelt beside her and hugged her to his chest. 'It's OK,

you brilliant, brilliant girl. Why are you crying now you're safe? That's so illogical.' He rubbed her spine in comforting circles.

'My dad . . .'

'My parents are working on him right now. They'll save him. In fact, listen.'

Rose closed her eyes, breathing in the reassuring scent of his soap. She could hear the whop-whop-whop of a helicopter.

'That's the bird that's going to take your dad to hospital. The Feds are probably already at the main gates. All we have to do is stay up here out of trouble.'

She looked across the vast lot of parked containers like some ugly patchwork quilt worked by a giant. 'They can't reach us up here?'

'If they do, we'll see them first, won't we, and we can run.'

Rose's throat went dry at the prospect of leaping the canyons between boxes. 'I hope the Feds get here first.'

Damien chuckled. 'Say that again.'

'Say what?'

'Admit you need the FBI.'

She huffed a put-upon sigh. 'All right, I admit it.'

'Say "Damien, you were right".'

'Don't push your luck.'

'Why not?' He lifted her chin and brushed his lips across hers. 'I'm feeling very lucky right now.'

'I'm lucky to have you too. You saved me.'

'I didn't. You saved yourself; I just gave you a helping hand for the last little stretch.'

'It was the last bit that mattered.'

'I'm glad you think so.' He began to kiss her as if there wasn't a group of armed bad guys hunting them and the authorities about to descend. He kissed her like she was the only thing for him in the world, the only person that mattered.

244

It was like they were castaways on the vast sea of container boxes, content to pass the time in each other's arms while rescue made its slow way to them.

Rose wasn't sure how much time passed, but too soon for them both they were interrupted.

'Damien Castle? Rose Knight?' The tannoy system in the port crackled into life. 'This is Agent Stevens. We've got five men under arrest and we've also impounded the ship and crew. It's safe to come out now.'

Damien nuzzled her neck.

'Damien, we should go,' she whispered.

'Should we? Why?' He was much more interested in exploring that shivery place under her ear.

'Be . . . because I think the FBI have climbed into the control tower of that crane over there and are looking right at us.' The crane was slowly moving to bring a metal cradle into position so they could step into the maintenance cage and be lowered to the ground.

Damien looked up and scowled. Joe was grinning at them both from the control room.

'I take it all back,' muttered Damien. 'Who needs the FBI?'

Chapter 16

Rose dozed in the chair at her father's bedside. The monitor made reassuring beeping noises confirming that all was well with blood pressure and heart rate. To distract herself from the clinical surroundings she told herself it was a little like the ancient Chinese habit of keeping singing crickets in special little echo chambers to lull the listener, but the comparison wasn't really working. Her dad, however, had no problems sleeping. He had woken up a couple of times in the last twenty-four hours, the first time too groggy to take in what had happened; on the second occasion he had wanted to know how he'd got there and how she had escaped. He had kept very silent as he heard about the two doctors who had risked their lives to administer first aid and the generosity of the man who had paid for a helicopter to bring him to hospital.

'Are we safe?' he'd rasped.

Rose had lifted his head to give him water. 'We're safe. There's a police officer on the door.'

'Who's paying the bill?'

'I said you had medical insurance. You have medical insurance, don't you, Dad?'

His eyes slid to the window. 'I might've let it lapse.'

Reaching for calm, she replaced the beaker on the bedside table. 'Then I don't know who's paying. That's your problem.' She felt much better for saying it. In the past, she would have rushed in with reassurances, strategies for raising the money, but no longer. She was sixteen; he was her dad; the responsibility was firmly his.

He had still dropped back to sleep though, shelving this problem with all the other difficulties.

There came a tap at the door and then Damien put his head round it. 'Got a moment?'

Beaming with pleasure, she leapt up to join him in the corridor. She hadn't seen him since they were rescued from the top of the containers. He and Joe had been busy with the FBI sorting out the evidence and making sure that none of Melescanu's people got away.

'How's your dad?' he asked.

'Doing well.' She finally relaxed now she was back in his arms.

'My parents and Uncle Julian want to meet you.'

'And I want to thank them.'

He led her to a visitors' lounge with an undrinkable-coffee-and-unhealthy-snacks machine. 'Mum, Dad, Julian—here she is: the girl I told you about.'

'Nice to meet you.' Rose found her polite reply was quickly stifled by a hug from Uncle Julian.

'So you're the one!' he declared. He had the comforting smell of expensive aftershave and French pastries. 'Damien's girl. His classy chick, as he told me.'

Rose laughed but was transferred before she could think of a suitable comeback into a more gentle hug from both of Damien's parents.

'We were so worried about you,' Grace told her. 'I'm so pleased Damien found you before those awful men.'

'So was I. You should be very proud of him. He was so brave.'

'We are, dear. And of you. How's the patient?'

Rose gave Grace and Lawrence a rundown of the latest medical reports on Don.

'It'll be a long and difficult recuperation,' said Lawrence.

'I'll have to tell Agent Hammond to make sure the federal authorities factor that into your relocation package,' mused Grace.

'Relocation package?' Rose turned to Damien. 'What do they mean?'

Damien raised his eyebrows. 'You haven't been told?'

'Told what?'

'You're being moved out of here later today to a more secure location. They can't be sure they've rounded up all of Melescanu's organization so they're playing it safe. We aren't allowed to know where you're going.'

'No, I hadn't been told.' She felt quite cold, her anchor slipping once more. 'For how long?'

Tactfully his parents and Uncle Julian drifted over to the coffee machine and began to argue over their selections. Damien pulled her down with him onto one of the upright armchairs. 'I'm sorry—I thought they would have told you by now. We weren't even supposed to come and see you now but I decided to pretend I didn't get that memo.'

She closed her eyes and sat with her head resting on his chest. 'I'm really really sick of this.'

'So am I—but we can't play fast and loose with your safety. You've got a lot of people very angry. You didn't just squash one hornet; you knocked down the whole nest and then hit it with a stick. Melescanu is going to be blaming you very loudly in prison and we can't be sure that the people he owes money to won't decide to see things his way.'

And she thought she had been so clever. 'Will you keep in touch?'

'Of course. I'll write to you via Agent Hammond—she's

248

the one working out this deal. As soon as it's safe for you to come out of hiding, I'll be over like a shot. I've got two tickets for the MetLife Stadium that I haven't been able to use yet.'

'Go with Joe, this weekend.' Rose smoothed the fabric of his T-shirt over his pectoral muscles. He seemed to shiver a little, which encouraged her greatly.

'It won't be the same.'

'I know. But they shouldn't be wasted.'

Joe burst into the visitors' lounge. 'Hi, Rose.' He gave her a kiss on the cheek and ruffled her hair. 'Time to go, folks. The Feds have just entered the building.'

'You were on lookout?' Rose hopped off Damien's knee.

'Yep. Again. Damien's getting quite bossy in his old age, ordering me around to keep you safe. I hope they send you somewhere with lots of interesting archaeology.'

She dug deep to sound brave. 'Southern Colorado or Louisiana would be OK.'

'Lots of pots?' asked Damien, seizing and not letting go of her hand.

'Lots. Dusty. Fragmented. Boring looking. Very, very interesting.'

'Rose heaven.'

She leaned in so only he could hear. 'No, not my idea of heaven now, Damien.'

'We gotta go,' warned Joe.

Damien took a final quick kiss. 'We'll be together again—I promise.'

She watched her visitors hurry out of the far door as the federal agents appeared at the other end of the corridor. 'I'll hold you to that,' she whispered, knowing she'd need something to look forward to in her exile.

Two weeks later . . .

Rose ate her Thanksgiving dinner alone in the canteen of the little general hospital in Tonopah, Nevada. It was possibly the most uninspiring turkey dinner she had ever eaten. She had come to the conclusion that the Feds were punishing her father by sending him here: it was the of the most isolated and arid desert towns in the west of America, famous for stargazing because of the lack of man-made light. Surrounded by rocky hills and dry valleys, it had a barren beauty, but for two New Yorkers like her and her dad it was a profound culture shock. Little wonder that Ryan had passed on the chance of joining them in their exile; he probably suspected what kind of location the Feds would pick.

She flicked through the brochure for the local high school. She was supposed to be enrolling under the name Holly Walters on Monday after the holiday, but couldn't quite summon up any enthusiasm for it. She hadn't been able to transfer her academic record because it marked her out as too extraordinary. The Feds had fabricated a GPA for a bright but unremarkable student heading for a mid-range university. Her grade advancement had been voided and she was expected to enter junior year, spending another eighteen months in high school before graduating.

'It makes it easier to justify the expenditure on relocating you,' said Agent Jameson. 'The department won't query paying for transfer costs for schooling for under-eighteens. Save us the headache, Rose.'

So she had agreed. She now had to work out a way of saving some of her ambitions from the wreck of her life. In that she felt sympathy with Samson, the Old Testament character of immense strength, who exited the story pulling a temple down on his head, as well as those of his enemies. She had collapsed Melescanu's temple but was still in danger of being hit by the falling masonry.

250

At least her dad was making a decent recovery. He should soon be coming home to their apartment near the main street. He had a job lined up for him when he was mobile as a warehouse clerk to a solar panel business—boring but steady. She gave him three months before he rebelled against that particular arrangement.

A woman appeared at the far end of the canteen, propelling herself along in her wheelchair. Rose recognized her from the careers talk at her old school. She put down her fork, uncertain how to read a personal visit by a senior federal agent.

'Holly Walters?' Shrewd dark eyes scanned her—a kind of human X-ray.

Rose nodded, playing the game of acknowledging her new name. 'Can I help you?'

'My name is Hammond, Agent Hammond.'

'I know. I remember you.'

'Good: that makes this much easier. Mind if I join you?'

Anyone was welcome on this lonely family holiday, even the FBI. 'Be my guest.'

'How're you getting on here?'

Rose shrugged. 'It's fine.'

'You're quite the favourite person in the New York branch of the FBI at the moment. The evidence you provided us with is gold.'

'I'm glad. Can I get you something?'

Hammond shook her head. 'I'm eating later. We liberated twenty young women and children from the *Southern Star*, did anyone tell you?'

'No.'

'They were being kept in appalling conditions. You probably saved some of their lives.'

'Oh, that's good.' A warm glow took away some of the lonely chill she had been feeling.

251

'Did Damien or Joe mentioned what they were doing with me that day at your school?'

'Er, no.'

'I'm thinking of establishing a branch of the YDA here in the States. You know what the YDA is, I think?'

'Yes. They told me a little about it—and I found out some more myself.'

Hammond smiled. 'I bet you did. Well, Holly, how would you like to be my first student?'

'Me?'

'Yes. I understand you are particularly interested in forensics—skills that apply to present-day crime scenes as much as they do to archaeological sites.'

'I am!'

'The only problem is I haven't yet had a chance to find premises and engage staff.'

'Oh. How long would I have to wait?' It had sounded too good to be true.

'Well, here's the thing: I was thinking I'd send you as a scholarship student to the branch in London so you can see how the place runs. Then, when I'm ready to open the one here, you can advise me on the programme. What do you say?'

Rose was renowned for having a quick brain but for once it stopped in its tracks. 'Me? London? With Damien?'

Agent Hammond smiled. 'I don't know about the "with Damien" part of that, but yes, you, yes, London. You could even revert to your own name as the risk of anyone finding you there is small. You'll have to be careful, of course, but the YDA will show you how to do that. After all, going undercover is one of the training areas. So there's my offer. How long do you need to think about it?'

Damien couldn't concentrate. The class was in fact a fascinating one—the methods for extracting DNA evidence from crime scenes—but his eyes kept sliding to the window overlooking the Thames, brain fading out to merge with the cold rain lashing the glass. The white dome of St Paul's huddled among the buildings of the city. A few seagulls perched on the railing outside, glaring into the room as if the YDA students were personally to blame for the wintry turn to the weather.

'Damien, can you answer the question please?' Dr Waterburn, the mentor of the Owls, was clearly waiting for him to say something. Her foot tapped impatiently.

Joe gave him a sympathetic look, Kieran looked as if he wasn't listening either, and Nathan was trying to mouth the answer to him.

'I'm sorry, Dr Waterburn. I tuned out there for a moment. Could you repeat the question please?'

'I have. Three times.'

'Twice actually,' muttered Kieran. 'The third time was phrased as a supposition rather than an enquiry: "I suppose you think that hair follicles are beneath your attention."'

Raven kicked her boyfriend, but at least he had given Damien a clue. 'I certainly don't think hair follicles insignificant.' He had a sudden memory of one of his conversations with Rose. 'I'm excited that we can solve crimes on less and less physical evidence. Soon we'll need little more than a microscope to catch the bad guys.'

Dr Waterburn's manner changed as she treated him to a warm smile. 'That's very true, Damien, and a very enlightened attitude; but I'm surprised that you, as a Cobra, have realized that. Your mentor, Mr Flint, is always telling me how we'll never do away with the need for the ones who have to go kick down the door, as he put it.'

'I've had reason to rethink the matter recently.'

The door to the classroom opened and the YDA boss, Isaac

253

Hampton, strode in. 'Dr Waterburn, sorry for interrupting. Our new student has arrived and has said she doesn't need any time to unpack. In fact, she was most insistent she join your lesson immediately.'

Damien looked to the door but no one followed Isaac. His interest slackened. His gaze went back to the miserable view from the window.

'Ah, the new Owl. I've been looking forward to meeting her.' Dr Waterburn peered over Isaac's shoulder. 'Do invite her to come in.'

'I will but I think she's a bit shy. It's OK—they don't bite.' Isaac smiled encouragingly to the timid new student.

She'd have to toughen up, thought Damien absent-mindedly, if she was going to flourish here. He then corrected his thought: no, they'd have to help her to adjust. Being strong wasn't the same as being always confident.

The YDA's newest recruit finally stepped into the room and gave them a shy wave. 'Hi, everyone.'

'Rose!' Damien shot out of his seat and vaulted the table in front of him. 'What are you doing here?' He didn't let her answer as he was already kissing her silly in front of the whole class.

'I didn't get a welcome like that when I joined the YDA,' grumbled Kate to Raven, her lab partner.

'I'll make up for that if you want,' murmured Nathan, from the table behind her.

Isaac tapped Damien on the shoulder, very pleased how his surprise for Damien had gone down. 'Hey, Mr Tough Guy, we need you to stop being so . . . er . . .'

'Sappy,' supplied Raven.

Isaac winked at her. 'Sappy. Just for a moment. Everyone, this is Rose Knight. Most of you know her from Damien and Joe's most recent mission which we briefed you on last week. You'll understand that she has some unpleasant people who might be looking for her so I want you to be careful. Her presence is not to leave these four walls, not to be mentioned on social media, and not to be discussed on your phones. Are we clear?'

The replies of, 'Yes, Isaac' came from all quarters.

'OK then. The Feds claim she is by far and away the most intelligent American teenager they have ever seen—sorry, Joe, no offence.'

Joe held up his hands. 'None taken.'

'So I'm expecting Kieran finally to have some competition. It'll do him good.'

Kieran raised a rather arrogant eyebrow until Raven threw a rubber at him.

'Good. I'll leave you to it, Dr Waterburn.' Isaac quit the classroom.

No way was Damien going to torture himself through another fifteen minutes of DNA analysis.

'I'm really sorry, Dr Waterburn, but I have some urgent business with your new Owl.' He towed Rose out before anyone could stop him.

'Damien, the class!' protested Rose.

'You know all that stuff already.' He looked for an empty room, settling finally on the library. Rose would like that.

'I might do—but you don't.'

'I can ask you to give me special catch-up lessons.' He closed the door behind them and pulled her over to the section on forensics. 'Right: now you're home.'

Rose finally noticed where he had brought her. 'Oh, Damien, that's so sweet of you.'

'Here's my library tour. Computers—tick; books—tick; devoted boyfriend—go on: fill in the blank.'

'Devoted boyfriend—tick,' she said softly. 'Overawed but very pleased to be here girlfriend . . .'

'Tick.' Damien kissed her. 'What do you think of the tour so far?'

'Perfect.'

He framed her face in his hands, tipping her head to just the right angle. 'I never knew libraries could be so interesting. You've really shaken up my ideas about things, Rose. I'm in love with a gorgeous geek princess.'

'In love?'

'Yes. But I think we'll have to keep on repeating the experiment, just to check.' He kissed her again.

'Oh, the empirical method. Basis of modern science.' She smiled up at him. 'And my observation is that the reaction results in the same emotion in me.'

'That's very, very good to know.' He rested his forehead on hers. 'Welcome to the YDA, Rose Knight.'

Discover a thrilling world of

romance with **Joss Stirling**

Coming
July 2016

ALSO BY
Joss Stirling

Want to know where it all began? Read on for an extract of Struck . . .

A black eye. Great.

Raven Stone studied it in the mirror, lightly probing the developing bruise. Ouch. The strip light flickered over the wash basin, making her reflection blink like the end of an old newsreel. The tap squeaked a protest as she dampened a cold compress.

'You look about seven years old,' she told her mirror-double.

Ten years on from the schoolyard of scraped knees and minor bumps, Raven considered the injury more a humiliation than a pain. She tugged a curl of her spiralling black hair over her face but it sprang back, refusing to hide the cloud gathering around her left eye. She wondered whether she could hide in her room until it faded . . . ?

Not possible. All the students were expected to attend the welcome-back supper and her absence would be noticed. Anyway—she threw the flannel in the sink—why give her enemies the satisfaction of knowing they had driven her out so easily? Cowardice was not part of her character résumé. She had far too much pride to allow it.

Raven stripped off her tennis kit and pulled on a towelling robe. She tossed the dirty clothes in the laundry basket by the door with a snap of the lid. It was tough keeping her promise to herself that she would be strong; easier when she had someone at her back. But the second bed in the room was empty—no heap of untidy belongings or suitcase as she had expected. What was keeping Gina? She was the only one Raven wanted to talk to about what had just happened. Raven flopped on her bed. How had it come to this in a few hours? Until the black eye, life had been skating along fine, a smooth place after years of rough. Westron, as run by the head teacher, Mrs Bain, had been weird sometimes, putting too much emphasis on wealth and parents, celebrity pupils and privacy, but teaming up with Gina, Raven had been able to laugh off most of those absurdities. She would have said no one in the school wished her ill. In spite of owing her place to her grandfather's presence on the staff, the other students had not appeared to mind her numbering among their privileged ranks. Now she knew better.

The realization had come out of nowhere, like the tornado spiralling Dorothy's house off to Oz. When Raven opened the door to the changing rooms, everything went skipping down the yellow brick road to Bizarre City.

Hedda's question had seemed so, well, *normal*. 'Hey, where's my Chloé tote?'
The other girls in the locker room getting ready for the tennis competition had made a brief search among their belongings. Raven had not even bothered: her little sports bag, a much mocked airline freebie, was too small to hide the bulky taupe leather shoulder bag. Hedda had been flaunting it all morning like a fisherman displaying a prize catch. The flexing, polished surface had gleamed like a sea trout in her manicured fingers: *so many pockets and you won't believe how much it cost!* Hedda had thought it a bargain but it had come with a price tag more than Raven's grandfather earned in a month as the school's caretaker. Something so pointlessly expensive had to be a rip-off.

'Hey, I'm talking to you, Stone.'

Raven felt a sharp tug on her elbow. Standing on one foot to lace her tennis shoe, she toppled to one side. Why had Hedda suddenly taken to using her surname?

'Whoa, Hedda, careful!' Raven balanced herself against the wire mesh dividing the changing areas and tied off the bow. 'You almost knocked me over.'

Stick thin and with an abundance of wine-red hair, Hedda reminded Raven of a red setter, sharp nose pointing to the next shopping bargain, a determined little notch in her chin that gave her face character. Hedda put her hands on her hips. 'Where have you hidden it?'

'What?' Raven was too surprised to realize what it was that Hedda was accusing her of doing. 'Me?'

'Yes, you. I'm not stupid. I saw you looking at it. It had my phone—my make-up—my money—everything is in that bag.'

Raven tried to keep a hold on her temper and ignore the hurt of being accused with no proof. She had had enough of that in the last school she had attended before coming to the UK. She tried for reasonable. 'I haven't done anything with it. Where did you last see it?'

'At the lunch table—don't pretend you don't know.'

The changing room fell silent as the other girls listened in on the exchange. A flush of shame crept over Raven's cheeks even though she knew she was innocent. Memories of standing before the principal in her old school rushed back. She felt queasy with the sense of déjà vu.

'I'm sorry: are you saying I stole it?'

Hedda tipped her head back and looked down her long nose at Raven. 'I'm not saying—I know you took it.'

Raven dragged her thoughts away from her past and focused on the accuser. What on earth had happened to Hedda? She had missed most of last term and had come back with what seemed like a personality transplant—from clingy, whingeing minor irritant to strident, major-league bitch.

Raven told herself not to back down; she'd faced false accusations before and this time she wasn't a traumatized little girl. What was the worst Hedda could do? Wave a mascara wand at her?

'So you think I took it? Based on what? On that fact that I just *looked* at it? Looking doesn't mean stealing.' Raven appealed to the other girls, hoping to find someone who would join her in shrugging off the accusation as absurd, but their expressions were watchful or carefully neutral. *Gee, thanks, guys.*

Then Hedda's friend, Toni, joined in the finger pointing. 'There's no point claiming you're innocent. Things were going missing all last term.'

'I had nothing to do with that. Some of my stuff was stolen too.'

Toni ignored her. 'We all noticed small things disappearing but didn't like to . . . I mean we *guessed* it was you but we felt sorry for you, so . . . ' Toni waved her hand as if to say *that was last term, this is now.*

'Sorry for me?' Raven gave a choked laugh. One thing she never wanted was anyone's pity. Even at her lowest moment after losing her parents, she hadn't asked for that.

Hedda got right up in her face. 'But taking my brand new Chloé? Now you've gone way too far. Give it back, Stone.'

Ridiculous. Raven turned her back on Hedda. 'And what am I supposed to be doing with these things I'm stealing?'

'Your grandfather has a new car—if you can call a Skoda a car.'

Toni snorted. Raven felt a surge of anger: taking a crack at her was one thing but Hedda had better keep her granddad out of it or there really would be trouble!

'So I, what? Steal from the rich to give to the poor? Now why didn't I think of that?' Raven's irony was lost on the literal-minded Hedda.

'Stop denying it. I want my bag and I want it now.'

Hoping that if she ignored the infantile rant Hedda would back down, Raven shook her head and dipped her fingers inside her jeans pocket for a band to tie up her hair.

'Don't you ignore me!' With a grunt of fury, Hedda shoved Raven hard into the mesh, right onto a peg that caught the corner of her eye. Even though the hook was padded by clothes, Raven saw stars. Clapping a hand to her face, she swung round, temper threatening to gallop away riderless.

'Look, Hedda, I don't have your stupid tote!' She gathered herself in the defensive stance she had been taught. Raven had to be careful, knowing she could do a lot of harm with the self-defence training her father had insisted she take. It had come in useful for fending off the predators who roamed the corridors in her American public school, but she guessed it would be frowned on at refined Westron and would earn her a reputation as a thug.

'Yes. You. Do!' Hedda shoved Raven in the chest with each word so her back collided with the mesh. Someone giggled nervously while two students hurried out to fetch the PE teacher.

That was outside of enough. It was time Hedda learnt there was one girl in the school she couldn't bully.

'I've had enough of your idiotic—' (push) '—accusations!' Raven thrust Hedda back a second time, measuring out exactly the same force as Hedda had used on her.

Then Hedda went for a handful of hair. Big mistake.

Joss Stirling lives in Oxford and is the author of the bestselling **Finding Sky** trilogy. She was awarded the Romantic Novelist's Association's Romantic Novel of the year 2015 for **Struck**.

You can visit her website at **www.jossstirling.com**.